~~~~~~

DEADLY

RETURN

~~~~~~~~~~~~~~~~~

The Seacastle Mysteries

Book 1

PJ Skinner

ISBN 978-1-913224-44-8

Parkin Press

INDEPENDENT PUBLISHER

Cover design by Mariah Sinclair

Discover other titles by PJ Skinner

The Seacastle Mysteries

Eternal Forest (Book 2)

Mortal Mission: A Murder mystery on Mars

Written as Pip Skinner

The Green Family Saga (written as Kate Foley)

Rebel Green (Book 1)

Africa Green (Book 2)

Fighting Green (Book 3)

The Sam Harris Adventure Series

Fool's Gold (Book 1)

Hitler's Finger (Book 2)

The Star of Simbako (Book 3)

The Pink Elephants (Book 4)

The Bonita Protocol (Book 5)

Digging Deeper (Book 6)

Concrete Jungle (Book 7)

Also available as box sets

Go to the PJ Skinner website for more info and to
purchase paperbacks directly from the author:
https://www.pjskinner.com

Dedicated to my sister Moo

Chapter 1

My divorce papers came through on the day I moved into the Grotty Hovel, a scruffy terraced house purchased for me by Detective Inspector George Carter, my erstwhile husband. The postman dropped the fat envelope containing the decree on top of the cardboard box I carried down the uneven path to my new front door.

'This looks important, love,' he said, grinning. 'Did you inherit a fortune?'

I managed a smile. A good postman is almost as important as a good hairdresser. I couldn't afford to alienate him at our first meeting. I stepped backwards to let him pass, and almost overbalanced as the heel of my boot sank into the flower bed. Recovering my dignity, I pushed through the door of the house and into the mildewed sitting room where I dumped the box on the floor and tried not to cry. *From smug married to impoverished singleton in the mere space of months.*

Only weeks ago, I had been the mistress of a spacious modern villa in the outskirts of Seacastle, and then, completely out of the blue my husband had asked me for a divorce. This turn of events shocked me to the core. It wasn't so much the divorce, but w*hat sort of investigative* *reporter didn't notice her husband having an affair?* He had organised everything, down to this new dwelling, without consulting me, and I found no stomach for the fight. Now, this pokey terraced house in the cheap end of town rammed home my new circumstances with its two-up two-down, 1970s-chic, flocked wallpaper, and swirly carpets.

I needed to regroup. There had to be positives to my new situation, even if I couldn't imagine what they were yet. At least I had somewhere to live, which was a lot more than many people could say. I took a deep breath and examined the room with the eye of an estate agent. If I stripped out the carpet and painted the walls a warm colour, the sitting room could be cosy with a roaring fire set in its neat tiled fireplace, and with my favourite knick-knacks spread around in the built-in bookshelves in front of my eclectic collection of paperbacks. Rather than empty all my boxes immediately, I would pile them up in one downstairs room and decorate the other. The emerging plan heartened me somewhat, and I went back outside to pick up more boxes.

When I had almost finished, I took a break, sitting on the crumbly brick wall which divided the overgrown front garden from the street, and reached for a cigarette. To my annoyance, my fingers did not caress the comforting shape of a packet of twenty Marlboro Lights; only one which held nicotine chewing gum. I hadn't picked a good time to give up smoking, but I wouldn't give George the satisfaction of seeing me starting again. I took out a piece of gum and chewed hard, trying to squeeze out the nicotine which would quash the cravings.

A robin bobbed into view along the gate opposite and opened his beak to trill his song into the cold air. I could see my breath, which meant the temperature hovered around zero. My fingers were like fish fingers from the freezer. I wished I had worn gloves. My jeans were no protection against the cold bricks, and my fashionable holey jumper let in the chill breeze against my rib cage. My warm Puffa jacket lurked inside one box, but which one? I stood again and jumped up and down to warm up my muscles.

As I contemplated the last of my boxes, still blocking the pavement outside the house, an ancient, covered van pulled in to the kerb opposite my house. The side of the van had 'Fletcher's Clearance' painted in new gloss over an old sign which had been whited out. The door of the cabin swung open, and a foot clad in a climbing boot dropped onto the step, resting there as if the occupant had changed his mind about getting out. A loud sigh emanated from the cabin and a stocky man with a close-cropped bullet head, as battered as his van, jumped down onto the street. He scanned the area as if expecting an ambush. His gaze alighted on me sitting beside my boxes, and he frowned, checking a piece of crumpled paper he held in his hand.

'Are those for collection, love?' he said, with a Cockney accent, gesticulating at my boxes.

'Definitely not,' I said. 'I'm moving in, not out.'

The man looked around him in confusion. Just then, a red Mini screeched around the corner and parked opposite the van. A plump woman in a tight suit almost fell out of the driver's door in her haste to exit the vehicle and lunged at the man with a set of keys.

'So sorry I'm late, Mr Fletcher. I had an appointment to show a flat on the seafront and my client never showed up.'

She thrust the keys into his hands and pointed at the house beside mine.

'That's the house. Everything still inside it is yours. Okay if I go now? I have another appointment.'

Without waiting for an answer, she got back into her Mini and drove off. I caught the man's eye, and we laughed.

'I'd better get going then,' he said. 'Do you need a hand carrying those inside?'

'No thanks. I'm almost finished.'

The man walked down the path parallel to me and started to empty the house of its furniture. I couldn't help smiling as we walked by each other. He had a military air and a rugged face with grey eyes that twinkled at me despite his air of sadness. A man of contradictions. Despite myself, I burned with curiosity to know his story. While he concentrated on loading his van, I wondered how to start up a conversation. Then he emerged from the house with a peacock chair and I stopped short in admiration.

'Wow! That's fabulous,' I said. '1960s or 70s.'

'It is?' he said, putting it down and examining it. 'I've no idea. I just sell the house contents in bulk to a dealer.'

'Could you sell that chair to me instead?' I asked.

'Do you want them both?'

'There's more?'

'Come in and have a butcher's.'

I skirted the privet hedge dividing the pathways and entered the neighbouring house, which had similar décor to mine. The man stuck out his hand, making me jump.

'I'm Harry Fletcher,' he said.

I took it in a firm grip, feeling his warm flesh under the rough calluses.

'Tanya Carter, I mean Bowe.'

He raised an eyebrow at me and my blood rose to my cheeks. With my heeled boots on, I was almost the same height as him, and he looked straight into my eyes without blinking.

'Are you sure?'

'Yes, I'm newly divorced. I'm not used to my old surname yet.'

'It's a good surname. It goes well with mine.'

Harry guffawed at my expression of panic.

'I'm not asking you to marry me. I just meant Bowe and Fletcher. Like bow and arrow.'

'Oh, I'm sorry. I'm not having a great day.'

'No worries. My jokes can be hard to appreciate. How come you know about chairs?'

'I have an antique shop. Well, it's vintage really.'

'There's a difference?'

I smiled.

'Only in age. Most of my stuff is from the 20th century. This house is like a time capsule from that era. I'd love to buy some of the furniture for my shop,' I said. 'If I pick out some pieces, can we negotiate over a cup of tea?'

'We can. Why don't you come in and look around?'

Harry stepped backwards to let me into the sitting room with its twin fireplace, which used the same chimney stack as mine. The carpets were stained and smelled of cat pee. I hoped they weren't flea-infested and resisted the temptation to scratch my ankle when I imagined I felt something crawling there. I distracted myself by examining the other peacock chair and the small matching wicker table and nodded in approval. A wooden lamp with a Bakelite figure of a bird sat on the floor. The flex needed changing, but the local electricians could rewire it in five minutes. I picked it up and put it on the chair and then moved between the small rooms.

One of the most satisfying parts of my hobby had been rescuing well-loved objects from people's houses and giving them a second life. Examining the relics of a past life always made me nostalgic. Something told me that the occupant wouldn't be needing furniture any more. *Had they gone to a care home or passed on?* I ran my hand over a small drop-leaf table covered in Formica.

'This too,' I said to Harry, who followed me around and transferred the selected pieces onto the small front lawn.

I wandered upstairs through the ice-cold house and found a Lloyd Loom chair with its original cushion, and a laundry basket of the same make in the bathroom. Luckily, the former owner had not repainted them, and they both had a weathered bronze sheen. I opened the laundry basket and leapt backwards in fright as a large black cat with a white bib stared up at me from inside.

'Oh my goodness. There's a cat in here,' I said.

'A cat. How—'

'I don't know. Maybe it jumped in and the lid shut. It's still alive though. It just hissed at me.'

Harry turned the basket on its side and raised the lid. He reached inside and yelped.

'Ouch. The little bugger scratched me.'

'It's probably just afraid. Give me a second.'

I ran back to the house and grabbed a pint of milk from the sideboard in the kitchen where I had left it. A discarded plastic bowl lay on the floor. I poured some milk into it and carried it to the other house to where Harry stood sucking his finger.

'Lift the lid again,' I said to Harry, placing the milk container on the ground in front of the basket.

'Do you think it will work?' said Harry. 'I know nothing about cats. I'm a dog man myself. Greyhounds.'

We didn't have to wait for long. A bedraggled black cat emerged from the basket and dove into the milk, sneezing as it entered its nostrils.

'He's thirsty then,' said Harry.

'How do you know it's a he?' I said.

'I don't.'

The cat lapped up the milk with desperation, looking around as if it expected the bowl to be removed. By the time it had finished, some of the tension had evaporated from its body. Then it looked around and, seeing me crouching nearby, hissed at me and ran back into the laundry basket. Harry laughed.

'I'm not trying to get it out of there again. It will die of cold and hunger in here. Why don't you take it home for now?'

I sighed.

'I've only just moved in, and even my cactuses die. I'm not sure I can be responsible for another life form.'

Harry guffawed.

'You didn't kill your husband too, did you?'

'I should have, but I didn't want to lower myself.'

A mewing sound came from the basket, and my heart melted.

'I'll take him for now,' I said. 'Let's leave him in the laundry basket. He feels safe in there. I'll carry it next door.'

Harry grinned.

'Maybe he'll be a good mouser,' he said. 'Any chance of that cup of Rosie? You can beat me down on the prices if you include a bickie.'

'Give me a minute to dig the kettle out of its box. I might even find the biscuits somewhere.'

I left Harry to finish emptying the house and carried the basket into my house. The cat mewed in question but stopped once I had placed the laundry basket on its side in the sitting room. Leaving it there, I opened all the boxes marked kitchen and found not only the kettle, but some relatively undamaged mugs, the tea bags, the instant coffee, the sugar, and some chocolate digestives. They were George's favourite, and not allowed on my latest diet, but I had removed them from their cupboard as a rebellious gesture. I boiled the kettle and made a pot of tea which I covered with a tea cosy decorated with a crown, a souvenir of the marriage of Charles and Diana.

Harry shuffled into the kitchen, glancing around and fiddling with his watch.

'Nice place you've got here,' he said. 'Don't you already have rather a lot of vintage stuff?'

I couldn't tell if he was joking.

'The furniture for my shop,' I said. 'I have to make a profit now it isn't a hobby anymore.'

'Are you sure you want to sell them?'

I grinned.

'Maybe not straight away. It will be nice to take things home without having to hide them from my ex-husband. George hated my taste. He told me all my stuff was junk.'

'My Cathy collected trinkets she kept in her grandmother's cabinet. They're still there, gathering dust.'

Something in his tone told me Cathy had died, but I didn't want to ask him, and invite misery into our, so far, rather fun conversation.

'They'll be worth millions one of these days,' I said.

'Who knows?' he said, sighing. 'How did you get interested in antiques?'

'Afternoon telly when I got made redundant. I got addicted to all those programmes about making money from stuff you find in your attic.'

'Do you work now?'

'Sort of. I'm trying to make my hobby into a career now I'm on my own.'

'The vintage shop?'

'Exactly.'

'Would you like me to bring your furniture directly to the shop? It's no problem.'

'That would be great. Now, how would you like your tea?'

Chapter 2

It felt strange to have a cat in my house. George had never let me bring a pet to our villa. He claimed to be allergic to both cats and dogs. I don't know if he told the truth about that, or indeed about anything. He had spent years hurting and belittling me when I suffered from depression and lost the job I adored in investigative journalism. The smaller I felt, the more he inflated with self-importance, offering me unsolicited advice about pulling up my socks and not moping around the house like a wet weekend. Was he cruel to me on purpose? I doubted it. The appalling misogynistic culture at the Metropolitan Police had infiltrated the man I once knew and replaced him with a cliched, hard man.

When George told me about being in love with Sharon, I actually laughed, as it sounded so unlikely. How could this unfeeling carbon unit have fallen in love? But she resembled me as a young woman, with her auburn curls and brown eyes. She even had the same slightly masculine figure with broad shoulders and slim hips. Is that why he chose her? Deja vu? I still looked the same, if slightly battered around the edges. The small wrinkles on my face and neck had not yet changed my appearance, merely blunted the effect. But it felt twice as galling to be replaced by myself. As for her, she must have been as blind to his faults as I used to be, or she would never have taken up with him. I felt sorry for her. She's not a bad person, if a little ruthless when stealing my husband. I might even get on with her given the chance. One day she would look across a crowded room and wonder how she made such a horrible mistake.

And the worst thing is, I wanted him back, despite everything. George didn't seem to realise that just because he had stopped loving me, it didn't mean I'd stopped loving him. I won't deny we were traversing rough seas, but no marriage sails calm waters for ever. When the passion fades, and the minor irritations of daily life together become magnified by repetition, rough patches are inevitable. But for me, George represented stability and old-fashioned values I held dear, and his affair was totally out of character. I attributed it to a middle age crisis, like buying a fast car. If I hung in and didn't complain, maybe he'd tire of her and return to me. My sister Helen claimed I must have caused the aberration in his behaviour, but I'd never done anything right as far as she was concerned. I was a train wreck who should pull up her socks and get a proper haircut.

She certainly wouldn't approve of my cat. I don't know why I agreed to take him home. I guess I was showing off. Meeting Harry made me feel many weird sensations. His arms gave me the shivers, the way they flexed when he picked things up. The way his eyes crinkled when he made a silly comment touched me. When he told me that his wife had died from cancer, I almost burst into tears. He said nothing about her battling it and didn't use any cliches. She just died and left him bereft of his best friend and the holder of his heart. We all think our pain is the worst, but it isn't. Nowhere near some people's suffering. I offered my condolences, but I could see that no words could touch his profound sorrow. I felt his loss like a dark chasm splitting his being. No wonder sadness hung over him like a cloud hovering over a hill. I hoped we would be good friends.

As for the cat, he had a foul temper and was only willing to emerge from his cave for food, a bit like George. He had been neutered and wore a tight collar. It needed to be taken off, or at least loosened, as it had sunk into his fur. I couldn't touch it then for fear of being bitten. I had to wait until he became less feral. Hades was a stopgap name, on account of his nature. If he ever emerged from his basket to engage with me, I could gauge if the name suited him or if he needed something less evil.

In the last hours of daylight, I busied myself emptying the sitting room again and pulled up a corner of the foul carpet. The wooden floorboards underneath cheered me up, and I tugged and ripped at it with a claw hammer. All the frustration I had bottled up came out as I fought with the glue and nails to free the floor from its gruesome covering. Finally, I stood back and admired my handiwork. The floor needed sanding and re-polishing, but I had the tools for that at my shop. Vintage furnishings often need spit and polish to prepare them for their reincarnations. I had always been good with my hands and physically strong, something I hid in the days when it hadn't been fashionable. George liked to do everything at home, in theory anyway. As he never had any time, I would wait for months for the smallest task to get done. When he stopped mentioning it, I would do it myself without telling him. Thank goodness I didn't have to pretend anymore.

I found the box with bed linen in it and made up my bed. The bedroom faced the small back garden, a jungle of brambles and nettles which had surrounded two small fruit trees and reverberated with the shrill sound of sparrows. I thought I could hear a robin in there, trying to compete. The light faded fast, and soon the garden disappeared into a black hole of darkness, the birds silent and huddled in the bushes. I resolved to buy a bird feeder to hang out of reach of the cat. My cat, unless someone came to claim him. Panic gripped me as I imagined having to give him away again. He might be a nightmare, but he was my nightmare now, and I wouldn't give him up without a fight.

I made some tea and cheese on toast from the meagre rations I had bought in a local Spar, and sat in the small kitchen listening to the radio and frowning at the news. Then I changed, shoved a tape into the slot, and rolled up my sleeves. Don't judge me. Most of my favourite music is on tape. With Led Zeppelin in the background, I cleaned the shelves in the kitchen cupboards of what looked like congealed mouse droppings and golden syrup. I unpacked the boxes containing a set of 1950s crockery I had taken from my stock. It suited the tired décor and gave an old world feel to the room. I resolved to go to the supermarket and hardware shop to buy supplies in the morning.

Tiredness hit me in a wave soon after, and I checked on Hades before heading upstairs. He hissed at me from the confines of his basket and I realised I could not let him outside until he felt at home in the house. I found some packing paper and laid it beside the back door, hoping he would know what to do there. I added cat litter to my list of supplies before trudging upstairs. The bathroom had a striplight I needed to get rid of and made my reflection stark and unflattering. However, I noticed a subtle change in my eyes, a glow of excitement, which surprised me. I brushed my teeth, sneaking more glances at this recent phenomenon. Could I make this work after all?

Quietness settled over the house, as I lay in bed and listened to the sound of cars arriving home late in my road. The stark silhouettes of the leafless fruit trees in the back garden stood against the yellow glow creeping in from the streetlights. Someone shouted in the darkness as my eyelids grew heavy and closed.

Chapter 3

The next morning, the raucous shouting of herring gulls woke me from an epic dream of which I couldn't remember anything. As it was impossible to go back to sleep, I cursed their noisy banter and left my comfortable bed. I had a shower and washed my hair and went downstairs, where I ate some more toast for breakfast. If I didn't get to the supermarket soon, I would look like a white loaf. The walk to my shop along the promenade added a few hundred yards to my commute, but the sea air and, yes, more herring gulls swooping over the sands lifted my mood. The chill in the air stung the tips of my ears where they had snuck out of my beanie, and the idea of leaving the house without drying my hair struck me as one lacking wisdom. I pulled my scarf tight around my neck and lifted the edge to cover my nose and mouth, increasing the pace of my footsteps as I neared the shop.

The town of Seacastle squatted on the southern coast of England, a backwater stuck halfway between Brighton and Littlehampton. It suffered by comparison with them, even though it possessed a handsome pier with a theatre at its entrance, a penny arcade along its boards, and a teashop resembling an ocean liner at the far end. A wide promenade with a cycle lane ran from one end of the town to the other along the shore and acted as a focal point for weekend walks in the almost constant breeze. Victorian wind shelters lined the promenade interspersed with food stalls and ice cream sellers. Seacastle had featured in the 'up and coming' pages of the property sections in the Sunday newspapers several times without believing its own hype. Once popular with Victorian visitors, the poor train service, and a reputation for being boring, had put off modern day trippers. The truth, as always, was more complicated. Despite its reputation as a place where old people who couldn't afford to live in Eastbourne came to die, Seacastle had recently become popular with couples who had young families and needed more space than they could afford elsewhere. On sunny days, the promenade featured a selection of people of all ages and, increasingly, all races, enjoying the facilities and sitting in the shelters.

The 'Second Home' vintage shop occupied a position halfway down the local high street, which ran parallel to the promenade and divided Seacastle into the posher and cheaper ends of town. It had a traditional wooden-framed shop front painted dark red with gold accents, and stood out from the other tired shop fronts around it, many of which were charity and pound shops. The sign above the window had an Art Deco feel, even though most of the contents were younger. Across the street, an Italian café, which had been the centre of social activity on the neglected high street, sat sad and empty with lacquered tables piled up on each other and old menus scattered on the floor. The cold air above the street vibrated with the calls of yet more herring gulls, which nested among the chimney stacks of the town and aimed their streams of faecal matter at any windows which dared to reflect them.

The doorbell jangled loudly as I entered the shop. An old-fashioned counter with a thick glass top over a velvet-lined display cabinet stood to one side of the entrance door. On the walls behind it, Victorian bracket lamps, wired and adapted to modern bulbs, overhung the desk. Sturdy hooks hung from the ceiling from which chandeliers and decorative lamp shades from various decades dangled at different heights, interspersed with old pieces of fishing net scavenged from the beach. The shop stretched out into a storeroom at the back and had a second floor containing two large rooms, one front and one back, which languished from lack of attention. They were sparsely arranged with pieces in no particular order, waiting for me to have a burst of enthusiasm or energy, or both. The third-floor attic sat empty as I had not found a use for the rooms yet. I had considered converting it into a flat, but that would take money, and the shop showed no sign of making a profit yet. Also, the thought of carrying furniture up the narrow staircase put me off.

I bought the property with an inheritance from my parents, to the derision of my older sister Helen, who considered herself to be the arbiter of good taste and sensible behaviour. She felt free to give me the full force of her opinions, some of them derogatory. Sometimes I wondered if being an only child would have been more fun than being judged for failing at everything by my smug-married sister, perfect in every way, but not forgiving or kind. Helen's reaction to George's betrayal typified her.

'Well, it's hardly surprising he's left you. It's not as if you make any effort,' she said.

But that was Helen. Not really a shoulder to cry on at the best of times. I avoided her when I could and tolerated her when I couldn't. It wasn't as if I could afford to lose her for good, as I only had a few friends left after the divorce. Most of George's and my friends had been police officers and their spouses, and they gravitated to George's side after he split up with me. I didn't begrudge them, and to tell the truth, I endured the company of most of George's friends because I had to rather than by choice.

One of my remaining friends, Ghita, dropped by the Second Home to dispense moral support, and to hear about the move to the Grotty Hovel. She planted herself in front of me, her arms crossed, as she interrogated me. Her plump, pretty face with its lively eyes framed by her thick black hair hanging down to her waist had adopted a stern look. Her short stature made her sensitive to being ignored and gave her the habit of standing on her tiptoes to get noticed. The wooden floor of the shop became dusty ten minutes after sweeping, so I had disguised it since her last visit with several well-patched, over-lapping Persian rugs. She poked at them with her toe, her disapproval obvious.

'Trip hazards,' she said.

Ghita worked part time for the council, when she wasn't running the local weight watchers club, Fat Fighters, and knew all about health and safety. She always smiled and encouraged people and had endless patience for the problems of others, but got irritated if you inquired about hers. She had moved to Seacastle to look after elderly relatives who had died soon afterward, leaving her the proud owner of a flat in a block overlooking the beach. Her family could not persuade her to move home again and spent a lot of energy trying to convince her to marry. But Ghita resisted.

Not long after Ghita arrived, the shop bell rang as Roz burst through the door, pink cheeked with the effort of trotting down the high street, her pink and blue hair piled in a messy bun.

'Brrr. It's freezing out today. Did I miss anything?' she said.

Roz Murray resembled a cross between a mermaid and a Valkyrie. Tall, at almost six-foot, her husband Ed owned a fishing boat, on which she often disappeared for days. She went by the nickname Foghorn, owing to her indiscreet habit of sharing everyone's secrets and any town gossip. In fact, whispering a secret to Roz guaranteed that everyone in town would hear about it in three minutes flat and could be quite useful. She completed our stalwart, if disparate, trio of childless women. We had strong opinions and different politics, but our shared sense of humour kept us bonded despite our distinct characters.

To their bemusement, I did not seem at all fazed by my move to the Grotty Hovel and on the contrary, extolled the virtues of the little house and showed them photographs of my new lodger crouching in his basket, his eyes aflame with hate.

'I thought you hated the house. And these photos of the cat are terrible,' said Ghita, screwing up her eyes. 'But he looks adorable with that white patch of his.'

'You've got some rubbish photos on that phone of yours,' said Roz. 'I wish you'd get a smart phone. You're such a Luddite.'

'Have you given him a name yet?' said Ghita.

'Hades.'

'Isn't that a funny name for a cat? What about Patch or Spot?' said Roz.

'Hades as in hellcat.'

'I don't like it,' said Ghita. 'Does he come when you call?'

'He hasn't emerged from his laundry basket so far, and cats don't come when you call them anyway.'

'That's true,' said Roz. 'Only dogs do that, and husbands.'

She grinned and Ghita arched an eyebrow at her.

'I'll put on the kettle,' said Ghita and disappeared into the small kitchen under the stairs. Roz put her arm around my shoulders and gave me a squeeze.

'How are you holding up?'

'Oh, you know. Divorced, abandoned, replaced.'

'George has no taste. Did I tell you what I heard about Sharon the other day, only—'

Roz stopped in mid-sentence and stared at the window of the shop where a good-looking man sheltered his eyes with his hand to peer into the depths. He spotted me and waved. A furious blush suffused my neck and face as I waved back. Roz spotted the change in the colour of my cheeks, and her eyebrows flew up.

'You cheeky baggage,' she said. 'Here's me feeling all sorry for you and you've been flirting with a new man already. Ow.'

I had thumped her on the arm to shut her up as Harry pushed his way through the door with one of the peacock chairs.

'Morning,' he said. 'I've got your bits of furniture here. Where do you want me to put them?'

'Oh, um, anywhere you can find room,' I said. 'I'll sort them out later.'

Ghita emerged from the little kitchen with a tray of mugs, teaspoons, instant coffee, tea bags, sugar, and milk. Her mouth fell open when she saw Harry and she pursed her lips in a fake whistle behind his back. I shook my head at her, but Roz elbowed Ghita and they both giggled and smirked as if a boy had tugged their pigtails. Harry seemed oblivious to their interest and brought in the rest of my purchases, whistling tunelessly, and making room for them on the shop floor. When he had finished, and stuffed his payment into his jeans pocket, I invited him in for a coffee. He beamed.

'I'll move the van,' he said. 'Or they'll tow it away.'

When he returned, we all sat around in the shop's selection of chairs and sipped our beverages, commenting on the weather and the strength of the wind and the annoying habits of the seagulls, like a group of pensioners in deckchairs on the promenade.

Then Harry stood up and swallowed.

'I've been wondering,' he said, almost in a whisper.

All three of us craned forward, which seemed to spook him. He glanced at the exit, but then changed his mind.

'Yes?' I said.

'Well, it seemed to me, with you being so knowledgeable and all that…'

He tailed off and bit his lip.

'About?' I said.

Roz had leaned so far forward that she almost fell off her chair with anticipation. Ghita shoved her back into it and shook her head.

'What I mean is, maybe you'd like to come on a house clearance with me and advise me which pieces have some value? You can keep the things you like for your shop, and we could come to an arrangement about what you pay me for them.'

He stood there shuffling his feet and looking uncertain.

'When's your next clearance?' I said.

'Right now, if you're game,' said Harry. 'Sorry about the late notice, but I hadn't decided to ask until I got here and saw your shop.'

'Oh, I don't know,' I said. 'I'm pretty busy today.'

'No, she's not,' Ghita blurted out. 'She's available.'

'She'd love to, wouldn't you, Tanya?' said Roz, grabbing my arm and pinching it. 'Ghita, get her coat from the hooks at the back.'

'What about the shop?' I said.

'Don't you worry about the shop,' said Ghita, handing my coat and handbag to me. 'I've got the day off and Roz has got nothing better to do. We'll manage.'

'If we get overrun with clients, we'll text you,' said Roz.

'Okay then,' said Harry, beaming. 'I guess that's settled.'

'I guess it is,' I said. 'Not that I got a say in it.'

'I parked the van on Shelley Road. We'd better hurry or I'll get a ticket.'

Chapter 4

Harry and I trotted past the dustbins on the pavements outside their owners' houses to the side street where he had parked the battered van. While I caught my breath, Harry inspected the windscreen. He wiped his brow with a mock handkerchief.

'Phew. No ticket. That's good news,' he said, as he clambered into the cabin, and reached across to open my door for me.

I used the running board to get into the cabin and heaved myself onto the front seat. It was made of brown leatherette and released an odour of cigarettes as I sat down. I wrinkled my nose and tried not to think about smoking. I didn't want to take out a piece of nicotine chewing gum and have to explain when he couldn't have one too. It mattered what he thought of me, but I could not explain why. I left my coat on, as the temperature in the cabin threatened to freeze me cryogenically, and reached for my seatbelt. It would not budge even when I tugged sharply at it. Harry noticed my struggle and leaned across me.

'Let me get that,' he said. 'It's a knack.'

He pushed the holder away from the seat, and the belt released. He smelled of burnt toast and warm days in bed, and I tried to ignore my racing pulse. I pulled at the belt and pushed the buckle into the holder. Harry fastened his own and said *'clunk click with every trip'*. I glanced at his battered face with its sad grey eyes. His jaw had set as if he was struggling with emotion. A reserved atmosphere had crept into the cabin, which I tried to dispel by chatting, a bad habit of mine, but I could feel the subtle change.

'Where are you going today?' I said.

'Don't you mean we?' said Harry. 'I thought we'd agreed to work together.'

'I don't know about other trips yet. Let's see how we get on first.'

'You're right. I might not enjoy working with you.'

Harry stared straight ahead, his knuckles white on the steering wheel, changing gears with a stiff arm. I forced myself to speak.

'Don't let's start off on the wrong foot. I'm excited to try this out. I'm just cautious about relationships of all sorts right now.'

'You are? So how come you let the cat move in with you after just one drink?' said Harry, but a wide grin creased his face.

I snorted.

'Caught in the act,' I said. 'But it was love at first sight.'

'Fair enough.' Harry's arms relaxed, and he pointed up to the crest of a hill at the back of Seacastle. 'We're going up there,' he said. 'The old Conrad place.'

My eyes widened.

'I know it. I went to school with their daughter, Melanie. She was in the year below me, though.'

24

'What was she like?'

'A little weird. Hard to like. I don't think we were kind to her, to tell you the truth. She disappeared after leaving school, but no one told us where she had gone. I don't know if she's alive or dead.'

'We all know people like that. Many of my mates from the army went AWOL after they demobbed.'

He sighed, and his sadness returned. I wondered how many of them suffered from PTSD or worse. I had met many damaged ex-soldiers in my former life as an investigative journalist. Surviving the army unscathed seemed to be a rare privilege for those who had seen active service. We drove in silence until the gates of the Conrad House came into view. Harry manoeuvred the van through the tight gap, and the van bumped its way up the badly maintained driveway. The Victorian pile emerged from the unkempt lawns like a stale wedding cake on a velvet green table cloth. Three cars had been parked haphazardly outside the building, making it hard for Harry to back the van up to the front entrance.

'Is there a coffee morning here today?' I said. 'I thought the place was supposed to be empty.'

'So did I.'

As I opened the door of the van, a bull terrier emerged from the bushes and rushed at me with its teeth bared. I pulled the door shut again.

'Bloody hell. It's the Hound of the Baskervilles,' I said.

'All bark and no bite,' said Harry, opening his door and jumping out. The dog barked hysterically as Harry got out, but it skidded to a stop and backed away when Harry moved forward. He beckoned me out of the van, and I slid out of the door, landing heavily, and twisting my ankle. I hopped around, rubbing it, while Harry rolled his eyes.

'You're more dangerous than the dog,' he said.

'I hurt my ankle.'

'Your ankle or your pride?'

'Thanks for the sympathy,' I said. 'What if I'd broken it?'

'I'm sorry. My army mates never admit they're hurt. It's seen as weak. Are you okay?' he said, his tone softening.

I put my weight on my ankle and grimaced.

'I guess so.'

'Let's go then.'

We approached the house and Harry pushed open the heavy front door. A padlock hung from the badly attached staple. The hasp stuck out from the door frame, catching my shoulder as I walked in. I squeaked and rubbed it hard to dissipate the pain, sure that I would receive zero sympathy from Action Man. I could hear loud voices coming from the room on the right-hand side. We approached cautiously, and I blinked twice as I took in the scene. Fiona Conrad, the bottle-blonde wife of the owner, stood at the window with a younger woman and a strikingly handsome man. The tall, brunette woman turned to look at us and I recognised her immediately despite the passage of time.

'Melanie?' I said. 'When did you get back? I thought, I mean, we thought—'

'You thought I had died? Understandable, but unfortunately for some people, not true.'

'That's a wicked thing to say,' said Fiona Conrad.

'As if you'd care,' said Melanie,

Fiona Conrad rearranged the silk scarf tied around her neck. I noticed a glance that passed between her and the handsome man. He tapped his nose and winked at her.

'You haven't changed much, unfortunately,' said Fiona. 'I've got to go. We'll speak later.'

She left before Melanie could reply, her heels clattering across the tiled hall. Melanie rolled her eyes.

'Silly woman. She's not that much older than me, you know, but she looks ancient.' She stared at me, narrowing her eyes. 'Oh, my goodness, it's Tanya Bowe, isn't it? I remember you from school.'

'Yes, that's me. How long have you been back?'

'Not long. We've visited a few times this year to see my father. He's getting on a bit,' said Mel. 'By the way, this is my husband, Greg.'

He leaned forward and took my hand, turning it over to kiss the back. Melanie rolled her eyes.

'Get a grip. Tanya won't fall for your charms.'

She pointed at Harry who had hung back to watch the show and pretended to be interested in a table lamp. 'Does he belong to you?'

I suppressed a smirk. Harry stepped forward and shook Melanie's hand.

'I'm Harry Fletcher. We're here to do the house clearance for you.'

'House clearance? Oh, yes, I forgot…'

'Your parents told me they had already removed the items they wanted to keep. Do you want to save anything for yourself?' said Harry. 'Just let me know and we can put them aside.'

Melanie looked around her and shrugged.

'Take it all. I like modern furniture, not all this old junk. It's not my taste at all.'

'Okay, so we'll get on with it, if it's alright with you?'

'Sure.'

I recovered enough to remember my manners, and I knew Roz would kill me if I failed to include her in this amazing reappearance.

'Um, I know it's been an age since we were at school together, but if you'd like a coffee sometime to talk about the old days?'

Melanie raised an eyebrow.

'Seriously? Those old days?' She sniffed, but then her eyes lit up. 'Actually, that would be nice. Can you rustle up some people from school?'

'I often meet with Ghita Chowdhury and Roz Murray, who used to be Roz Taylor. And there's Joy Wells who runs the local pub. I think she was in your year.'

'That would be great.'

Melanie handed me a business card.

'Call me and let me know where and when, and I'll pop into town.'

I rummaged in my handbag for one of my own cards, but Melanie had gone, taking Greg, and leaving a waft of expensive perfume behind her. Chanel Number 5, I think.

'The socials seem to be over,' said Harry. 'Let's get started, not that there's much left in here. I've got some labels. Can you use them to identify anything that's worth more than a few quid, and I'll start putting things in the van? Oh, if you want anything particular, can you let me know and I'll put it in last?'

I nodded, struck speechless by my amazement at seeing Melanie after such a long time. *What would the girls make of it?* Roz would have a field day, and Ghita would try to find something nice to say about her.

I refocussed and worked my way methodically around the room, lifting dust covers and peering into the gloom underneath them. The Conrads had obviously abandoned most of the remaining pieces of furniture without a thought when they moved out. Perhaps their new house did not have enough room for so many chairs and side tables. A lot of them were what I thought of as dark brown furniture, late-Victorian pieces with beef-gravy coloured varnish which were deeply unfashionable, and no better than firewood in most cases. I put a label on a cute pair of Art Nouveau stools which had been overlooked in the drawing room, before heading up the stairs. The bannisters were made of highly polished wood and I thought I could remember sliding down them once, perhaps at a birthday party. For a moment, I was tempted to try them out, but Harry had hurried ahead of me, all business, so I refrained.

The second floor yielded little of interest either. Two acceptable standard lamps which would need rewiring, and a heavy trousseau box with oak carving. I spotted a small staircase leading up to the loft, but hovered uncertainly until Harry turned up.

'Do you think there's anything up there?' I said.

'Highly unlikely,' said Harry. 'But as you said earlier, furniture goes out of fashion, and the Conrads seem to be snobs, so you never know.'

Harry climbed the steep staircase, which protested with loud creaks, and tried the door.

'It's locked,' he said, jiggling the handle.

'There's a key hanging on a hook down here. Why don't you try it in the door?'

I removed the key and handed it upwards to Harry. He inserted the key into the lock, which opened with a click, and the door swung open to reveal a narrow passageway with further doors leading off it. It was like stepping into a walk-in freezer, and I could feel the hairs on my arms stand up in protest. I followed my breath into the first door on the right and gasped in surprise. They had not touched the room in years. An attractive iron-framed bed stood in the centre, with pristine linen still folded around the mattress, which sagged in the centre. Some long dead flowers stood stark and dry in a water-stained glass vase, and a thick layer of dust covered everything.

'Blimey, it's like a scene from a horror film.'

'Flowers in the attic,' I said. 'Creepy.'

Harry opened the opposite door and his eyebrows flew up.

'Take a butcher's in here,' he said. 'Is this the sort of thing you're interested in?'

My eyes widened as I stepped through the door. I stared at the treasure trove of Art Deco pieces piled up under the eaves of the long room, which seemed to run to the end of the roof.

'Wow,' I said. 'Jackpot.'

Chapter 5

Ghita picked at the chocolate curls on the cake she had brought for our meet up with Melanie Conrad. She licked her fingers with an expression of bliss.

'Yum. This is gorgeous. I don't know how they make it for the price.'

'Don't do that. What if she notices?' I said, moving the cake across the table and out of Ghita's reach.

Ghita pouted and Roz sighed.

'You'd think the Queen was coming to tea. It's Melanie Conrad. No one ever invited her to their parties when we went to school with her.'

'Do you remember why?' I said.

'She sat at the front of the class and sucked up to the teachers. But then I did too,' said Ghita.

'That's because you're as blind as a mole,' said Roz. 'She did it because she thought her poo didn't smell.'

'Don't be catty. Give the woman a chance. We've all changed a lot since school,' I said.

Roz sniffed.

'You've had too much therapy. It's made you soft,' she said.

'Do you mean nice?' I said.

'No.'

'She's here,' hissed Ghita.

Melanie entered the shop wearing large sunglasses with her coat collar up, a picture of elegance and style.

She came straight to me and air kissed me on both cheeks.

'Your shop is adorable,' she said, removing her sunglasses and looking around.

'Thanks. Would you like a tour? And we can hang your coat up while we're about it,' I said. 'It's quite warm in here with the heater on.'

We headed for the back of the shop. Melanie went upstairs to peep at the other floors while I hung up her coat. Roz elbowed Ghita.

'Did you see those sunglasses? Who does she think she is? Jackie O'?'

'Maybe she doesn't want anyone to recognise her.'

Roz grunted.

'And why would she do that?'

'Everyone's got secrets,' said Ghita.

'Even you?' said Roz.

Ghita looked away. Mel returned, and I took her arm, leading her over to the girls, saving Ghita from having to reply.

'You girls remember Mel, don't you?' I said.

'Of course. Welcome home,' said Ghita.

'How could we forget?' said Roz, but she smiled.

We were seated around an Art Deco table gleaned from the hoard I had acquired in the attic room of the Conrad house. I waited for Mel to recognise it, but she only ran her finger across the top as if checking for dust. She settled into her seat, scanning the jumble of furniture on the ground floor with a jaundiced eye, until she spotted a lacquered chinoiserie box.

'Oh, that's lovely,' she said, reaching out and opening it.

I held out my hand, and she gave it to me.

'It's got a secret compartment, right here at the bottom,' I said, pressing the release.

'How fantastic! May I buy it?' said Mel.

'Take it home with you and I'll look up the price later.'

'Thank you. It's gorgeous.'

'Are you back for good?' said Ghita, pouring us cups of tea and coffee.

'It depends,' Mel said, flicking her hair back.

'On what?' said Roz.

'Oh, you know.'

Roz looked as if she might reply that she wasn't psychic. A common retort of hers. I frowned at her and shook my head.

'Your parents must be thrilled,' said Ghita.

Mel smirked.

'Oh, I wouldn't say that. Not everyone's pleased to see me. I've got some loose ends to tie up from my past.'

'Are they social issues? Roz knows everything about everybody,' said Ghita.

'I doubt she knows anything about me.'

'True, but it wouldn't take me long. I'm like a bloodhound. Just point me in the right direction,' said Roz.

'If I get stuck, I may well do that,' said Mel.

Roz grunted. I knew she felt rejected. She would go out to sea with her husband Ed and sulk until she recovered. I knew my friend's coping mechanisms well.

'What's your plan?' I said.

'I need to sort out my relationship with my parents first. Some of my ideas have gone down like a lead balloon.' She looked around at the shop, wrinkling her nose. 'I'm not sure my next one will go down well either.'

'What's that?'

'Why don't you convert the front room of the first floor of the shop into a café? People could sit around and chat amongst your stock. It would defray your costs and showpiece your best bits.'

I frowned.

'Speaking of lead balloons. That is one that won't take off either,' said Roz.

'I think it's a good idea,' said Ghita. 'There isn't another café for miles now that the Italians have retired and gone home to Rome.'

'It seems like a massive amount of extra work for bugger all income.' I said. 'Don't I need a licence?'

'Not for tea and coffee,' said Ghita. 'I can check the requirements at the council standards office tomorrow if you want me to.'

'Actually, I think Mel is right,' said Roz. 'It will give clients a chance to try out your wares. And we'd have a legitimate excuse for hanging around here all the time if we helped in the café.'

Mel beamed.

'Thanks, Roz,' she said. 'That means a lot coming from you.'

The shop bell jangled as Joy Wells burst in, panting with exertion. As usual, she wore one of her 1950s style dresses with a pinched-in waist and tight bodice. I always wondered why she chose that era, but she had the figure for it.

'Ladies, sorry I'm late. Ryan had a problem with his wheelchair and it took ages to work out what was wrong. I couldn't leave him immobile and alone.'

'Joy, this is Mel. Do you remember each other from school?'

'Nice to meet you, Mel. I'm getting a feeling of déjà vu, but I can't place you,' said Joy.

'Do you want a coffee, Joy?' said Ghita.

'No, I just stopped by for a moment to meet Mel. I have to buy some spares for the wheelchair. I hope we'll see you at the Shanty for a drink sometime, Mel. We're always there.'

'That would be nice. Once I get settled in, I'll definitely visit you.'

Joy left again, and Ghita refilled our cups.

'Anyone need more cake?' she said.

'I don't think anyone actually needs cake,' said Roz. 'But yes, please.'

'Don't you find it hard to stay so slim?' said Mel. 'I find it a constant battle as I get older.'

'You could join the Fat Fighters,' said Ghita.

'The fat fighters? Are they some sort of plump vigilante group?' said Mel.

Roz guffawed, and Ghita looked crestfallen.

'It's my club,' she said. 'For losing weight, or keeping it off. We do exercise classes and talk about diets. I guess it sounds silly.'

'Not at all,' said Mel. 'I was only joking. I'm crass sometimes. It sounds like fun. Maybe I could come along. I'm keen to restart my life here.'

'And why did you come back after being away for so long?' I said.

'Our old housekeeper wrote to me and told me she was worried about my father's health. My parents had never met Greg, so I decided it was high time to mend my bridges. I wanted to see my father before he died, and I needed to sort out some family stuff.'

'It must have surprised them when you turned up.'

'Shocked, in the case of Fiona. My father suffers from mild dementia and didn't seem to realise I'd been away at all. He is happy to see me, though.'

'Where will you live?' I said. 'The house can't be habitable in its present state.'

'I'm staying at a local B&B for now. Eventually, I want to get some workmen in to sort out the house and open it up again. The garden has gone to seed, so I'd like to trace the gardener, Ronnie Barratt if I could. There are some exotic plants mixed in with the dross and he's the only one who can identify them.'

'Would he still be alive?' said Roz. 'You've been gone for a while.'

Colour rose in Mel's cheeks.

'Oh, yes, he wasn't much older than me.'

I noticed the pink hue, but didn't draw attention to it. Everyone is entitled to their secrets.

'Where's the B&B?' I said.

'In the old part of town, near the station, but I'm keeping the location under wraps for now. There are complications with coming home.'

'Hence the cloak and dagger appearance?' said Roz.

'Just the cloak,' said Mel. 'I'd hate to think daggers might be involved, although…'

'Although?' said Roz.

'Nothing. Life always chucks in a googly now and then,' said Mel.

Ghita's face lit up.

'Do you like cricket?' she said.

'Cricket? No. Why?'

The light extinguished as quickly as it had appeared.

'Oh, it's just that googly is a type of unexpected ball bowled in cricket. I thought maybe—'

'Don't be ridiculous, Ghita. No one likes cricket anymore,' said Roz.

'I do,' I said. 'I used to go with my father to watch the local club, although I mostly remember the match teas. Yum.'

'My husband, Greg, uses the term. I must have picked it up from him,' said Mel. 'He's posh.'

'I didn't realise you were married until I met him at Conrad House. Is Greg staying at the B&B with you?' I said.

'No, he, um, well.'

'It's complicated?'

'Exactly,' said Mel.

Chapter 6

The Fat Fighters Club qualified as an institution in Seacastle, having been open for ten years. For all of this time, Ghita had cajoled and encouraged the plump women of the town to exercise and eat healthy food with none of us losing so much as an ounce. Truth be told, we treated it more like a social club, and it had proved a lifesaver for me when the axe fell on my marriage. Ghita should have studied to be a counsellor rather than a town councillor. Her combination of tough love, and a soft shoulder to cry on, had healed many wounds among us middle-aged women, some casualties of the menopause and others, like me, of horrid divorces. Don't get me wrong, we partook in yoga, fight fit and Pilates classes and every other exercise fad going, but we couldn't resist the post-class coffee and cake to discuss the local gossip or our personal woes. Ghita sometimes cooked a curry for us, a massive treat. She really could cook up a storm.

The core group of attendees were Ghita, me, Roz, Joy, Grace Wong (from my competition on the high street), Flo Barrington (a forensic expert) and several other members of the local council who worked with Ghita. A selection of other ladies drifted in and out of our circle, either moving away or too busy to attend often. We always welcomed new members with enthusiasm, but the core group never varied. All of us had been with Ghita from the start. She never talked much about her personal life, but she suffered from negative family perceptions about her unmarried state. They constantly hatched plans to marry her off, but somehow, she had always avoided it. I planned to sit down with her and find out more, but life always seemed to get in the way.

After a relatively gentle hour of Pilates, Roz, Ghita, and Joy came to the Grotty Hovel for coffee. None of the women had visited my new abode before, because of reluctance on my part. I am not good at being the object of sympathy or even empathy, and I dreaded them pretending my terraced house compared to my marital home with George. Silly, I know, but there you are. I needn't have worried. Genuine cries of surprise and warmth greeted my cosy sitting room and back kitchen.

'It's so you,' said Ghita.

'I never knew why I didn't like your old house until I saw this,' said Joy.

'It had George in it,' said Roz, a wicked grin on her face.

I loved my friends.

'Have you thought more about opening your own café?' said Joy? 'It's such a great idea.'

'We all think it's a banger,' said Roz. 'Tanya's just being stubborn as usual.'

'I've met mules who couldn't compete with her,' said Ghita.

I sighed.

'But how will I run it as well as the shop?'

'If you built it, they will come,' said Roz, which made little sense, but everyone nodded sagely.

I gave up resisting the idea, and despite my reservations, I wasted no time before converting the front room at the top of Second Home. It took a backbreaking amount of work, when added to the refurbishments I had started on my terraced house. My savings were dwindling, despite the bargain prices of the new stock I had found with Harry. Increased footfall would increase sales and give me a chance of breaking even. I had an almost limitless selection of tables and chairs from different vintages to pick from. It seemed logical to group the vintages and materials so that a Habitat pine table from the late 1960s had spindle chairs around it and vintage Danish leather chairs surrounded a 1970s tiled table. I even had a 1950s Formica table with four scruffy Antelope chairs in one corner. Roz searched Gumtree for a second-hand, commercial coffee machine and found one the previous owner claimed to be in great working order.

'If I ever figure out how to make it work,' I said, prodding it with a cautious finger.

Ghita had scoured the charity shops and came back with an eclectic mix of cups and saucers.

'Aren't these adorable?' she said, washing them up in the sink. 'I only bought cups without chips on them, so complete sets were out of the question.'

'What will you call the café?' said Roz.

'How about The Home from Home?' said Ghita.

'Far too twee,' said Roz.

'Not bad,' I said. 'But how about the Vintage Café?'

'Or just The Vintage?' said Roz.

'I like it. Fancy a coffee at The Vintage? Yes, it's got a good ring to it,' said Ghita.

'The Vintage it is, then.'

News about the opening of a new café spread like wildfire in the under-served high street. Not even Roz's networking could compete with the power of word of mouth for spreading the news. The first visitors to the café were the other members of the Fat Fighters club. The women oohed and aahed as they looked around the room, taking in the dazzling mixture of styles and eras. Ghita had painted the room in a deep burgundy red and the sultry feel encouraged the exchange of confidences around the style islands. Even Mel made an appearance, although she soon left for 'an appointment that couldn't be broken'. She had been quite helpful in the café's design and had formed a bond with our threesome despite Roz's barely concealed hostility. I had grown quite fond of her, despite her prickly nature. A bit like Hades, I suppose.

I had given up trying to get the coffee machine to work, and instead made pots of filter coffee as a stopgap until I could find a technician. Nobody seemed to care, especially as the selection of cakes took most of the attention away from the beverages.

'I really shouldn't,' said Joy, as she savoured a piece of coffee-walnut cake. 'You'd better pack me a piece for Ryan in case he finds a crumb on my clothes. Sherlock Holmes has nothing on him when it comes to covert cake eating.'

'It's hard to resist,' said Grace Wong, who'd popped along from the Asian Antique Emporium, which she ran with her husband Max, to see what all the fuss was about. 'You'd better sign me up for another package of classes, Ghita, or I won't be able to fit my summer clothes.'

'My evil plan is working,' said Ghita, rubbing her hands together. 'More cake, more classes, Bwuhahahaha.'

'Who needs summer clothes when you've got cake?' said Flo Barrington, the forensic scientist, pulling at her waistband. She had known me all of my married life and was one of the few shared friends who hadn't abandoned me after George left.

While Ghita and Roz gossiped and refilled customers' cups upstairs, I sat at the desk downstairs directing people to the café or showing potential customers my stock. Roz rang up another order on the cash register and called me on WhatsApp to beam at me and give me a thumbs up. I felt discombobulated with the early success of my new venture. I suspected that once the cost of the cakes, beverages and extra electricity were considered, I would not see much of a profit, but at least people were coming into the shop. Many of them had never frequented a vintage shop before and had biased opinions about second-hand goods. Perhaps a sugar rush would give them rose-coloured glasses. I had hung the most beautiful of my lamps and decorative items around the café, in case they tempted anyone to buy them.

The day flew by. I looked at my watch and wondered if I should shut up the shop. The telephone rang when I was about to wander upstairs to catch the tail end of the gossip, making me jump. I picked up the receiver and put it against my ear.

'Tanya? Is that you?'

'Harry? Is something wrong?'

'I'm sorry to be the bearer of bad tidings, but it's your friend, Mel. She's had an accident.'

'An accident? Oh, no, that's awful. What happened? Has she gone to the hospital?'

'I'm afraid she's dead. They found her at Conrad House. They're saying she fell down the stairs.'

My hand flew to my mouth, stifling a shout of fright.

'Are you sure? Who told you?'

'I drove by Conrad House and noticed the ambulance turning up the driveway with its siren going. I followed it up to the house and asked a policeman I found outside the house what had happened.'

'Thanks for calling me. I'd better tell Flo, the forensic pathologist. She's upstairs in the café, but they'll need her to examine the body before it's moved.'

I replaced the handset and freed the latch on the shop door. Then I ran up the stairs and met Flo coming down, shoving her phone into her handbag.

'So, you heard then?' I said.

'Seems like Mel Conrad has had an accident at the old House. Terrible business.'

'Horrible. Come back soon. It was great to see you.'

'I will, I promise.'

After Flo left, I descended the stairs again and sat at the desk, doodling on a piece of paper in my agitation. When I realised I had drawn a staircase, I dropped my pen in horror. How could this be an accident? It made little sense. It wasn't as if Mel had mobility issues. Did young healthy people really fall down stairs? People who had turned up out of the blue and interrupted other people's plans? I couldn't believe it. The first thing to do would be to find out what George thought. He might be my ex-husband, but we had to talk sometime. A light knock on the door alerted me to Flo's presence outside. She carried her heavy evidence case in front of her in both arms, and panted, struggling to get any words out.

'Flo? What's wrong?'

'I got to my car and found it had a flat tyre. There's no way I can change it myself, and I really don't have time to wait for the breakdown guys. Can you drive me to the Conrads' house? I know it's an imposition.'

'Not at all. Give me a second to warn Roz and Ghita, and I'll be right there.'

The women were not only shocked but also agog, and not a little jealous of my mercy mission to take Flo to the scene of the crime.

'This could be right up your street,' said Roz.

'Maybe it will get your creative juices flowing again,' said Ghita.

'The woman is dead,' I said. 'It's not a movie.'

But my heart raced because of the excess adrenaline coursing through my bloodstream.

'Get out of here. We'll close up,' said Roz.

'But we demand all the details next time we're here,' said Ghita.

I put on my coat and jammed my beanie on my head before retrieving my handbag from behind the counter. Flo and I hurried to the side street to find my Mini. I carried the case of forensic equipment, as Flo had still not recovered her breath and I put it on the back seat. Flo forced her plump body into the front seat of the small vehicle with considerable effort. Her long black hair with its grey streaks had come loose from its habitual scrunchy and she looked like a frazzled witch.

'Let's go,' I said. 'Don't forget your belt.'

Flo tugged at the webbing and let it out through the adjuster before shoving it into the buckle. She breathed heavily, gasping a little, and seemed distressed.

'Are you alright?' I said.

'Yes, it's just that...'

She tailed off and rooted in her handbag for a tissue.

'Were you two friends?' I said. 'I'm sorry I didn't know. This must be very upsetting.'

'No, it's not that. I didn't even like her. But she asked me for help last week and I refused. This could be my fault.'

Chapter 7

Flo flashed her identification card at the young policeman who stood guard at the gate to Conrad House. I recognised him as PC Brennan of uniform. He nodded at her, then stared at me for an instant before his eyes lit up in recognition and he waved us through. There were two squad cars, an ambulance, and a Ford Granada which I recognised parked in front of the building. George's car. Not a surprise, considering he would be the primary choice as SIO (Senior Investigating Officer) for any major investigation in the town. Murder cases were uncommon in Seacastle, but they still came up a few times a year, and their frequency had increased. I had always enjoyed my non-official role as George's sounding board for complex cases like these. My career as an investigative journalist had given me a keen instinct for rooting out the truth. George might base his cases on evidence, but my ability to understand motives far outstripped his and he knew it.

I parked my Mini in a spot on the drive way unlikely to get blocked by any further arrivals. Then I helped Flo to get the evidence bag out of the back seat and carried it to the door for her. I peered through the front door at the activity within while one technician helped Flo to get into a jumpsuit and bundle her hair into a net. The padlock hasp which had dug into my shoulder on the last visit now hung loosely from the closed padlock after being levered off the frame. A white sheet, covering what I presumed to be Mel's body, lay at the bottom of the stairwell, but, with the area in shadow, I couldn't be sure. Someone tapped me on the shoulder. I turned around, expecting to see Flo wanting to enter, but found myself nose to nose with George Carter instead.

He frowned at me, but his eyes twinkled too, as if he had caught me doing something naughty.

'Hello,' I said. 'Fancy meeting you here.'

'I was about to say the same thing. Thanks for bringing Flo. We're trying to get the scene photographed and go over it with a fine-tooth comb to make sure we don't miss anything.'

'Are you sure it was an accident?' I said. 'Only it seems peculiar she should die so soon after returning to her childhood home. Maybe she stirred up old wounds.'

'Who told you we are calling it an accident? We haven't ruled anything out yet, hence the careful evidence gathering. What do you know about old wounds?'

'Nothing I can put my finger on, but Mel came to have coffee at the shop last week and she mentioned unsolved issues at home. We went to school together, you know. Who found the body?'

'The former housekeeper.' He examined his notebook. 'A Sarah Bingley. She says she had an appointment to see Mel, but she found the door padlocked, and looked through a side window to see if she could see anyone in the house. She noticed a shoe on the floor beside what looked like a foot, and that's when she called it in.'

'But if Mel fell down the stairs, who padlocked the door?' I said.

'We don't know yet, but we'll find out. Someone may have closed it by mistake, thinking no one was at home.'

'Do you need a statement from me?'

'Not if we treat her death as an accident. I'll let you know.'

'Which one's Sarah Bingley?'

'She's over there having a sweet tea to help with the shock.'

'Do you mind if I talk to her? Mel was fond of her, and I'm sure she'd like to know that.'

George raised an eyebrow.

'I wasn't born yesterday, and I know you pretty well by now. Don't interfere with my investigation.'

'I thought it was an accident.'

'And don't get cheeky with me. I can arrest you, now we're not married.'

I swallowed.

'I had noticed,' I said, and walked off to hide the tears that threatened to escape.

'Tan? I'm sorry.'

I kept walking, seething with resentment at his stupid joke and at my reaction to it. I headed for the woman perched on the step at the back of the ambulance. Sarah Bingley did not fit the archetype of the typical rosy cheeked housekeeper. Stick thin with lips pinched in permanent disapproval, she glared at me as I approached her.

'Ms Bingley? My name's Tanya Bowe. I'm a friend of Mel, or I was, anyway.'

'You were? She never talked about you to me.'

'I hadn't known her for long. She helped me to set up my café on the high street.'

Not technically a lie.

'That woman needed a friend. She had troubles in abundance.'

I cleared my throat.

'Do you think her death was an accident?' I said.

'No. But what difference does that make now that the Plod have leapt to a conclusion?'

'You're not the only one with doubts.'

'And what can you do about it?'

'The Senior Investigating Officer is my ex-husband.'

Sarah Bingley guffawed.

'A woman with influence in high places? Don't make me laugh.'

'Trust me, I can work this out, but I need somewhere to start. Can you tell me why you were meeting Mel?'

'We had business to discuss.'

'What sort of business?'

'Nothing that concerns you.'

'Can you think of anyone who would want to hurt Mel?'

'There is a long queue of suspects. Most of them were interested in her money.'

'How do I get the list?'

'If I were you, I'd go to the funeral. They'll all be there gloating, and you can take your pick, but personally I'd start with the husband. He's not all he seems, and they do say you start with the nearest and dearest, don't they?'

She had hit the nail on the head. Most murders were over domestic issues of some sort. Mafia hits and drug cartels were mostly confined to Netflix as motives. I thanked her and went to sit in the Mini, listening to Sigur Ros and waiting for Flo to finish. The orchestral music soothed me and slowed my heart rate to normal. The sound system had cost almost as much as my beloved second-hand car, but it was worth it. I made a list in my head of the people who might be involved in Mel's murder, but soon gave up from a lack of information. Sarah Bingley was right. The funeral would be the perfect place to question people without arousing suspicion.

I dozed off until Flo rapped on the window, waking me from a weird dream about Harry and a standard lamp.

'All ready?' I said. 'Find any clues?'

'You know I can't tell you that,' said Flo. 'Mind you—
'

'Mind me what?'

'Oh, nothing scientific. I just can't see how anyone would tip over a banister that's greater than waist height, no matter how awkwardly they fell.'

'So, you think someone pushed her?'

'I didn't say that, did I?'

'I spoke to the housekeeper who found the body.'

Flo's eyes widened.

'And what did she say?'

'She claimed they were supposed to meet at the house, but someone had padlocked the main door before she arrived.'

'How did she find the body?'

'She spotted it through a window.'

'She must have good eyesight. I needed arc lights for the crime scene photos, as there's no electricity supply to the house. Anyway, I'm starving. Let's get some fish and chips on the way home.'

'Remind me to save a piece for Hades. He'll be shredding the furniture in protest by now.'

'Who's Hades? He sounds like a devil,' she said, winking.

'Hilarious. Actually, he's a cat I adopted on a whim. He's difficult to get close to. So far, so wild.'

'Try Feliway. It's a plug-in thingy that is supposed to calm cats down.'

'I'll try fish first.'

Chapter 8

Despite Flo's suspicions, Mel's autopsy did not produce any evidence of foul play, and, several days later, the police released her body for burial. By that time, news of her death had percolated through the town and made headlines in the local newspaper. Roz and Ghita were in their element, and demanded several reruns of my mercy mission to Conrad House with Flo. Roz's over active imagination went into overdrive when she heard about the housekeeper's suspicions, but I did not want to become embroiled in Roz's conspiracy theories. Mel's untimely demise struck me as bad karma, but I found it hard to attribute it to sinister causes. After all, George had designated Mel's death as accidental and he was nearly always right, no matter how annoying I found it. Flo also seemed convinced by the results of the autopsy.

'She's gone. We need to move on,' Flo said, when asked.

I wanted to, despite my intuition and Roz, insinuating that something wasn't right. My illness had destroyed my confidence in my ability to spot an anomaly, and I still fought to recover it. I knew I should let sleeping dogs lie, but this one kept leaping to his feet and barking.

Unable to decide either way, I confided my doubts to Harry over a coffee upstairs in the Vintage. He had quickly become a favourite at the shop, treating everyone with the same mixture of kindness and humour. I fancied him like mad, but his status as a recent widower made me cautious. Also, I badly needed a male friend to restore my faith after George had wounded me deeply by his desertion. I had always assumed we'd muddle through and grow old together, but George had other ideas.

'Do you think Mel's death was an accident?' I said. 'The police have released Mel's body and shut the case, but from what we witnessed, I'm not convinced.'

He rubbed his chin.

'Falling down the stairs happens mostly to old people and drunks. Was Mel a drunk?'

'I don't know. I never smelled booze on her breath.'

'It just doesn't ring true to me. Turning up after all those years away must have upset the apple cart as regards people's plans for the Conrad fortune. That Fiona woman didn't seem pleased to see her for a start.'

'And what about her husband? George always said they concentrated on the nearest and dearest first.'

'I thought he seemed too interested in Fiona. I don't care what the police say about an accident. It doesn't sit right somehow,' he said. 'Mel was in line to inherit a fortune, and it's just too convenient her dying like that. Also, what about her not letting people know where she was staying? It makes little sense. Surely, she should have been excited to be back and telling people where to find her so they could catch up? She had secrets, big ones. Maybe someone wanted them to stay hidden.'

'Maybe they did,' I said. 'Who inherits if Mel is dead? Her husband seems like the obvious candidate, or maybe her mother, as her father is still alive. William is not long for this world. Maybe Fiona Conrad needed Mel out of the way so she could inherit instead?'

'Why would a mother kill her daughter, though? It seems unlikely.'

He had a point. We needed more information. If Mel had been murdered, we had to search for suspects and motives. A frisson of excitement coursed up my spine.

'The Conrads have set a date for the funeral,' I said. 'Will you come with me and ask some discreet questions? We might root out some of those secrets.'

Harry did not answer for a moment, and I crossed my fingers. Finally, he said, 'I'm not keen on funerals, but I'll make an exception in this case.'

'Me either, but Mel's death seems too well timed to be a coincidence. I want to put my doubts to rest, or if not, find evidence we can follow to work out what really happened.'

'The wake is definitely the most likely place to find all the suspects in one place.'

'And, if we're lucky, some of them may down too many sherries and be indiscreet.'

'I'll meet you at Conrad House after the service, if that's okay. I don't do religion any more. Not since my Cathy…'

'Perfect. I doubt you'll be missing much. The vicar never met Mel, so she'll just mutter some flannel about Mel being loved by everyone and kind to animals.'

Harry chuckled.

'You're a caution,' he said. 'I've got to go back to work.'

Ghita and Roz had a field day when I told them I'd be attending Mel's wake with Harry.

'First date at a murder scene, and second date at a funeral. It's very Addams Family, isn't it?' said Roz.

'It is not a date,' I said. 'We're investigating Mel's death.'

'Never mind the circumstances. What are you going to wear?' said Ghita.

'Aren't you two coming?' I said. 'Maybe you could do some sleuthing too.'

'I can't,' said Roz. 'Ed's a crewman short, so I'll be marooned on the high seas.'

Roz often accompanied her husband in his small fishing boat. She pretended to hate it, but her eyes always shone after a day out at sea with him. I took her complaints with a large pinch of salt.

'Me neither,' said Ghita. 'I've got a distant cousin's wedding in Birmingham. All my relatives can have a go at me for not being married yet.'

'It's not compulsory,' said Roz. 'Only dying is unavoidable.'

'You're obviously not a Hindu,' said Ghita. 'We have to get married. It's our sacred duty.'

'It will be fun,' I said. 'More fun than a funeral anyway.'

'I doubt it.'

When the date of the funeral came around, I put on a black shift dress and a red coat with a pair of black knee-length boots.

'What do you think, Hades? Too much with the red coat? I know it's not a fashion show, but Mel would appreciate the flash of colour.'

Hades glared at me from inside the Lloyd Loom basket. I had half filled it with old blankets to enable him to jump in and out of it easily, after he had turned up his nose at the expensive bed I bought for him online. He still spat at me when I tried to stroke him, fury clouding his green eyes. He had even turned his nose up at the battered cod I brought him. *A cat who won't eat fish? He's just bloody minded, and two can play at that game.*

'Mind the house for me, pussycat.'

I smiled as I shut the door of the house as I imagined the poor burglar who tried to invade Hades' space. *Better than a Doberman.*

As predicted, the church service drowned in platitudes, and the real Mel remained veiled to the grave. I made a mental list of the people I needed to talk to later, at the wake in Conrad House. I recognised Fiona Conrad and Mrs Bingley, and Greg Summers sitting stone faced at the front of the church. The old man sitting beside Fiona, and looking frail and devastated, must be William Conrad.

The only person who seemed affected by the service sat at the far end of a pew at the back of the church. Fresh tears stained his face, and his eyes showed the damage associated with prolonged crying, being red rimmed and puffy. When the coffin rolled into the curtained off area containing the crematorium, he almost tripped over in his haste to leave the church. I got the impression he hadn't wanted anyone to see him, but perhaps he just didn't want to watch her body leave the planet.

The local press had arrived and took photographs of everyone leaving the church. I recognised the photographer and shuffled to her side, kissing her hello.

'What a sad business,' she said, tucking a wisp of hair behind her ear. 'How well did you know Mel Conrad?'

'We went to school together. I'm thinking of writing an article about her. I wondered if you might let me have copies of these photos.'

'You're working again? No one told me. That's fantastic. I can send them to your Dropbox.'

I tried not to panic. *What on earth was a Dropbox?*

'Um, that would be great. I need to check if it's still available,' I said.

She smiled and handed me a card with the name Jasmine Smith on it. It didn't ring a bell, but I had thousands of contacts before I lost my job.

'Just let me know which email you are using and I'll upload them for you,' she said.

Someone would know what this meant. I tried to smile, and she walked away, camera to her face.

Harry had already arrived at Conrad House when I got to the wake in a convoy of vehicles. He made a face at me over the shoulder of Mel's husband, who dabbed his tearless eyes with his handkerchief. I gave Harry a discreet thumbs up and headed for the distressed man I had spotted at the funeral. He had ensconced himself on a window seat overlooking the rose garden, and appeared deep in contemplation of the still bare bushes. When I approached him, he glanced around, his body tensed for flight. I put a hand on his forearm.

'Don't go,' I said. 'I'm Tanya, a friend of Mel's. I don't think we've met.'

'Mel didn't have any friends,' he said, sniffing and rummaging through his pockets for a tissue. I took a packet from my handbag and offered one to him.

'Thanks,' he said. 'Imagine coming to a funeral without a tissue, and crying a river. You must think I'm an idiot.'

'Far from it. You're the only person who seems genuinely affected by Mel's funeral. What's your name?'

'It's Ronnie Barratt.'

'Nice to meet you. How did you know our girl?'

Ronnie lifted his head, and a faint smile ghosted across his face.

'My girl. Mel was mine. Well, for a while anyway. Then she disappeared. I hadn't seen her in twenty years until—'

'You came!' said Fiona Conrad, pushing her way through the mourners. She grabbed me in a tight hug, her cloying perfume almost suffocating me. *Had she spilt the bottle on her black Chanel suit?* I shrugged at Ronnie who shot Fiona a look of pure hatred, and stalked away, getting lost among the other mourners.

'I had to,' I said. 'Mel meant a lot to me. How do you know Ronnie? Did you meet him while he and Mel were going out?'

Fiona's eyebrows shot up and an expression of disbelief crossed her face.

'Ronnie with Mel? Who told you that? He used to be the gardener at Conrad House years ago, when she was a teenager. That's the full extent of his contact with her.'

Was it possible she didn't know about them? Fiona's face showed no trace of guile, but neither had any sign of grief marred the perfectly applied mascara or the outlined trout pout. *How old was she?* Even without the enhancements, she appeared far too young to have a daughter that age.

'I'm so sorry for your loss,' I said. 'It must be doubly hard having only got your daughter back after being parted for so long.'

Fiona's eyes narrowed.

'She isn't my daughter. Not that it's any of your business. I'm William's second wife.'

I slapped my forehead. How could I have forgotten something so obvious?

'Forgive me. No wonder you look so young.'

Fiona smirked.

'Diane died when Mel was four. I married William soon afterwards. I'm younger than him but we've all got to make an effort dear, to keep our men on side.'

'And when did Mel marry Greg?'

'Greg? That loser? They were getting divorced. I got the impression she couldn't stand him.'

She walked off, leaving me mystified by her hot and cold moods. I felt a gentle pinch on my arm, and Harry materialised at my side.

'Did you rub Mrs Conrad up the wrong way? She had a face like thunder when she left you.'

'That woman is impossible to fathom. What's Mel's husband like? Fiona seemed to think they were heading for a breakup,' I said.

'His heart seems intact. He's more intent on sourcing tickets for the Ashes than mourning his wife.'

'Curiouser and curiouser. I'm going to speak to William Conrad. He looks broken by the whole thing.'

'Don't look now, but Fiona is already speaking to William. There's something funny about their body language. If you eavesdrop, you might pick up some interesting titbits.'

'Fiona's face is a picture. Have you seen her expression?'

'The whole family dynamic is completely screwed up. Do you still think Mel fell down the stairs by accident?'

'The odds are getting longer.'

Chapter 9

When I got home, I slumped onto the sofa with a glass of Merlot. My cravings for a cigarette had increased exponentially with the stress of Mel Conrad's wake. It qualified as one of the most unpleasant experiences of my life. If it hadn't been for Harry, I would have gone home after my run-in with Fiona Conrad. What a nasty, grasping woman! There was no love lost between her and Mel, but could that have been sufficient motive for murder? Ah, yes, murder, she wrote. I had been steadfast in ignoring my internal voice shouting itself hoarse at me over the past few days, but now my conviction had crumbled. George normally excelled at sniffing out a murder, but the distraction of having a new and nubile girlfriend may have scrambled his circuits. He had got it wrong for once. Mel's death couldn't be an accident.

I wondered if my circuits were any better. Fighting my way through a clinical depression had changed me in fundamental ways, affecting my ability to laser focus on a problem without losing interest. Self-sabotage, I guess. Could I still track down a killer? It couldn't be that different to investigating frauds, and scams, and corrupt politicians. George had access to forensics, but I had my nose for foibles. People couldn't help giving themselves away. Men were prone to flattery, women to sympathy, everyone liked praise, deserved or not. I would model myself on an old-fashioned sleuth, like Poirot without the moustache, and discover who killed Mel. Whatever she did, she didn't deserve to die, and I didn't intend to let her fade away without a fight.

First, I needed a cup of tea and one of my trusty notebooks. I had a gorgeous one my sister Helen had given me for Christmas. She didn't qualify as a great sister most of the time, but her taste was impeccable. The purple notebook had an embossed design of raised flowers in delicate colours. I would write my notes in that one, ignoring the fact I had an entire stock of similar notebooks on my bookshelf, unsullied by a single written word. A classy notebook always intimidated me. In the past, I used to worry whether I had anything brilliant enough to write within the sacred pages. Now, I was just a washed-up journalist with a pile of empty notebooks whose corners were curling up with age. It was time to lose the fear of polluting the pages, and stop wasting time. Who knows? I could even dare to cross things out.

I started with the basics. In order to murder someone, you've got to have had a powerful motive. Nobody kills someone because they forgot to lower the toilet seat or because they finished the milk and didn't buy more. Well, nobody normal anyway. I assumed that somebody with a powerful motive killed Mel. And what were the motives of the average person? I put world domination to one side as there wasn't much call for that in Seacastle. Desperate people acted for reasons of hate, jealousy, greed, avarice, and revenge. How had Mel aroused such passions in such a short time? Why had the murderer chosen that time to kill her? Had she reawakened feelings from the past?

I had no answers to those questions, because as I sat down to make a list of potential suspects, I heard a thump upstairs, which made the hairs on my arms stand on end. My first instinct was to glance over at the Lloyd Loom cat basket, but Hade's black form lay snuggled in a blanket, his chest rising and falling as his paws unsheathed for a kill in his dream. I crept to the bottom of the stairs and stood there holding my breath while I listened for more sounds, but nothing disturbed the heavy silence. I grabbed a walking stick with a knobbly head from the stand beside the front door and ascended the stairs, avoiding the one with the creaky floorboard. The noise had come from the tiny spare room. Perhaps something had fallen off a wall.

I wasn't great at DIY. I had been plotting an ambush in order to get Harry to come and fix some things in my house, in exchange for tea and biscuits. Hades liked Harry and would sit on his lap, purring like an engine. Traitor! Harry would know what to do with an intruder. He wouldn't talk about his days in the army, but he'd been around. I hadn't pressed him about his life yet. I had plenty of time and his defences would drop eventually.

Another sound came from the spare room. Light leaked out under the door. I found myself unafraid, just annoyed. I lifted the stick, knob upwards, and pushed open the door.

Chapter 10

The next morning, I went downstairs and put on a kettle, closely followed by Mouse who stumbled after me and collapsed into one of the kitchen chairs, his mop of black curly hair resembling a ball of wool after a cat had attacked it. He gazed at me through his blue eyes, wary, reminding me of Hades.

'Are you hungry?' I said, as if a teenage boy is ever going to reply negatively to this question. 'I can do us a fry up if you like.'

This had a magical effect. A big grin appeared on his face.

'Yes, please. I could eat a horse.'

'I can offer you bacon and eggs with a side of fried bread. Why don't you make us a pot of tea?'

'Me?'

I pretended to look around the kitchen.

'I guess so. There doesn't seem to be anyone else here.'

Mouse dragged his tall, slim frame around the kitchen touching things like a blind man, until I took pity on him and gave him a tour, showing him the cupboard for the tea and coffee, another where I kept the crockery and lastly the kitchen drawer which contained the cutlery.

'You know you have to warm the teapot?'

'Of course. Do I look stupid?'

I ignored the rudeness and flipped the bacon. The delicious smell made us forget our tiff and dream of breakfast. Soon we were sitting at the little Formica table digging into our meals and slurping out tea. I waited until Mouse sat back and rubbed his stomach before I asked him questions. I'm a believer in food being the fastest way to a man's heart, even a lost teenage basket case like Mouse.

I should explain that Mouse and I were not strangers. My ex-husband, George, had contracted a short-lived shotgun marriage in his teens after getting his girlfriend pregnant. Mouse, whose real name was Andrew Carter, was the product of their union. George had left shortly after the birth of the baby, but had always paid child support, even if the mother wouldn't let him be involved in Mouse's life. She had died a couple of years back from breast cancer, and Mouse had fended for himself, refusing all offers of help. He despised George and tolerated me, and had ended up in a few scrapes with the law. He hot-wired cars for fun with some friends, until he ended up in the cells one night. I don't know what George said, or did, to him, but he never did it again.

Mouse had to go to computer studies classes as part of the plea bargain to avoid jail time and had found his true calling in the coding class. His wizard-like abilities at the keyboard had led to his nickname of Mouse, a nickname that spread to all the people who knew him, except his father, who insisted on calling him Andy, not something that helped their already fraught relationship.

The man who ran the computer courses told George that Mouse had the talent to become a top-class hacker. I don't really know what that means. I'm a bit of a Luddite myself. I still have a Nokia phone which exposes me to ridicule among my friends, but I don't see the point of having a smart phone. What for? So hacking is something outside my comfort zone. I have an old computer from my days as a journalist, but it needs replacing and I'm not comfortable with modern technology. Even as I mulled on this, I knew I needed to do something about my terrible ignorance. The world had moved on, and I had to catch up.

'What's the code for your Wi-Fi?' said Mouse, fiddling with his smart phone.

'Um, I haven't got internet yet. I only moved in a few weeks ago.'

'A few weeks ago? And you haven't got internet connected yet?'

His eyebrows almost met as he stared at me in disbelief.

'Well, you know. I got divorced from your father, my friend died, and so on. It's been a trying time. Anyway, that's not important right now. May I ask what you are doing here? I don't remember inviting you to stay, and breaking and entering is still a crime, isn't it? I could give your father a call and find out if you are unsure.'

I made the mistake of taking out my Nokia.

Mouse's eyes opened wide, and he guffawed.

'What is that?' he said. 'Are you from the Stone Age?'

A gurgle started in his throat, and he got an attack of the giggles that spread to me. I couldn't stop. *How could I be cross with this orphan?* George had abandoned us both. I had a spare room, and I needed to learn how to re-join the modern world. Maybe karma was good and bad.

'You can stay for now,' I said. 'But you'll have to pay rent.'

His face fell.

'Not that sort of rent. I need a teacher. I've fallen off the world, and I want to get back on. And somebody murdered my friend Mel. I'm sure of it, but the police say it's an accident. I have to have access to the internet if I'm going to solve this case. What do you say?'

He rubbed his chin in a droll manner.

'A murder, Holmes? Where do we start?'

'I don't know. That's why I'm asking you. And I'm Sherlock, you're Holmes, or you could be. There must be a million things we can do on a computer these days, and I don't know how to do any of them.'

Mouse rubbed his hands together.

'We'd better get started then. I heard you opened a café at Second Home. Can we use the internet there instead, for now?'

My face fell.

'I haven't got internet there either.'

Mouse shook his head.

'Oh, my stars, it's worse than I thought. You can't have a café without internet. No one will come.'

'It's been full so far,' I said.

'That's novelty value. They'll come for the cake, but they stay for the internet. You'll get writers and consultants sitting up there with their laptops and drinking lattes.'

'That's another thing to put on your list,' I said, trying not to laugh. 'My coffee machine doesn't work yet and I don't know if it has broken down or we are just too dumb to make it function.'

'Let's make a list,' he said. 'Your phone is crap, so we need to trade that in for a better one if we're going to make this work. Where's your computer? Why can't we put the list in there?'

I bit my lip and pointed to the alcove in the bookshelves that I had designated as my office space. My ancient laptop languished there, still shut, with the cable in an untidy knot on top of it.

Mouse's eyes opened wide, and he slapped his forehead.

'This is going to be more of an intervention than a teaching assignment. That is basically scrap.'

I sighed.

'I've been through the mill the last few years, you know. I cut myself off from the world, and not using a computer made sure no-one could bother me. The same with my mobile phone. I'm not stupid though. I can pick this all up if you show me what to do.'

Mouse shrugged.

'It's none of my business, and I wasn't criticising you. Lots of old people have trouble with technology.'

What a cheek!

'Oy! Less of the old. I'm ill, not old. I've had depression, but now I'm better. Let's make a list of the things we need, and I'll raid my bank account. Choose a notebook.'

I pointed at the shelves of A5s. Mouse grimaced.

'They're rather flowery for me. Haven't you got something less pink and purple?'

'No. I'll buy one later. Just make a list of everything I need to get up to scratch in one of mine and we'll go shopping.'

'I'll put it on my phone.'

It took about an hour to make a comprehensive list of the equipment and services we needed, by which time Hades had purred his way onto Mouse's lap and sat looking smugly at me; the dirty maggot. I pretended I hadn't seen him and concentrated on finishing the list. I crossed my fingers that my new clientele would buy expensive vintage gifts for Valentine's Day. Mouse located a technician for the coffee machine and offered to call a barista friend of his to train us up on the different coffees and how to prepare them. Then I remembered Joy could use one, so I said we'd ask her first. I knew a few of Mouse's friends and I wasn't too keen on them using my café as a base.

We walked into town along the promenade. A smell of seaweed blew in from the beach, dotted with glinting rock-pools at low tide. Seagulls fought over the stale bread being thrown into the air by an old man in a purple Sikh turban. A gorgeous brindle greyhound begged us for strokes, straining at his leash while his owner tried to light a cigarette. Mouse lavished attention on the dog, his face animated. My heart went out to him. He might be dodgy, if George had told me the truth, but Mouse needed love as much as oxygen. If he let me, I would be there for him, no matter what.

I assumed we'd be going to actual physical shops, but Mouse led us to an internet café where we paid by the hour to use a scruffy terminal. To Mouse's amusement, I cleaned the keyboard with a Dettol wipe before I would touch it. The January sales turned out to be a Godsend for cheap electronics and deals from internet suppliers. Mouse navigated the net with the consummate ease of an expert, and soon we had purchased a new laptop, and signed up to a combined internet and smartphone deal for me.

After a couple of hours at the computer, I dragged Mouse to visit Second Home, where Ghita manned the cash register.

'I hope you've made lots of money today,' I said. 'Because Mouse and I have emptied the coffers.'

'Actually, I sold that Art Deco table to a collector, and I raised the price when he talked down to me.' She paused and examined Mouse from under her giraffe-like eyelashes. 'I don't think we've met.'

'Mouse is my stepson,' I said. 'He's been away, but now he's going to live with me.'

Mouse glanced at me and I nodded at him, getting a shy smile in return. Ghita gave a pleased gasp and came around the counter to give him a spicey hug. She always smells of curry and incense and sweet spices. It's like being hugged by a delicious takeaway. Mouse blushed and stared at his shoes. She put her hand under his chin and looked into his eyes.

'Oh my,' she said. 'What a lady-killer. I hope we'll be seeing lots of you in here.'

Mouse regrouped.

'I've just organised Wi-Fi for the café, so that I can hang out there. Maybe I'll make coffees too.'

'Maybe you will,' I said. 'How did the wedding go?'

'One long guilt trip with lots of delicious food,' said Ghita. 'How was the wake?'

'An unpleasant ordeal with lots of suspects,' I said.

Chapter 11

Mouse's move into the Grotty Hovel proved to be the best decision I'd made for years. It raised my spirits and gave me a new energy for life. The technician who installed the internet told me he'd never seen anyone smile so much. I guess you can't hide happiness. While Mouse did not qualify as the perfect housemate, I took all the extra laundry and housework on the chin, for the joy his presence brought to me. He opened up a world of online access and research which I had only dreamed of before. I couldn't believe how far the world had moved on while I mouldered in my misery. I felt renewed.

A few days later, I found myself alone at home when a loud knock on the door disturbed my attempts to Google Greg Summers. I jumped up and went to open the front door.

'Aren't you going to ask me in?' said George.

'Sure. Come in and make yourself at home,' I said, returning to my desk and shutting my laptop, hoping he hadn't noticed the search on the screen.

George entered cautiously, ducking through the door as if he might bump his head, despite being less than six feet tall (a lot less according to me). His enormous head swivelled on his neck as he cased the sitting room. I noticed his enlarged bald spot catch the light and smirked to myself.

'It's cosier than I expected,' he said, walking over to my desk. 'Since when have you started using a computer again? I thought you hated the things, like me.'

Ah, the one thing we had in common. Twin Luddites. Gone now.

'I joined the twenty-first century. I've got a smart phone too.'

George shook his head.

'Wonders never cease.'

He picked up a Brighton supporter scarf, which Mouse had left lying on the sofa, and sneered.

'Got a new boyfriend?' he said.

'Actually, that belongs to your son.'

'My son? What on earth does Andy want now? Did he ask you for money?'

Fury almost made me blurt out something I'd regret. I counted to ten in my head.

'Mouse is staying with me for a while. He helped me get set up on the laptop.'

'That boy is trouble. You should ask him to leave as soon as you can.'

Like you did?

'That's harsh. A lot of teenagers go off the rails for a while. He seems like a changed person.'

'You'll see. Wait until you meet his friends. Don't say I didn't warn you.'

I changed the subject; afraid Mouse might come back and hear something.

'Have you got any leads on the Mel Conrad case?' I asked.

'The what?' said George. 'There is no case. The woman fell down the stairs and broke her neck.'

'But I'm sure there's more to it,' I said. 'She had secrets.'

'Secrets? I suppose you think the butler did it. Honestly, Tan, don't you think it's time you grew up? You're not a journalist anymore. Those days are over. You should get a proper job and stop procrastinating. I'm not subsidising you any longer.'

'You don't understand. Something's not right here. You should know me better by now. I have a feeling for these things. Don't you remember when I used to help you with cases?'

'Help or hinder? Knock yourself out,' he said. 'Ring me when you've identified the murderer.'

I attempted to will him out of the front door, but George insisted on taking a tour of the house, which tried my patience further. I didn't complain, since he had paid for it. There's no point in creating an unnecessary argument. Since I didn't offer him a coffee, he took the hint and left, but not before warning me off his son again. I put it down to jealousy and ignored him. Hades loved Mouse, and he was an excellent judge of character, unless it came to me, of course. He still hissed if I tried to stroke him, so I just waited him out, buying expensive cat food and tolerating him the best I could.

After George had left, I felt insulted and bereft. I tried to rationalise the mix, but the only remedy had to be solving the mystery myself. Mel's murderer would not get away with it if I had anything to do with it. I opened my laptop again and searched for the spreadsheet Mouse had set up for me. I had used the original versions of Microsoft Word and Excel while I still worked at the magazine, and I soon became competent at them again. I scanned the list I had made of people I could speak to about Mel. Nobody stood out as a candidate for her murderer, but I needed to establish some motives before I could consider whether they had the means and opportunity to carry out their plan. I needed to discover where Mel had been staying so I could search her room. But who would have that information? Maybe they had cleared it out already? But maybe not.

Flo owed me a favour, and I called it in. I dialled her number twice before she answered it. That told me all I wanted to know about her willingness to share. Finally, she took my call.

'George told me not to talk to you about Mel,' she said.

I laughed.

'I'm not asking for any information about the case. Mel took a rather expensive box from my shop and never paid me. I hoped to recover it, but I don't know where she stayed before she died. Can you help me, please? I'm not made of money, and that box would be the perfect gift for Valentine's Day.'

Flo sighed.

'She had the business card of a B&B in her handbag, but if I give you the address, you must promise me not to tell George where you got it.'

'I promise.'

'You can do me a favour in return. Do you have her husband's contact details? He hasn't been in contact yet, and we should make sure he gets her belongings.'

'Isn't that odd?'

'I'm not sure how close they were. Her recent texts were all from someone called Ronnie, not that she answered them.'

'If I remember rightly, he was the gardener from Conrad House. They must have been in contact after all.'

'Now there you go, getting information out of me despite myself. Just get Greg's number for me.'

'I will.'

'That would be great. Now that they have ruled her death an accident, no one seems too interested, not even her husband.'

'I could take Mel's stuff to him if you like. Harry and I were planning on a trip to London with some stock. We can take the things you got from the murder scene, as well as the belongings in the guest house.'

'I'll have to ask George, but I don't see why not. We don't need them anymore. Shall I read out the address?'

'Can you text it to me?'

Flo snorted.

'Since when have you been able to text anything?'

'Mouse Carter has moved into the Grotty Hovel with me. He's made me get a smart phone. This is the new me.'

'George's son? Isn't he a delinquent?'

'He used to be, but he's older now. I guess he grew up.'

'I'd be careful if I were you. He may be using you.'

'I'm using him too, you know. Anyway, he needed my help. I've never had a teenage son before. It's a revelation.'

'On your head be it. Just don't let him prey on your kindness.'

'I won't.' I took a gamble. 'That reminds me. Will you tell me why Mel wanted your help?'

I could almost hear the cogs whirling in Flo's head. Finally, she answered.

'It doesn't seem relevant now, but I can't tell you while I'm at work. Can we meet up for lunch one day and I'll tell you then?'

My mobile beeped a couple of minutes later and the address of Mel's B&B flashed up onto the screen. I sent a thumbs up emoji to prove how much progress I'd made, but I didn't get a heart in reply. Instead, Flo sent a brief text telling me to collect Mel's belongings at the station's reception desk where I would have to sign for them. I crossed my fingers not to run into George again and set my alarm for the morning.

Chapter 12

The next morning, I left Mouse sleeping off a late night with his mates, and I hurried along hedgerows, with their light coating of frost, to the police station. I needed to get a move on, as I had organised a rendezvous with Harry in an hour and a half outside Mel's guesthouse. He wanted to visit London to deliver some stock to one of his cousins, so we had agreed to take Mel's stuff to Greg and do a bit of low-key sleuthing at the same time. I pushed my way through the swinging door into the suffocating heat of the police station. It had a fuggy smell like dirty uniforms and sweaty feet. I wrinkled my nose in protest. The young constable on reception recognised me and gave me a cheery greeting.

'I've got that stuff for you, Mrs Carter. Give me a minute.'

She disappeared into the back room and returned with a sealed transparent bag with a contents list stapled to the top. I tried not to be irritated that she still called me Mrs Carter.

'D.I. Carter says you're not to open the bag, on pain of death,' she said, dangling the bag in front of my face. 'In case you were thinking of it. I know I would be.'

'It's definitely tempting,' I said. 'But I won't touch it. I'm taking it up to London to the victim's husband's house.'

'It's odd he had no interest himself, isn't it? I'd have thought a grieving husband would want his wife's things back. Shows what I know.'

'All people react to grief differently. I guess he has no interest in her possessions now she's gone.'

'Still. It's dead cold, isn't it? I'm glad I'm not married to a man like that. My Jimmy's a treasure.'

'You're a lucky girl then. Keep him locked up, so no one steals him.'

'They wouldn't dare. I'd arrest them.'

She winked at me, and I hoped she'd never be disappointed by him. It's hard not to turn cynical when your own love fades.

I set off for Mel's guesthouse with the bag tucked into my rucksack. Before I put it away, I couldn't resist twirling it around and trying to look at the contents. I recognised Mel's crocodile handbag and matching shoes from her visit to the café, and a shiver ran down my spine. The temptation to open the bag had not gone away, but my fear of reprisal from my ex-husband was stronger.

I made my way north through town to the Dunromin guesthouse, which sat in the middle of a terrace on a road behind the railway station. The road to the station ran uphill, and I could see my breath as I strode along fast to keep warm. By the time I arrived, my cheeks throbbed pink. The outside of the house had seen better days. Weeds grew through the cracked concrete which covered the small front garden and the paintwork on the windows had split and peeled. An enormous toy rabbit had been dumped outside beside the dustbins; its head slumped on its chest like a wino after a hard night on the tiles.

I pushed the gate open and headed for the gaudy yellow front door with the hand-painted guesthouse sign affixed to the right. The doorbell played the tune to the Birdy song made famous in resorts like Torremolinos. I couldn't imagine anywhere further away from Spain than this drab corner of Seacastle. A tiny woman, with reading glasses balanced on the end of her nose, opened the door, and peered out at me.

'Are you the Mormons?' she said. 'Because I don't hold with them foreign religions.'

I frowned.

'I should think not,' I said. 'What's wrong with the Church of England?'

She kept a tight grip on the door.

'I'm a Baptist.'

'And you're a credit to your church. I'm sure you'd be pleased to help a lost stranger.'

She glared at me.

'The station's back that way,' she said, pointing. 'You walked straight past it.'

I shook my head.

'Sorry. I wasn't clear. I meant a stranger who has lost something. One of your guests took something from my shop on credit, but she hasn't paid me yet.'

The little woman drew herself up to her full height, which meant her eyes were level with my breasts. She folded her arms.

'Are you casting aspersions on my guests? All my regulars are quality people, I can assure you. I vet them myself.'

I tried not to sigh.

'We seem to have got off on the wrong foot. Mel Conrad and I were friends. I've—'

'Why didn't you say so?'

She peered at me.

'I don't know you, but Mel was a friend of mine too. Do you want to come in?'

Without waiting for a reply, she turned and walked down the passageway. I followed her, closing the door behind me.

'What is it you want exactly,' she said, as she laboured up the stairs.

'I need to collect Mel's stuff for her husband, and look for my celluloid box.'

'Is that the Chinese one? She showed me that after she found it at your shop. I'm sure she planned on paying for it.'

'Oh, I wasn't concerned about that. I hadn't told her the price yet. I'm reorganising my antique shop and I didn't have the price to hand.'

'It's on the mantelpiece I think.' She pushed her glasses up on her nose, before peering at me in the dim landing light. 'Her husband came here before, you know. Soon after the murder. He searched her room for ages, but he took nothing away with him. I wondered at the time why he didn't take her stuff with him.'

'Now that is odd. Are you sure it was Greg Summers? Have you met him before?'

She pulled her cardigan tighter over her chest and her eyes narrowed.

'No, I hadn't. Why would he lie about being married to Mel?'

'I've no idea. Um, can you tell me what he looked like?'

She shut her eyes as if searching her mind for the memory.

'Mousey man with a skinny, wiry body. Looked as if he spent a lot of time outdoors. He had that toughened skin on his arms and face from being out in the sun and rain. Is that him?'

Ronnie Barratt. What on earth was he looking for?

'Sounds like it. I'll get on then, will I?'

'She didn't bring that much with her. I don't know how long she planned on staying. Do you need any help?'

'No, thanks. I've got this.'

I tugged a suitcase from underneath the bed and removed her clothes from their hangers. Mel used the same perfume as Fiona, which struck me as peculiar, and the aroma hung around in the wardrobe. I guess it was the only thing they had in common. Maybe Mel used to steal it as a teenager. I wish I'd known her better. I felt like I was wading through treacle. Helping George with his cases made me imagine I'd know what to do to, but I didn't. *How do I know if something's a clue? Or that someone's lying. Or that someone is dangerous?* Baddies don't have name badges, as George used to say. I pulled open the drawer

79

of her bedside cabinet. Bottles of nail varnish and makeup remover pads and other girly stuff filled the drawer to bursting and made it difficult to open. I jerked it out too far, and the drawer fell out of the chest onto the floor, scattering the contents.

As I tried to reinsert the drawer, I spotted an envelope which had fallen down the back of the cabinet. I placed it on the bed while I picked up the items and refilled the drawer. Then I sat on the bed and looked at the envelope which was addressed to Ms Conrad. It hadn't been opened, but I didn't think Mel would mind if I had a look inside. It contained an official-looking letter, which I hesitated before unfolding to read. In it were the results of a genetic test, it didn't state for who, just that the test had revealed no familial relationship between the two samples presented. I folded it and put it in my handbag. Maybe Greg needed the test for some reason? A transplant? Still, she had kept it, so I put it in my handbag to examine later.

Then I realised I hadn't yet found my lacquered box. I started in the bathroom and rechecked the bedroom, searching on top of the wardrobe and lifting the mattress. Having checked under the bed and tipped the drawers upside down, I felt sure it had vanished. Could Ronnie have taken it? What conceivable motive did he have to remove it? I spotted a Ziploc bag in the dustbin with an empty can of Fanta sealed inside. It struck me as odd, so I picked it up and put it into my rucksack. I looked at my watch and realised Harry would be waiting for me. I had a last look around the room before staggering downstairs again, carrying Mel's suitcase.

'You're going then?' said the landlady.

'My friend has offered me a lift to London, so I'm going to take Mel's stuff to her husband.'

'Doesn't he live here?'

'No, but he came to the funeral. Um, I couldn't find the box. You didn't put it somewhere for safe-keeping, did you?'

'If it wasn't on the mantlepiece, I can't answer for it. I guess her husband took it with him.'

'Maybe.'

But which one?

The landlady wiped a tear from her cheek as I left.

'The end of an era,' she said. 'Why do the good die young?'

Cliché city. I wondered if she had been a football manager in a previous existence. I dragged the suitcase onto the pavement and looked around for Harry, longing to see him again. This enigmatic man, jolly on the outside with the sad centre, which sometimes oozed out of the cracks, fascinated me. A loud horn blast alerted me to his presence.

'Oi! No sleeping on the job,' he said, leaning out of the cab and winking. 'Let's get this suitcase on board and leave before the traffic warden turns up.'

'Did you remember to bring Greg's card?' I said.

'Is the Pope a Catholic? I've put the address from his business card into the GPS. Jump in and we'll get on the road.'

The cabin reverberated with music when I got in. Fleetwood Mac.

'Do you want me to turn it off?' said Harry.

'Don't you dare. I love this album.'

'Me too. No singing, though. Driver's prerogative.'

I laughed.

'Okay, but can I talk instead?'

'Not yet.'

We didn't speak until we were halfway to the capital. I'm not very good at silence and my foot tapped on the floor, but I let the music wash over me and managed not to hum. Then Harry glanced over at me, a suppressed grin on his face, the corners of his mouth twitching comically.

'What's so funny?' I said.

'You are. I just wanted to see how long you could keep it up.'

'And?'

'I'm seriously impressed by your self-control.'

I punched his shoulder, and he gave me a fake look of shock.

'Don't hit the driver,' he said. 'By the way, how's your love life going?'

I must have looked stunned, because he snorted with laughter.

'With Hades, your live-in-lover? Has he melted into your arms yet?'

The wicked twinkle in his eyes disarmed me. I swallowed.

'Actually, I've got two men living with me now.'

It was Harry's turn to look shocked.

'You got another cat? Or…'

He trailed off, and I left him hanging for a few precious seconds.

'My stepson, Mouse, moved in with me. Or he could be my ex-stepson, or something weird like that. He's George's son from his first marriage.'

'How old is he?'

'Eighteen, going on full-blown crime wave.'

'I've got a nephew like that. How come he moved in?'

'He had nowhere to go after George threw him out, and he's a computer wizard, so I thought we could be mutually beneficial to each other.'

'Am I going to meet him?'

'Would you like to?'

'Does Hades like him?'

'Hades is all over him like a rash.'

'Cats are like that with mice.'

'Hilarious.'

Harry grinned.

'I'd love to meet him. Can I come over for supper one evening?'

And just like that, we got over our shyness with each other. Mouse was the key to our lock.

Chapter 13

Harry's cousin had a warehouse in Bermondsey in the East End of London. They had converted most of the former warehouses into expensive flats, but Tommy's still fulfilled its original purpose for furniture storage. Tommy was as worn and scruffy as many of his wares. He wore a jumper which had 'more holes than wool' according to Harry, and a pair of ancient corduroy trousers with the nap worn off. He greeted us with enthusiasm and gave me a big hug 'because you're so beautiful'. Harry avoided his insinuations about his new van mate and forced Tommy to get on with the job of emptying the contents. We turned down a cup of tea, disappointing Tommy who was up for a natter, and promised to return another day when we had less pressing business.

The van headed for the outskirts of the City, where Greg kept an office in a new building of steel and glass nestled among the Victorian shop fronts. We found an off-street parking lot, and left the van in the care of the sleeping attendant, who had a hot water bottle on his feet and snored like a motorbike without a silencer. A keen north wind blew down the street and made me wish I'd worn a thicker coat. The door of a nearby Nero swung open, releasing the intoxicating smell of Italian coffee, as two giggling girls carrying trays of takeaway coffees came out and disappeared down the road. I could have done with a latte, but Harry did not appear to notice the smell or my begging puppy dog eyes. We soon arrived at the brand-new building where Greg had his office. It mirrored the other office blocks in its highly reflective windows.

'Swanky,' said Harry, gazing upwards. 'This guy is one of life's winners. No wonder Mel liked him.'

We pushed our way through the revolving doors and approached the reception desk, where we inquired if they could alert Mr Greg Summers to our presence. The clerk raised a bored eyebrow and sighed.

'He left.'

'Will he be back today?' I said.

'He abandoned his business, leaving a trail of unpaid bills and furious investors, so no, I doubt it.'

'When did this happen?' said Harry.

'Officially, last week, but his bankruptcy has been on the cards for months now. He kept telling everyone he had something big coming soon, but whatever it was, it never materialised.'

'Is there anyone who can tell us more about Greg's business?' I said.

'There's his erstwhile partner. I have his card here if that's any good to you.'

He dug under the desk and pulled out a box full of well-thumbed cards.

'Here you go. But if they owe you money, you can join the queue.'

'Thank you,' said Harry, and he led me out of the shiny lobby. 'Why don't you call the guy on your smart new phone? What happened to your Nokia, by the way?'

'Mouse called me a Luddite and made me change it.'

'I'm liking the sound of this rodent.'

Greg's partner, Frank Byrne, told us to come to a nearby pub where he intended to eat lunch and drown his sorrows. The Duke of York lurked in a backstreet near the parking lot. Inside, the warm air smelled of stale beer, but the comfortable seats invited long stays, and the ladies' room had hand cream, a big plus in my eyes. Frank Byrne occupied a snug behind the main bar. He had already ordered himself a steak and kidney pie, and ate with the ferocity of a man who skipped breakfast, his jowls wobbling like a bulldog with his nose in a dish of dog food. The only other people in the bar were a courting couple who were sharing a chicken-in-the-basket, feeding each other chips, and dabbing each other's noses with ketchup. I rolled my eyes at Harry to disguise the fact I felt jealous of them.

'Mr Byrne?' I said, approaching the trough.

'Are you the lady who called me just now?' he said, wiping his mouth with a napkin.

'Yes, that's right. I'm Tanya Bowe and this is Harry Fletcher, my associate. We're interested in Greg Summers.'

'Delighted, I'm sure. Although I'd be even more delighted if you could tell me where the rat is hiding.'

'We were about to ask you the same question,' said Harry.

'Can't help you I'm afraid,' said Frank Byrne, returning his nose to the trough.

I tried not to show my disgust, but Harry, being made of sterner stuff, had already pulled up a chair.

'I'm sorry about Greg,' he said. 'It must have been shocking to find out the man you worked with couldn't pay his bills.'

Frank Byrne shook his head.

'I can't say it shocked me. We were flying by the seat of our pants from the beginning. Commodity trading is notoriously up and down, you know. We had loads of money for ages until we didn't.'

'That must have been a blast,' I said. 'I bet the girls loved you.'

'You've got that right. Well, the girls mostly went for Greg. He had the looks and the money. I only had money.'

'Oh, I wouldn't say that,' I said, crossing my fingers. 'I bet you had your share of fun too.'

He beamed.

'Thank you. I did. But it's all gone now. We made the wrong bets, and the money disappeared faster than we made it.'

'Greg told me he had a big deal coming up. Do you know what sort of deal he had in mind?'

Frank licked some gravy off his blubbery lips.

'No idea. I think his wife had some property or something. I'm foggy on the details, but he planned to sell it and make a mint.'

'What did she think about that?' I said.

'I can't tell you, but if she had any sense, she would have refused.'

'Maybe she did,' said Harry.

'Well, I certainly saw no money coming our way, so she must have,' he said.

Harry pushed his chair back.

'Thanks for taking the time to speak to us,' he said.

'No bother. Take my card. I'd appreciate it if you could tell Greg to give me a tinkle. We have unfinished business.'

'Do you have his home address? We've got some of his wife's things in the van.'

'Sure.'

He wrote it down on a napkin with a smear of pie on it. I couldn't take it from him, but Harry stuffed it in his pocket with thanks. Once outside, I took a deep, cleansing breath.

'Well, that was disgusting,' I said.

'It reminded me of Animal Farm,' said Harry. 'Do you want to get some lunch?'

'I thought you'd never ask.'

'I'm not a monster. I just wanted to get the unpleasant business out of the way, so we could enjoy lunch without sound effects.'

'Fair enough. Pub or Prêt?'

'We passed a Prêt on our way to the Duke of York.'

Despite the hour, we found a table at Prêt, and I bought myself an avocado wrap. Harry bought a ham and cheese baguette and soon we were munching our way through them. Afterwards we shared a fruit pot and drank strong coffees. I could feel the life force flooding back into my veins. I'm not much use when I'm hungry.

'Money sounds like the motive to me,' I said, biting into a fat blueberry which spat its pulp at Harry.

'It's a powerful reason. But how would Greg benefit if Mel died? William is still alive. I would've thought killing William made more sense.'

'Perhaps she threatened to divorce him, and he thought he'd get nothing. Fiona said they weren't getting on. If you believe anything she says.'

'Fiona, hmm. She's not off our radar either. Who gets everything when William dies, now that Mel is out of the picture?'

'And where does Ronnie fit in?' I said.

'Ronnie? I hadn't even considered him as a suspect until you told me about his visit to Mel's guest house.'

'Maybe he murdered Mel because he was jealous. He might have pushed her down the stairs by accident while they were arguing.'

'The more we know, the less we understand.'

'Do you fancy an almond bake?'

'Are you always hungry?'

'I can't lie.'

After lunch, we drove to the address given to us by Frank Byrne. Greg lived in a pretty house in Fulham, but I noticed an estate agent's 'For Sale' board outside as I got out of the van.

'He's moving out,' I said.

'I guess he doesn't have any choice.'

Harry knocked at the door for us. He had chatted to Greg at the funeral about tickets for the Ashes, so they had bonded (so he told me). No one came to answer it.

'Do you think he's moved out already?' I said.

'Maybe.'

'What will we do with her things?'

'We could leave the suitcase here. There's still furniture inside, so he must be coming back.'

'But when?'

'Try the door again.'

I pressed the doorbell hard and felt it click and heard a buzzing in the hallway. Minutes later, a bedraggled Greg Summers opened the door a crack and peered out. His eyes opened wide as he spotted the suitcase on the ground between us.

'Hello, Greg,' said Harry. 'We met at Mel's funeral in Seacastle.'

'Harry? Did I invite you to stay with your wife? It's all such a blur.'

I snorted despite myself.

'We've come to deliver Mel's belongings to you. She left them at the guesthouse.'

'Oh, won't you come in? I'm sorry, the place looks as if a bomb went off. I'm in the middle of packing.'

We all shuffled along the hall to stand in the sitting room among the bubble wrap and the piles of flat cardboard boxes waiting to be assembled with parcel tape.

'We won't stay long,' I said, holding out the plastic bag containing Mel's handbag and its contents. 'Harry has the suitcase she left at the guesthouse in Seacastle. And there's this bag of personal belongings the police gave me.'

Greg took it from me and tipped it out on the table. He sifted through the contents as if looking for something.

'That's weird,' he said. 'My keyring isn't here. She borrowed it to use for Seacastle keys. The fob is a large bronze letter S for Summers.'

'It may be at William's house,' I said. 'If I come across it, I'll make sure you get it. I'm sorry about Mel. What a tragedy for you on top of everything else with your business and so on.'

His face fell.

'How do you know about that?'

'We met Frank near your office building,' said Harry.

'Ah, another loose end. I'm in a dreadful pickle. Mel's death was the last straw.'

'Have you been in contact with the Conrads?'

A bitter laugh issued from Greg's throat.

'After the wake, Fiona made it crystal clear that she never wanted to see or hear from me again. No great loss really, except for financially. We stood to inherit William's fortune when he died, but Fiona got what she always wanted. It's a cliché, isn't it?'

'What is,' I said.

'Much younger secretary marries millionaire soon after first wife dies in an accident. I think I've read that script before.'

'I hadn't,' said Harry. 'But the optics aren't great.'

'We'd better get going,' I said, desperate to leave and discuss this revelation.

Greg grabbed my hand and looked into my eyes.

'She liked you,' he said. 'Do you want any of her stuff? I'll have to give it to the charity shops now.'

'I don't want any of her clothes, but I gave her a Chinese lacquered box which had sentimental value for me. I'd like it back, but I couldn't find it when I packed her things.'

He dropped my hand and shook his head.

'If it wasn't in her room, I can't help you,' he said.

'Never mind. It will turn up sometime,' I said. 'I hope you can rebuild your life after all this.'

He reached over to a sideboard and picked up a small album of photographs.

'I wonder if you might take this instead. They are all photos of her childhood. It means nothing to me. Maybe you could give it to her father if you don't want it.'

'Thank you. I will.'

'Give me your number, and I'll let you know if the box turns up,' he said.

Once we were outside again, Harry turned to me.

'Did you know William's first wife had died in an accident?'

'No, I didn't. As far as I know, she died of cancer when we were young. I never considered it suspicious before.'

'It may not be, but we need to find out more about Fiona.'

'The person who knows most about her, besides William, is probably Sarah Bingley, the housekeeper. She's not the easiest person to deal with, but I think she'll speak to me. Maybe Mouse can do some research on the net too.'

'I've got to meet this kid. He sounds great.'

'You've invited yourself to supper, so any time you like is good for me.'

'By the way, what does the box you gave Mel have to do with anything?'

'I don't know, but if Greg's telling the truth, Ronnie Barratt removed it from Mel's room. That's a pretty odd thing to do. I wonder what she had in it.'

'I think we should find out.'

Chapter 14

I went to bed with my mind still whirling. It had been a long day, and I felt no nearer to finding the truth behind Mel's death. The Harry conundrum made my attempts to organise the facts in my head even harder. He had stayed with Mouse and me for a Chinese takeaway and quizzed him on all things sport and computer related. To my relief, Mouse had responded with enthusiasm. He can be cagey around adult men. I blame George. They had joined forces to tease me about my hopeless grasp of the 'interweb', and my failed attempts at seducing Hades. The brat took one look at Harry and did figures of eight around his legs, purring like a Maserati. Soon he had wangled his way onto Harry's lap and sat there smirking at me. I never thought I'd be jealous of a cat, but there you are.

After Harry left, Mouse and I cleaned up the cartons and transferred the remains of the food to Tupperware boxes in the fridge. Mouse switched on the television to catch a late movie and curled up on the sofa with Hades.

'You like him, don't you?' he said.

'Don't you?' I said. 'Harry's a lovely man.'

'I meant like him.'

'I know what you meant. Bed is calling. Night night.'

Of course, I liked him. Who wouldn't? But it was way too early to embark on a relationship. I knew George has moved on, and I should too, but I thought we'd be together forever, and it's hard to abandon your fantasies, even when they are tarnished and battered. Anyway, Harry needed to like me too, for anything to happen, and even though he appeared to be an open book on most subjects, a firewall protected his heart. I guessed he'd give me the password when he was ready.

Were we any closer to finding the killer? We had uncovered some strong motives floating about in the family soup. I had a feeling we were missing some vital pieces of information. Following the revelations from Harry's and my trip to London, Mouse had promised to dedicate himself to getting a background on Greg Summers and Fiona Conrad. When I got the chance, I needed to talk to Sarah Bingley. Perhaps if we invited her to the Vintage, I could corner her for a chat. She was the person who contacted Mel. Without her, Mel would still be alive. And now I thought about it; either Sarah was the last person to see her alive, or the first to see her dead? But what plausible motive could she have for killing Mel? I guessed we'd soon find out.

Chapter 15

The next day, I opened Second Home at ten and discovered to my glee that Ghita had sold a couple of large pieces of Art Deco to the same client, a dealer called Max Wong. He and his wife, Grace, who was a member of Ghita's Fat Fighters Club, had an antique shop up the posh end of the high street, with even posher prices. I knew if I looked in the window of their shop, I would spot my wardrobe and dressing table set at double or triple the price I had sold it. I had no problem with that. Harry gave me the furniture from Mel's attic at a bargain price in return for my help with the pricing on the things he kept. Both of us were benefiting from our collaboration, and things didn't look so bleak on the financial front. We needed another clearance soon to restock the shop, now that Ghita had sold those articles. A sizeable gap advertised their absence, and I had nothing suitable to fill it.

I rang Sarah Bingley and asked her if she'd come and have coffee with me. I used the pretext that I had something to show her, intending to bond over the photograph album. She agreed to come after lunch. Then I spent about an hour doing the books before Roz turned up with Ghita in tow. Roz did her imitation of a bloodhound after a powerful scent, sniffing her way around me for evidence of foul, or other, play.

'If I'd had sex, I would have showered,' I said, annoyed at her intrusive manner.

'Don't be mean,' said Ghita. 'I know you hate to eat in front of the starving, but I need all the details.'

'Never mind the hanky-panky,' said Roz. 'I need clues and motives. How am I going to solve the mystery if you won't spill the beans?'

I sighed.

'I promise to tell you everything if you'll watch the shop for an hour later, while I talk to Sarah Bingley, the Conrads' housekeeper.'

'It's a deal,' said Roz.

'I've got a shift at the council this afternoon,' said Ghita. 'But I'll owe you a morning if you keep me posted on your progress.'

'Okay, but this is top secret. No blabbing to anyone. The case is closed, and no one must know we are investigating it. If word got back to George, he'd be livid.'

After I extracted pinkie promises from them both, I regaled them with a slightly exaggerated version of my previous day's sleuthing with Harry, and they made sounds of enthusiasm in all the right places. Ghita found Frank Byrne particularly disgusting, and then almost cried when I told them about his lonely search for love. (Trust me, she loves that stuff). They were both equally shocked at the precarious state of Greg's finances.

'But he seemed so, so…' Ghita trailed off.

'Rich?' I said.

'Yes. Wealthy. With that accent and those expensive clothes. His cashmere jumper would have cost me a month's rent.'

'That bloody box is concerning me,' said Roz.

'In what way?' I said.

'Nobody knew it was missing, but now everyone does,' she said.

Before I could ask her what she meant, a gaggle of women came in, gasping for coffee and cake. Roz and Ghita showed them upstairs, and soon I heard the tell-tale hiss of the Gaggia, and the shouts of laughter as Roz spread the gossip on thick. The bush telegraph had nothing on Roz. Her antennae were more sensitive than air traffic control at Heathrow. The lack of bush telegraph she had picked up on Mel so far surprised me.

I popped out to buy some supplies for the café, and lunch for us girls, while Ghita watched the shop. Sarah Bingley turned up just as we were drinking a coffee. The doorbell jangled as she entered, and Roz sent her up to the café, as Ghita had already left for work. Sarah Bingley stalked up the stairs with an odd heron-like walk. Then she settled herself into a chair, her skinny legs too long to fit comfortably under the table. At her request, I made her a cup of tea, but she refused cake.

'You said you had something that might interest me?' she said.

I smiled. *Straight to the point then.*

'We were in London yesterday and passed by Greg and Mel's house to leave her belongings with him. He gave me a photograph album.'

Her dull eyes came to life.

'Of Mel? Oh, how wonderful. Can I see them?'

I handed the album to her, and she touched it with reverent fingers, as if I had presented her with a holy relic.

'Mel kept it all these years? She must have hidden it well when she still lived at Conrad House. Fiona did her best to eradicate every trace of Mel's mother, Diane.'

'Why?'

Sarah cackled.

'That woman set her cap at William from the first minute she came to work for him. He was as gormless as the next man and found it flattering to have a pretty young woman sucking up to him. But no matter what Fiona did, he had no intention of ever leaving Diane.'

She leafed through the pages, running her fingers across the photographs of Mel and Diane, as if trying to feel the essence of their existence. Mel wore a massive smile in every single photograph. Both she and her mother gazed at each other in mutual admiration in several of them. Sarah lingered over one of herself and Mel on a beach. Sarah's arms were wrapped around Mel's chest and they were laughing into the camera. The Mel I remembered from school had always been sullen and sarcastic, but that must have been after her mother's death.

Sarah sniffed, and I offered her a tissue. She wiped away her tears and blew her nose brusquely, as if caught indulging in self-pity. I waited.

'I always thought Fiona had murdered Diane, you know, when she got impatient.'

'Maybe she realised she would never have William while Diane lived?'

'I can't prove anything, though.'

'And Mel? Do you think Fiona got impatient again?'

Sarah gave me a sly glance.

'The police called it an accident.'

'And what do you call it?'

'One accident is a tragedy, but two is a coincidence too far.'

'My George says there's no such thing as a coincidence.'

She raised an eyebrow.

'Aren't you divorced?'

I coloured.

'Yes, but it's quite recent. I forget sometimes.'

'Replaced by a younger model? Does she look like you?'

I felt the cold cruelty of her question cut me to the quick. Sharon could have been my clone. She looked and acted like me before my depression. The only difference obvious to me was her lack of honesty. I could never have cosied up to a woman I planned to replace. Rage bubbled in my veins as I pictured Fiona doing the same to Diane. Had Diane realised she held a serpent to her bosom? Had Fiona killed Mel to prevent her inheriting William's fortune?

'A bit,' I said. 'A lot.'

I noticed her gazing at a picture of Mel and a small boy, with an almost maternal fervour. A spark of recognition hit me.

'Gosh! Is that Ronnie Barratt?' I said.

'Who?' she said, picking up her keys as if she intended to leave.

'The gardener. With Mel in that photo.'

She ignored me, appearing preoccupied with the keys, sifting through them with her bony fingers, and rubbing the edges. I nudged her.

'Oh, yes, of course. Sorry, I was miles away.'

'I can imagine. They look like wonderful memories,' I said. 'Did you ever get married?'

A shadow passed over her face.

'No.'

She didn't elaborate, instead she sighed and closed the album.

'Happier days,' she said.

'Would you like to make some copies?' I said.

'I don't know how.'

'Mouse, my stepson, is a computer whizz. Leave it with me and I'll get him to scan them or something so the chemist can print them.'

'I'd be so grateful. Can you call me when they are ready?'

'Of course.'

She gave me a stiff hug before leaving, and I steeled myself for the inevitable torrent of questions from Roz before going downstairs.

Roz fixed me with her steely gaze and patted the seat beside her.

'Tell me everything,' she said.

When I had finished, I handed the album to Roz and let her leaf through it without comment. She guessed the identity of Diane without prompting and noted the plump happiness of Mel in every photograph just as I had done.

'Do you think Fiona did it?' she said. 'She's got the obvious motive.'

'I don't know. Greg seemed to have a motive to keep Mel alive rather than dead, so I'm discounting him, for now. But I'm not convinced we have all the information yet.'

'There's the Chinese box,' said Roz. 'Why did Ronnie Barratt take it from Mel's room?'

'I'm not sure it was him who took it, though.'

'You won't need his address then?'

'You have it?'

'Of course. Have you forgotten that Mel wanted to find him and asked me to help? Why? There are plenty of gardeners around who know how to identify plants.'

I jumped up and snapped my fingers.

'How could I have forgotten?' I said. 'I noticed her blushing when she mentioned him.'

'You didn't say so.'

'I didn't want to embarrass her. And we didn't know she'd be dead a short time afterwards.'

'Do you want it then?'

Chapter 16

I had my first run-in with Mouse today. It was inevitable, really. I had not appreciated just how much upheaval having a teenage boy in my house would cause. It's not all bad. I have been stuck in a rut ever since my illness, and Mouse has brought me back to the real world with a bump. But this felt different. He invited some friends round to my house without telling me, and they emptied the fridge. I know teenage boys eat like ravenous wolves, but I hadn't anticipated letting the entire pack use my house as a free restaurant. On my drive home, in between mulling over my meeting with Sarah Bingley, I had fantasised about heating the left-over lasagne and eating it with some peas. Saliva had even collected in my mouth, as I imagined the taste of the creamy sauce and the layers of pasta and meat.

The devastation in my sitting room took me aback when I entered, and should have pre-warned me as to the absence of my supper. Dirty plates and cups littered every flat surface, and an improvised ashtray full of roll-up butts made the air reek. The sickly-sweet smell of pot had not dissipated sufficiently to avoid my olfactory senses. Trying not to overreact, I stacked a pile of dishes and took them with me to the kitchen. Then I opened the fridge, figuring I'd wash up after eating my supper. But they had ransacked the fridge. No lasagne, no milk, no butter, nothing except a couple of eggs and some ancient carrots rolling around in the vegetable drawer. I almost cried with self-pity. After the day I'd had, this abuse of my hospitality hit deeper than it might otherwise have done. I sat at the table, glaring at the fridge for a couple of minutes and chewing savagely on a piece of nicotine chewing gum.

Then I shouted up the stairs for Mouse. He bounced down the steps, but stopped halfway down when he noticed my expression.

'What's up?' he said.

'How can you ask me that? Have you seen the state of my sitting room?'

He avoided my eyes.

'I was going to clean up,' he said.

'When? Also, I don't appreciate you inviting people to my house and emptying my fridge without asking me. Neither do I appreciate you leaving the sitting room covered in plates and cups. I am not a maid, and this is not a hotel.'

He chewed his cheeks, frowning.

'That's not fair,' he said. 'I'm sorry about the food. I didn't know they would help themselves and once they started, I didn't know how to stop them. They fed me for months after George threw me out.'

That took the wind out of my sails a bit.

'And the drugs?'

He shook his head.

'I wasn't born yesterday, Mouse. The sitting room stinks of weed. And you and your buddies didn't even bother to clear up after you.'

'I can move out,' he said. 'If you want me to.'

'Don't go overboard. I don't think I'm asking for too much from you. But this is an abuse of my generosity. I can't afford to feed your friends.'

'Neither can I,' he said. 'I have no income, and my savings have run out.'

'Why didn't you say something?'

'I was embarrassed.'

I sighed.

'Let's clear up the sitting room. And then we'll set some ground rules.'

After we restored order, we sat at the kitchen table.

'I can't pay you much,' I said. 'But would you like to run the Vintage for me? You can have a basic salary and a cut of the profits, but if I see you giving anyone a free coffee, I'll take it off your pay.'

'Okay, that would be great. I've got ideas for the place.'

'Please run them by me first. And no more unannounced visits here by your friends. While I pay all the expenses, this is my house, and the contents of the fridge are off limits. Your friends may come over and drink coffee and tea, but they can't smoke indoors. They can stand on the pavement like everyone else. If I smell weed in here again, I'll ban them.'

Mouse sighed.

'But they won't come if they can't smoke.'

'And…'

He shrugged.

'Can you give me an advance, please?'

'Sure. Why don't you show me how to research something on the computer, and I'll give you twenty quid to keep you going?'

'What do you want to know?'

'Can you search the records of births, deaths and marriages online for the dates of the Conrad marriages?'

'I don't know. Probably. Why are you interested?'

'Honestly. I'm not sure what I'm looking for. But I think Fiona Conrad may have had something to do with the mysterious death of her predecessor. Can you find out stuff about Mel's marriage to Greg Summers while you're at it? I'm not convinced Greg's motives for marrying Mel were kosher, either.'

'That's a lot of work.'

'Can you take the laptop to the café with you? That way, you kill two birds with one stone. Oh, by the way, is there anyway of copying photographs if I don't have negatives?'

'Sure. Do you want paper copies or digital?

'Paper copies.'

'I can scan them and load them up to the machine in Boots. How many copies do you need of each photo?'

'I don't know yet. I'm working my way through the suspects, and I'm guessing most people will want copies. I'll give you the album when I'm finished with it.'

'Do you still think someone pushed Mel down the stairs?'

'I'm pretty sure.'

'Why does it matter to you? I thought you hardly knew her.'

'Justice matters to me. I'm not sure you know this, but before I became ill, I used to work on *Uncovering the Truth*.'

Mouse's eyes opened wide.

'You? Holy shit. I'm addicted to reruns of that programme. I watch it with my mates.'

I beamed at him.

'At least they have good taste.'

'What did you do on the programme?'

'I investigated miscarriages of justice and scams, mostly cases where rich or powerful people had got away with murder, sometimes literally, because of who they were.'

'You were one of the investigative journalists? But why have I never seen you on the screen?'

'I suppose you could call it another miscarriage of justice. I did all the work and then the celebrity presenters got to do the gotchas for the camera. They didn't have the nous or the time to do the research.'

'I suppose they got all the money too.'

'Most of it. But I loved my job. It just got a bit much for me after a while. I worked myself into the ground, and the next thing I knew I collapsed with exhaustion.'

Mouse bit his lip.

'I'm so sorry. Dad never told me any of this. He told me you had women's problems and were so pathetic that he couldn't bear living with you anymore. He didn't tell me you had clinical depression.'

'There's nothing to be sorry for. Your father is a dinosaur, and he hides from his feelings. One of these days, he's going to fall hard. I hope Sharon can cope.'

'Don't you hate her?'

'Hate's a strong word. It's not her fault George was looking for a reason to leave and she happened to be available. I'm sure she thought she was saving him from a miserable marriage. And, in a way, she'd be right. Neither of us were happy. I thought we were going through a rough patch, like many marriages. I didn't realise it would end in divorce. George didn't either.'

'You're too nice. I'd stab him.'

'Don't be silly. You couldn't stab a cushion. Anyway, I'm not that nice. I'll ban your friends if they empty my fridge again.'

'Speaking of fridges. Are you hungry?'

'Is that a real question?'

'Shall I pop around the corner and get us some fish and chips?'

'Now you're talking.'

I gave him another tenner to buy the fish and chips, and sent him out to get them while I washed up the dirty crockery. I mourned my dishwasher, but the tiny kitchen had neither the space nor the plumbing for one. As I washed the plates, I mused on the grief of Ronnie Barratt and the colour rising in Mel's cheeks when she talked about him. I had missed something important, and I intended to find out what.

Chapter 17

When Greg handed me the photograph album, I never imagined how useful it would prove to be in my investigation. It gave me the perfect excuse to show the photographs to every suspect in Mel's death without arousing suspicion about my motive. The sight of the young Mel revelling in her childhood opened people up to emotions and memories they couldn't hide from me. After his reaction to my being hugged by Fiona at the funeral, I had little hope that Ronnie Barratt would want to meet me. However, like Sarah, he jumped at the chance to see the photographs of Mel.

Now that Mouse had taken charge of the Vintage, he had also added an electronic lock to the front door, making it easier for me to absent myself for an hour or two. Customers had to ring the doorbell when he looked after the shop by himself and was making coffee upstairs. Roz and Ghita still hung out at the shop, preferring it to sitting at home on their days off, but now I had made enough money to pay Mouse, their babysitting of me ended.

I agreed to meet Ronnie at the café on the pier, which had recently reopened after refurbishment. The double layer of round windows and the snub nose facing out to sea gave it the appearance and feel of an ocean liner. A lower level functioned as a regular restaurant with popular favourites and an entire menu of elaborate ice cream sundaes. The mezzanine level faced out to sea and served as a place to chat and drink coffee or tea with friends. The sea view beat the Vintage hands down, but then the prices were sky high compared to our more modest ones. They had covered its walls in a gorgeous fish-themed wallpaper in gold and blue colours. Inflated puffer fish and deep-sea dogfish swam among the gilded seaweed and coral. Velvet-covered scallop-shaped couches surrounded low tables with seashell motives.

I arrived ten minutes early for our meeting and sank into one of the velvet couches to gaze out at the sea. Outside, the seagulls dive bombed a small fishing boat bobbing in the waves, their raucous cries filling the cold air. Below me, the clinking of cutlery on plates and the indistinct murmur of conversation filled the restaurant. I was miles away when I felt someone touch my arm. Ronnie Barratt stood silhouetted against the window, his thin frame emphasised by his loose clothing, his black hair greasy and unkempt.

'Have you been waiting long?' said Ronnie, sliding onto the couch.

'No, I just got here. Doesn't it look wonderful?'

He shrugged and ran his hand over the velvet covers.

'I think I preferred the place in its former scruffy state, but I guess it won't be long before it frays around the edges.'

'That happens to the best of us,' I said.

He nodded, and I noticed the black bags under his eyes and his still haggard face. I made a note to go easy on him.

'Do you have the photos?' he said.

'Right here. They're in this little album.'

He took it from me and turned it over a couple of times, a shy smile on his face.

'I can't believe it,' he said. 'I gave her this album for her tenth birthday.'

They had been friends for decades. No wonder Mel's death had shocked him so profoundly. He made his way through the pages, screwing up his eyes to peer closely at the photographs, until he got to the one of him and Mel laughing together. Then he stopped and put down the album for a moment, fighting back his tears. I waited for him to control himself. Gradually his chest stopped heaving, and he picked it up again, gazing at the photograph.

'That's such a fantastic picture,' I said. 'I didn't realise you knew her for so long.'

'We grew up together. We were like two halves of an apple.'

'You told me at the funeral that she was your girl. What did you mean, exactly? Did you go out together?'

'We did, but her father didn't approve of us being together, so our relationship had to be secret.'

'Did he try to stop you from seeing her?'

'He threatened to disinherit her if she continued to see me.'

'Did you stop?'

'No, we were in love. Money meant nothing to her in those days.'

'What happened?'

'We got married at sixteen.'

I tried not to look shocked. He stared into the distance as if visualising the day.

'But didn't you need permission from Mel's parents?' I said.

'Fiona signed the form for us.'

My jaw dropped almost to the table.

'Fiona? I thought she hated Mel.'

'So did I. But it made sense for Fiona to help us. If William cut Mel out of his will, Fiona would be the first in line to inherit his fortune. She only ever cared about the money. Mel and William were just collateral damage in the Fiona show.'

'But why did Mel leave Seacastle without you? What happened?'

He shrugged.

'I don't know. I've never found out. She just disappeared one day without leaving a forwarding address or a note. She broke my heart into a million pieces. I've never got over it, to tell you the truth.'

'Did you divorce her?'

'No. As far as I know, we're still married.'

'But what about Greg? Wasn't he married to Mel?'

Ronnie rolled down his bottom lip.

'He thought so, but she was still married to me.'

'Could he have found out?'

'Maybe. I suppose it's possible somebody told him when he came down here.'

I sat open-mouthed, thoughts chasing each other around my brain. How would Greg have reacted if he found out he wasn't married to Mel after all? He must have been furious. Would he have fought with her and pushed her down the stairs?

'Did you know she had come back to Seacastle?'

'She let me know she would be coming.'

'How did you find out about Greg?'

He frowned and twisted his fingers.

'I don't remember.'

A blatant lie. There was no way he forgot how he learned something so shocking. Was Mel's marriage to Greg a motive for murder? I changed the subject.

'Mel told me she had to talk to you about the rare plants in the garden. Did she contact you before she died?'

To my intense surprise, he burst out laughing.

'The rare plants? That's classic Mel.'

'What do you mean?'

'We used that as a code between us.'

'Can you tell me what it meant?'

His face grew serious again.

'We thought Fiona had murdered Diane in the rose garden.'

'Did you see her do it?'

'No, but we used to joke about it a lot. Diane died when Mel was only four years old. Mel didn't really remember her.'

'You haven't told me whether you saw Mel.'

'I was supposed to meet her, but she died before we could see each other again.'

'I'm so sorry.'
'Me too.'

Chapter 18

The next morning, Harry picked me up from the shop to help him with a house clearance. As always, my mood lifted when I saw his twinkling eyes and stocky frame through the window. Before setting out, we sat in the van drinking coffee from our insulated coffee mugs. I had bought them on a whim from a friend's shop. Mine had a Frieda Kahlo design, and his had Diego Rivera. Harry loved them, but I didn't explain their relationship. It felt too intimate. Anyway, I had other things on my mind.

'You'll never guess what,' I said. 'Ronnie Barratt married Melanie when they were sixteen.'

Harry choked on his coffee, making me laugh and try to slap his back.

'Does that mean her marriage to Greg wasn't valid?'

'I guess so. Quite a motive, wouldn't you say?'

'It gives Ronnie a motive too, though. Jealousy. Maybe they fought when she came home?'

'I've been thinking about that. But Fiona is not out of the frame. She helped Mel to marry Ronnie.'

'And why would she do that?' said Harry

'To ensure William would disinherit Mel.'

'It must have crushed her when Mel reappeared.'

'But did William write Mel back into his will? I think we ought to find out.'

'Will William talk to you?'

'I'm hoping the photo album with be my golden ticket. It's worked so far.'

'I'm constantly amazed at your sleuthing skills. You must have been fantastic at your job.'

I beamed.

'Thanks. I used to feel like Columbo. I even used his methods.'

Harry put on an American accent.

'Oh, just one more thing.'

I laughed.

'Exactly. Drink up, we should get out of here.'

The semi-detached house in the outer suburbs of Seacastle belonged to a widow who had recently moved into a care home suffering from advanced dementia. Her smug middle-aged son, dressed in skinny jeans and a faux leather jacket which smelt of sweat, waited for us outside. He gave me a once over and dismissed me in the same glance. I had a feeling he had judged me to be past my sell-by-date, and I gave him and his smelly armpits a wide berth. Harry shook his hand and turned over five twenty-pound notes, which the man counted twice before accepting. He handed over the front door key with a sneer.

'I thought rag-and-bone men were a thing of the past,' he said.

'I prefer to be called a junk dealer,' said Harry, unfazed. 'I'm assuming you'd like me to take as much as I can from here.'

'You can burn the lot for all I care. My mother owned six cats. The place is swimming in fleas and cat hair.'

'Have you rehoused the cats?' I asked.

'Not exactly. They're still running riot inside. I'm having them all put down tomorrow. Filthy moggies.'

He smirked. What a bastard. Harry shook his head at me, and I swallowed a retort.

'Are you sure we can have everything?' he said. 'What if we find something valuable?'

'You won't, but if you do, you can keep it. The old dear had no taste. I just want the house cleared so I can tart it up and sell it.'

'What shall we do with the keys when we're finished?' I said.

'Just shove them through the letterbox.'

'Will do,' said Harry.

'By the way, I put a padlock on the back door because it doesn't shut properly. If you go in or out using that entrance, please don't forget to lock it again. You'll need to use the key, though.'

'Sorry?' I said.

'The padlock needs a key to lock it. You need to shut it first and then toss the keys through the mail flap in the front door.'

'Thanks,' said Harry. 'Are you sure you removed everything your mother wanted to keep?'

'She doesn't recognise me. I could buy her a poster of Bon Jovi and she'd be happy.'

'I'm sorry,' I said.

'It's a cruel disease, but we never got on anyway. She's been dead to me for years. I just want to sell the house and move on.'

With that, he turned on his heel and left us both open-mouthed. I bit my lip, close to tears.

'We can't let him kill the cats,' I said.

Harry wrapped a muscular arm around my shoulders and bopped me on the nose with his other fist.

'Don't worry, partner. We'll round them up and take them to the cats' home.'

'But how will we carry them?'

'I expect she's got carriers to take them to the vet. If not, we going to improvise.'

'What a nasty piece of work. I can't believe he intends to kill them all.'

'Not uncommon, I'm afraid. Let's see if there's anything to salvage. I only gave him a ton, so we ought to make it back, and have a contribution for the cat's home too. Fingers crossed.'

'Don't bet on it. Heaven knows how long the cats have been shut in. They may have left their own legacy.'

'Yuck. It doesn't bear thinking about,' said Harry, opening the front door and pushing aside the piles of junk mail. 'Let's get going.'

A fetid odour of cat's pee mixed with rotting cat food met us as we entered. My stomach flipped, and I tried not to gag. We turned left into the sitting room where a misshapen couch occupied one wall faced by two armchairs with thick covers on them. The layer of cat hair over all three pieces made me squeamish, but I took the corner of the cover and peeled it back to reveal an almost new tapestry cover underneath.

'Not bad,' I said. 'Original covers.'

'Aren't these left over from the seventies?' said Harry.

'Yes, but that's the point. Vintage is all the rage at the moment. Parker Knoll is the best known make for these wing chairs. People like them. These will sell from my shop as soon as I put them in the window.'

Harry rolled his eyes.

'I know nothing,' he said in an Italian accent.

'Stick with me, sunshine, and all will be revealed.'

'Please don't take your clothes off; I'm trying to work.'

I snorted.

'Have you seen the cute Georgian desk hiding under that tablecloth?' I said.

'I don't mind the furniture doing a striptease, as long as we can make money from it.'

'Are you insinuating that I am past my prime?'

'You're the one who's insinuating.'

And so forth. Our childish banter reminded me of hitting boys in the playground so they would chase us, and then squealing in indignation when they caught us. I tried to picture Mel in the playground with us, but even the photographs hadn't dredged up any memories of her for me. Then I spotted a glimpse of a marmalade flank as one cat made a break for the stairs, followed by several of its brethren.

'Did you see that?' I said. 'They've sped upstairs. Maybe we can corner them up there.'

'Let's see if we can find any carriers in the kitchen or utility room.'

The stench increased as we entered the kitchen and passed into the utility room. Trays of cat litter lay in rows on the floor.

Upstairs, we found a couple of decent wardrobes and a Victorian brass bed which had been badly painted white, but easy to clean up. Harry bounced on the mattress.

'This is lumpier than my granny's porridge,' he said. 'I wonder…'

He grabbed the material straps on the side of the mattress and pulled it off the bed. Underneath it, several packages swathed in bubble wrap lay on the spring bed.

'Would you look at that?' said Harry.

'What are they?' I said.

'Let's find out?'

Harry picked up the closest one and cut it open with his penknife. As he stripped off the layers of bubble wrap, I spotted a glint of metal.

'Oh, my goodness,' I said. 'I think we found the family silver.'

Harry continued to unwrap the packages and soon we had a Georgian tea tray, teapot, hot water pot, sugar bowl and milk jug all in the same design. I looked at the hallmarks.

'Made in Birmingham,' I said. 'Worth a mint.'

'We should call the owner's son and tell him,' said Harry.

'Or not,' I said.

'We can't keep them,'

'I didn't think we should. He told us he wasn't interested. The owner had six cats, and her son will put them down without giving them a chance. I think if she had the choice, she'd donate the money to the cat charity.'

Harry rubbed his chin.

'I like your logic,' he said. 'Can you sell them in your shop?'

'Not really, but Max and Grace down the road could sell them for us if we give them a commission. They charge far more than me, so we could get full value for them.'

'Fine. That's what we'll do.'

When we had finished removing the silver and a couple of pieces of furniture from the house, I went to the back door to lock it, but the padlock wouldn't close. Then I remembered the instructions we had received, so I asked Harry for the key.

'Isn't that padlock the same as the one on the Conrad front door?' said Harry.

'I think so. I didn't get a close look. Let's get out of here. This place gives me the creeps and I think there's a flea crawling up my shin.'

Later, as we sat in a pub after eating delicious steak and kidney pies with perfect chips, I rang Sarah and asked her for the telephone number of William Conrad. I told her I wanted to extend my condolences to him and show him the same photographs I had shown her. She seemed reluctant, but a couple of minutes later, my phone pinged and his contact details came up on my screen. I signalled Harry to stay quiet and tapped on William's number. After a few rings, his quavering voice came on the line.

'Hello? If you're selling something, I'm not interested.'

'Mr Conrad? It's Tanya Carter, Mel's friend.'

'Tanya who?'

'I used to be called Tanya Bowe before I married. I went to school with Mel.'

'What do you want?'

'Greg Summers gave me an album of photographs belonging to Mel and I wondered if you might like to see it?'

'Can you send it to me?'

'Oh, no. I'm afraid it might get lost in the post. Can I come and visit you?'

'No, that wouldn't do at all. Is there somewhere I can find you instead?'

'I have an antique shop on the high street, near the old Italian café.'

'What's it called?'

'Second Home. We've got a café ourselves, upstairs, if you fancy a coffee.'

'I don't drink coffee. It stops me sleeping, but I'll have tea, thank you.'

'When can we expect you?'

'My wife has booked a hair appointment at eleven o'clock on Thursday morning. She's normally in there for at least an hour or two when they do her greys. Can I come then?'

'I'll look forward to it.'

He hung up.

'That's interesting,' I said. 'I got the distinct impression that William didn't want his wife to see the photos.'

'Maybe you can find out why?' said Harry.

'Maybe I can.'

Chapter 19

Mouse arrived home from partying in the early hours of Thursday morning, and, having already resolved to treat him with a little more tolerance, I left him to sleep in. Teenage boys are far less mature than they appear physically and I should learn to pick my fights. I peeped in through his door and watched him sleep for a little while, his mop of black curls and bowed lips making him resemble a prince from a fairy tale. I felt an unreasonable rush of love for this delinquent boy I inherited with my divorce from George.

I opened Second Home at ten o'clock and waited for Grace Wong to turn up. It wasn't a long wait. She turned up excited and breathless at about five minutes past ten with a little fold up trolley. She kissed me hello, her eyes darting around the ground floor, checking my stock for bargains to buy, for which she would charge double in their shop. I didn't resent their profits. I lacked the gumption to charge so much and preferred a steady stream of income rather than limited cash-flow from time to time. She spotted the cardboard box on the gate-legged table in the middle of the Turkish kilim rug.

'They're all yours,' I said. 'Get what you can for them and bring me a fat wad of cash.'

Grace pulled out the ornate silver sugar bowl and removed a hand lens from the pocket of her harem pants. She examined the hallmarks and beamed at me.

'I have a client who will pee his pants when I tell him what I've got,' she said. 'They could do with a bit of a polish, though.'

'I'm sure Max is a dab hand with the Duraglit,' I said, grinning.

'He likes to give things a good rub,' she said, her eyes twinkling with amusement.

We folded down the flaps and loaded the box onto the trolley. Grace left with a wave and a smile. She had grown on me since the first time she'd come into the shop and looked down her nose at my stock. Her impression of me had improved with the quality of my stock, although I suspected her attitude might change if I started copying their inflated prices. Her husband Max was harder to read, but I intended to get to know them better now that I had to work full time in this tricky market. I had nowhere near their breadth of knowledge, and I could rely on them to be honest with me about pricing. That said, I suspected that the ease with which I could check how much they were making on my ex-stock kept them that way.

The thought of a nice milky coffee tempted me upstairs, but I held off making one, anticipating William Conrad's arrival. I put the album on the coffee table. Mouse had already made copies of all the photos on a USB stick so my paranoia about losing it had diminished.

I surfed the internet for a few minutes on my smart phone and got a text from Harry asking for updates. My new phone had proved easy to use despite my fear I would be too backward to make it work. I had even tried a game called Candy Crush, which I had a feeling would soon become addictive.

The doorbell rang, and I trotted down the stairs to open the door for William Conrad. He had been a dashing man in his youth, and spent time in Malaysia on the tea plantations. Now he looked like a white raisin, shrunken, shrivelled and much diminished by age and illness. I offered my hand for him to shake, but he kissed it instead and gave me a wink. Not dead yet then.

'Hello, my dear. I hope I'm not late. Fiona must see a particular stylist who she's been with for years and years. The stylist postponed the appointment by fifteen minutes this morning, so we had to go in later.'

'I quite understand,' I said. 'I've had the same hairdresser for years and no one else will do.'

'Sometimes I think women are more faithful to their hairdressers than their husbands,' said William.

'You may be right,' I said.

I changed the sign in the door to read shut and showed him the stairs up to the café.

'Always the stairs,' he said.

I followed him up. Was that a reference to Mel's death? It couldn't have been an attempt at a joke, could it?

'What sort of tea would you like?'

'Just builder's tea. Strong with milk,' said William.

'I'll make a pot. You can add your own milk. The album is on the table if you would like to look at it.'

He tottered over and picked up the album, leafing through the pages before he had even sat down. I watched him out of the corner of my eye while I filled the stainless-steel pot with boiling water and made myself a latte. He gazed at the photographs as if transfixed, crooning over the ones of Diane, and gently stroking them with his finger. A tear escaped from his right eye and ran down his cheek. He took out a creased handkerchief and dabbed at his cheeks. I pretended I hadn't seen him, and waiting until he had replaced the hanky in his pocket before bringing over the tray.

'Aren't they wonderful?' he said to me. 'I didn't know Mel had kept them all. She left in such a hurry. I'm glad she had them to keep her company all these years.'

'Why did she leave?' I said. 'One minute she was at school with us, and the next she had left. She didn't say goodbye to anyone. She just disappeared.'

'I don't know. She was very strong willed you know.'

I let him look at the photos some more until he came to the one of Mel and Ronnie. He pointed at it.

'That's where the trouble started,' he said.

'With Ronnie?' I said.

'Yes. She wanted to marry him, but I forbade her. It couldn't have worked. She seemed to comply with my wishes. I thought she had accepted my explanation, but then Fiona told me they had married in secret. I couldn't figure out how. They needed one of us to sign the papers.'

'But then she left?'

'Yes. Nobody knows why. She didn't even tell Ronnie. I was relieved at first, but then the years went by with no word. I thought we'd lost her.'

'Why were you so against their marriage?'

'They were too young. It wouldn't have been right.'

'And then she turned up out of the blue?'

'Not quite. She called me and asked me to forgive her. She said she had married a man called Greg and had made a new life for herself. I presumed she had divorced Ronnie, but I don't know if she ever did. She came down here to see me and we made up. I thought I had my little girl back.'

He reached into his jacket. I thought he would bring out his handkerchief, but he handed me an old Kodak envelope filled with photographs.

'I kept these others locked away. Fiona doesn't like photos of my past life with Diane, so I don't look at them often.'

I looked through them and recognised some of them as being taken on the same day as the ones in the album. I admired some classic studio shots of Diane looking fabulous in a two piece and pearls. One photograph showed William gazing at Diane with a fervent expression on his face. Then I stopped and stared at the one taken on the beach. Mel and Ronnie stood together laughing beside Sarah Bingley, who looked a million years younger and beautiful with happiness. Something about the photo seemed odd to me, but I couldn't put my finger on it.

'What a great day that was,' said William. 'One of our last happy days together.'

'It must have been dreadful for you all when Diane died.'

'The shock nearly killed me. Thank heavens for Sarah. She kept me going. She's the one who redesigned the memorial rose garden after Diane's death. It's not much to look at now, but in the summer it's a blaze of pink blooms. It reminds me of her every year.'

'Did Sarah work for you for a long time?'

'Many years. But she didn't get on with Fiona. They had a big fight after Mel left, and it forced me to let her go.'

'That must have been hard,' I said.

'You can't imagine.'

'May I take a photograph of this one?' I said.

'Of course. They're all we have now, aren't they?'

'Would you like the album?' I said. 'I've taken copies of the photos.'

'That would be wonderful, but Fiona wouldn't understand if she found it. Can I collect it another day?'

'I'll keep it here under the desk. You can pop in any time and have a look at them until you can take it.'

He smiled.

'You must think me a foolish old man,' he said. 'But Fiona is good to me, and she's all I've got left now.'

I patted his hand.

'Your album is safe here. Come and see it whenever you like.'

He tottered out of the shop and headed down the high street towards the hairdresser. He had seemed a lot more compos mentis than I remembered from the funeral. Perhaps he had been dumbstruck with grief. It wouldn't be surprising, losing your only daughter like that, just when you got her back. Mel had talked about him getting frail, but perhaps she meant compared to back in her youth. My parents both died relatively young, so I envied anyone who still had theirs. Except Ghita. Hers seemed to use her as a punch bag.

I opened the photograph I had taken of Mel, Ronnie and Sarah on the beach and magnified the faces looking from one to the other as I tried to figure out what had struck me about them. It hit me like a punch in the face. The same ears, the same chins and lips, the same brown wiry hair. Sarah Bingley was Ronnie's mother. But why hadn't she said so? I remembered asking her if she was married, and she gave me a one-word answer. But I never asked her if she had any children. And why had he changed his surname? It seems like every time I found an answer, another two questions appeared. No wonder George spent his whole life frustrated and confused. I always thought I caused it, with my depression and inertia, but maybe the clues wouldn't come together for him either.

Chapter 20

I called a summit at the Shanty, the pub run by Joy and Ryan Wells. It sits on a small bluff on the outskirts of Seacastle, overlooking Pirate's Bay. The pub is awkward to get to and entails a walk along the bluff from the car park. The cliff is slowly falling down into the sea and the pub will follow the path before too long. Joy says it will see them out, but I'm not convinced. Apart from that minor inconvenience, the Shanty is the most welcoming, cosy, archetypical seaside pub I know. Even I have to stoop at the door, which Ryan swears they built so small to keep the heat in. He should know. He's a scientist, and George always claimed Ryan was a spook, but I couldn't get anything out of Joy about the M15 connection. Ryan looked like George Smiley with his swot's demeanour and the cloudy glasses. He had been in a wheelchair for years after an accident, but Joy wouldn't talk about that either, so I became convinced he had a shady past they covered up.

I walked over to the pub with Mouse, who had been quite happy to come for a drink to share his research with us. He spent a lot of time with his friends, and pretended to be a hard man, but if left to his own devices, he often liked to spend time with women. I guess he missed his mum. I usually enjoyed his company, but I had something on my mind, and I couldn't imagine how to broach the subject with him. My favourite bracelet had gone missing, and I had a sinking feeling about it. It had definitely been on the shelf in the bathroom when I left for work, and even though I searched high and low, I couldn't find it. I wanted to ask him if he had seen it, but I felt awkward. How could I avoid the appearance of blame? And what if he or one of his mates had taken it?

I knew that Mouse's criminal record had involved carjacking, but not if he had indulged in petty theft. Taking him in had been instinctive, but George had called me naïve. I should have asked him, but it would have seemed like a betrayal of Mouse's trust. I'd have to talk to him eventually, but now didn't seem like the time.

A stumble on the stony path jolted me out of my inner dialogue and I wondered how on earth Ryan manoeuvred his chair out of the pub. No wonder Joy spent her life buying new tyres and spare parts. Mind you, I also suspected Ryan of constantly tinkering with the mechanism to make it do more. He had already installed an elevator under the seat so he could speak to people face to face at the bar and not have to look upwards. We leant into the breeze blowing from the west down the Channel and turned to gaze at the wind farm far out to sea. The sun had started its steep winter descent to the horizon and the horizontal light caught the blades and towers of the turbines, making them appear like a field of rapeseed, golden against the sky. Mouse sighed at the beauty of it. I knew exactly how he felt.

We pushed our way into the pub and headed for the back corner table where Roz and Flo were already seated and deep in conversation. The glass fisherman's float, which hung from the ceiling over their table, caught a flash of light from the setting sun before it sank. Harry had also arrived, and he chatted to Joy and Ryan at the bar. I slid into the window seat and introduced Mouse to Flo, who beamed and enveloped him in a squidgy hug, which he did not seem inclined to leave quickly. Flo's hugs are the best. She smells so good. I pulled my eyebrows together and tried to look disapproving, failing miserably. He gave me a cheeky grin.

I had printed out William Conrad's photos and inserted them into Mel's album, which I carried in my bag. I took out the album and placed it on the table.

'Exhibit A,' I said. 'Essential viewing.'

Flo picked it up and leafed through it with Roz, asking me for confirmation of the cast of characters and nodding vigorously. Harry joined them and pointed out the bits he remembered from Conrad House. Mouse sipped a lager and ate a large packet of salt and vinegar crisps even though he had eaten just before we set out. He took out his iPad and went up to the bar to ask Ryan for the Wi-Fi code, and they were soon deep into conversation about something nerdy and technical, by the looks of the hand gestures. I loved how Ryan could talk to anyone. It made him the ideal landlord, and a rubbish businessman. Joy kept a tight rein on the finances, or the pub would have gone under years back from Ryan handing out free drinks to anyone he liked.

Ghita burst through the door, pink-cheeked from the wind, and ordered herself a jasmine tea at the bar. She doesn't drink much and says she's allergic to alcohol. I'm not convinced, as I've seen her have a glass of champagne on special occasions without adverse effect. She'd already perused the album various times at the shop, so I only showed her the recent additions from William Conrad's collection. Soon Joy couldn't resist our gathering either and we brought her up to speed too.

Then I hit the group with my finding.

'I think Sarah Bingley is Ronnie Barratt's mother,' I said.

Roz grabbed the photograph album and opened it at William's one of Mel, Ronnie, and Sarah. She peered closely at it again.

'You might be right,' she said. 'But why didn't she tell you that?'

'You are right,' said Mouse, who had returned from the bar, and was now flicking through tabs on his iPad. 'Ronnie Bingley changed his name to Ronnie Barratt after his eighteenth birthday.'

'Why on earth would he do that?' said Flo. 'It seems so random.'

'Maybe it's his father's surname?' said Ghita.

'Good call,' I said. 'Sarah told me she never married, but maybe Ronnie found out who his father was from his birth certificate.'

'Or from government records,' said Mouse. 'You have to be eighteen to access them.'

'Mystery solved,' said Roz.

'I also found the record of his marriage to Mel Conrad when they were teenagers. Fiona Conrad countersigned it.'

'Fiona Conrad?' said Ghita. 'I thought you said she hated Mel?'

'They were pretty hostile to each other when I saw them at Conrad House, but time may have changed their relationship.'

'And what about Greg?' said Roz. 'You told us they were on the verge of getting divorced. But what if he discovered Mel was married to Ronnie and not to him? Would he have murdered her out of jealousy?'

'Not jealousy, but greed is a possibility. He desperately needed money,' said Harry, who up to then had only been listening.

'Flo, I know you can't give us the skinny on current cases, but since the police ruled Mel's death an accident, is there any way you can tell us what you heard or found about the incident?' I said.

'I wouldn't be here if I couldn't speak at all,' said Flo, shifting in her seat. 'But George is not to hear about this.'

'Cross my heart and hope to die,' said Roz. 'I'll be as silent as a grave.'

I rolled my eyes.

'Don't you mean rave? If you blab about any of this, I'll kill you myself,' I said.

Flo drew herself up and closed her eyes as if to visualise the scene better.

'I found Mel in the stairwell under the first-floor landing. She had broken her neck in the fall, which would have killed her instantly. Her handbag had opened on impact and spread its contents all over the floor. I recorded some random items of makeup, her bank and store cards in a wallet, a packet of tissues, a business card for the guesthouse where she stayed, and a handkerchief. I think that's all.'

'Did you check the upstairs landing for clues?' said Harry.

'Of course, but I could see no evidence of a struggle. And the autopsy did not show any signs of violence on her body. She had marks on her upper arm, but they could have come from anything.'

'Like someone gripping it?' said Ghita.

'Perhaps,' said Flo. 'Difficult to tell though,'

'Maybe someone tried to stop her from falling and grabbed her arm?' said Roz. 'But why didn't they say so? Why did they leave her dead on the floor and shut the padlock? It's too weird for me.'

'We couldn't find any evidence of anyone else in the house with her that evening. There were a multitude of fingerprints, including yours, Tanya, and that's about it. No signs of a scuffle or unusual activity. No traces of drugs or alcohol. Nothing. The only witness was that annoying dog who refused to tell me what he knew.'

'He's all hat and no cattle,' said Harry. 'You should have bribed him.'

'He'd have frightened away most people,' I said. 'He is ferocious.'

'What have we got so far?' said Mouse.

'A bunch of suspects, multiple motives and scant evidence,' I said.

'A jealous husband, an estranged father, a greedy stepmother, a jealous, vengeful ex-husband or even still married first husband in a bigamous union, a dead mother, a lonely housekeeper, and a vicious dog? And that's not including the dodgy school friends. I think we all need a drink,' said Harry.

'Hear, hear,' said Joy.

Chapter 21

I chose the next morning to ask Mouse about the bracelet. I dropped it into our breakfast conversation as casually as I could.

'Um, I'm missing a bracelet. I don't know if you've seen it? I left it in the bathroom a couple of days ago, and I can't find it anywhere.'

Mouse's spoon stopped halfway to his mouth and colour rose to his normally pale cheeks. His eyes opened wide.

'Are you asking me if I stole it?' he said in a quiet voice.

I shook my head, avoiding his glare.

'No, of course not, I just thought you might have moved it or—'

He shoved his chair back and threw his cereal bowl on the floor, where it shattered into a million pieces. He swallowed twice.

'How could you? I've done everything I could to help you. Dad was right. You're a bitter old bitch who blames other people for her troubles.'

'But I'm not accusing you of anything.'

'Aren't you? It certainly sounds like it to me. I'm not staying here to be insulted by you. I'm the only fool who thought they misjudged you, but now I know better. Even Hades hates you.'

He ran upstairs and stuffed some clothes in a rucksack while I watched on helplessly, trying to calm him down. But he ignored me and stormed out of my house, screaming that he would never come back. I had been rooted to the ground with fear and shock for a while before I burst into tears. Even Hades seemed concerned by the commotion, peeping out of his basket, before going back inside. I left the kitchen as it was and threw on my coat, still choking back the sobs. The depth of my emotions, and his, had shocked us both, I think. It felt irreparable at that moment. What had I done?

The landline rang as I headed for the door, and befuddled with grief, I forgot to screen the number.

'Hello,' I croaked.

'Have you been crying again? George is worried about you.'

I slapped my forehead. Just what I didn't need right now. A call from my smug married sister.

'Hello Helen. How nice to hear from you! Are the kids well?'

'Don't think you can distract me. I can tell you've been weeping. Is your depression back?'

'No, I had a horrible shock that's all. I'm fine now.'

'You don't sound fine. Anyway, George asked me to call and talk to you.'

'Why didn't he ring me himself?'

'He told me you were being difficult.'

'Difficult? What about?'

She snorted. *Is there anything more annoying than an elder sister who condescends to you all the time?*

'Don't be silly, Tan. He told me you're obsessed with Mel Conrad's death.'

And how did George know? Ghita probably. Ghita was lovely and caring, but she never met a problem head-on, preferring to swerve it or hand it to someone else to solve. This went for her own problems too. We never heard about them, but her level of sighing and biscuit eating went up exponentially when she felt pressured.

'I'm not obsessed, just concerned. Ever since Mel's mother died of cancer, she had to deal with one disaster after another. I'm making sure nobody caused this one deliberately.'

Helen tutted.

'Diane Conrad didn't die of cancer. Who told you that?'

'I don't know. Maybe our form teacher at school?'

'Seriously? Diane died of a fall in the garden. An accident.'

'Another accident? That's two accidental deaths in the Conrad family. I'm not buying it.'

'For heaven's sake, give it a rest. Are you still taking your pills?'

'I stopped about six months ago, if it's any of your business. I'm just having a fraught day, that's all.'

'Would you like me to come and see you?'

My eyes filled with tears at this unexpected offer, and I had to force out the next sentence.

'I'd love you to come and visit, but only because I miss you.'

A long silence followed my admission. I missed her. I longed for the days when we actually had things in common, like giggling and Miami Vice. I liked Tubbs and she like Crocket. We never had the same taste in men, thank goodness. She coughed.

'I miss you too. I might even get down to see you one of these days and have a Mr Whippy on the promenade.'

She hung up before I could reminisce about our walks along the sea and the 99s we gobbled before they could melt. The boys we fancied. But I felt better, and I had the germ of an idea.

I got into my car and drove to the graveyard. By the time I'd got there, I had stopped crying, but my hands shook as I blew my nose. Why did I even ask Mouse about the bracelet? It had not been worth anything much, only sentimental value, and only to me. It had a small amount of nine carat gold, but the resale value would have been minimal. Mouse's reaction had scared me. Had George really told him I was a bitter bitch? I had felt sorry for myself for years, but only because my serotonin levels were on the floor.

I walked to the Conrads' grave and looked around at the quiet scene, so different to the one in my house. I hadn't returned since Mel's funeral and small shoots had already sprouted on the earth covering her grave. Somebody had planted a couple of snowdrop plants near the headstone. Their quiet beauty almost made me cry again. Mel's name had been carved into the family gravestone below Diane's. I took out my notebook and copied the date of Diane's death.

After I had paid my respects and had a wander around, I sat on the wall and called Flo.

'I need a small favour.'

'How small?'

'I need the file on Diane Conrad's death.'

'And how do you know one exists?'

'Because her death was unexplained, so she must have had an autopsy. The file must be somewhere in the bowels of the station.'

Flo sighed.

'It will take me forever to find. However, it's a slow morning here, so I'll do my best to get that for you right now,' she said.

'That would be wonderful,' I said. 'By the way, I had a bit of a run in with Mouse today.'

'Did you? I thought you two were like peas in a pod.'

'One of my bracelets has gone missing, and I made the mistake of asking him if he'd seen it.'

'Silly girl. Mouse suffers from ADHD, not sticky fingers. Did he get angry?'

'Steam came out of his ears.'

'He'll calm down. But, trust me on this, Mouse doesn't steal.'

'The bracelet's definitely missing, so it's awkward.'

'Leave it with him. If any of his mates took it, you'll soon find out.'

'Thanks Flo. I couldn't bear to lose him now. He's kind of special.'

'Peas in a pod, like I said. Text me her date of death.'

'I'll do it immediately. And…'

'I know. Don't tell George.'

Chapter 22

Mouse did not come back that night, or the day after. I wanted to call George and ask him if he knew where Mouse was staying, but I couldn't face the gloating. Mouse had managed before by sofa-surfing with his friends, so I assumed he had gone straight there and told them all about me and my horrible accusations. One of the few people that Mouse trusted picked me up to take me to a house clearance the next morning. I tried to be my usual chatty self, but the effort drained me and I soon sank into an exhausted silence. Harry did not help me. In fact, he seemed to enjoy my discomfort. I became quite angry with him and struggled not to blurt out something sarcastic.

Finally, he took pity on me.

'I had a call from your young rodent,' he said. 'He's not a happy bunny.'

'He's not happy?' I said, struggling to contain myself. 'What about me? I'm worried sick about him.'

'Are you though? Because he says you accused him of stealing from you.'

'And you believe him? I thought you were on my side.'

'I'm trying not to take sides. Do you want to talk about it?'

'Not really. I can see why he's angry, but it doesn't change the fact that he, or his friends, are the only possible culprits. My bracelet is gone, and I didn't lose it. George gave it to me for our first Christmas, and it held happy memories of that time. And I didn't accuse Mouse of anything. I asked him if he had seen it.'

'Do you think he's a tea leaf?'

'No, he's wild, but he's not a thief. I expect one of his light-fingered friends pocketed it. I'd do anything to wind back time, but I can't. Does he hate me?'

'I don't think so. Nobody could hate you. You're pretty wonderful.'

I bit my lip.

'Really?'

'Don't fish for compliments. You still made a complete horse's arse of the entire business. I expect he'll get sick of sleeping on sofas eventually.'

'As long as he doesn't tell his father. I couldn't bear George laughing at me.'

'You still care what George thinks?'

'No, I mean yes, I mean, I don't know what I mean. I suppose I relied on his approval for so many years, I can't get out of the habit.'

'You should. You use him as a shield.'

'A shield?'

'Against men. Anytime someone tries to get close, you quote George at them. He might as well be standing beside you, warding them off.'

'That's not true.'

'Isn't it?'

I hated Harry right then, but I swallowed my fury, and went for humour to mask my distress.

'Maybe. I'm making progress, though.'

'You are?'

'Well, I've got two men living with me now.'

Harry roared with laughter and banged the steering wheel with his hands.

'That's true. I'm tempted to join them, just to annoy George,' he said.

'Don't go getting any ideas. I already have to cook and clean for three. Four might tip me over the edge.'

He grinned and pulled up beside a boarded-up shop.

'Okay. We're here. Let's hope there's something worth coming for.'

'What is this place?'

'An old tailor's premises. It's been closed for years, but the owner wouldn't sell it. A mate of mine told me they might have some old sewing machines.'

'Sewing machines?'

'There's this charity in the East End. They recondition old machines and send them to Africa. I thought we might do a run to London to deliver them, if you're game? And there might be some stuff you can use.'

'That sounds like a better plan than sulking at home and quoting George to the hoards trying to break down my door.'

'You might enjoy a break from your self-loathing too.'

'Please don't lecture me. I rely on you to differ from the other well-meaning people interfering in my life.'

'Fair enough. I'm just trying to help.'

He jumped out of the van and forced the key into the lock, which had rusted from lack of use. He launched himself at the door and hit it with a grunt as it popped open with ease, spilling him onto the floor. I offered him my hand, trying not to laugh, and he dusted himself off, shaking his head.

'All that army training is pointless,' he said.

'I wouldn't say that. You've got the grunt down to a T.'

He rolled his eyes.

'Can you check if that blind works? They have cut the electricity off.'

Determined not to look foolish, I gave the cord a sharp tug, and the whole blind came away from the wall and landed on the window display, throwing the tailor's dummies and stands onto the floor.

'I love a woman's delicate touch,' said Harry.

I couldn't help guffawing at that. I bent over and picked up the dummies. They were works of art in their own right, padded and covered in heavy cotton, which had faded from years standing in the window. Definitely something people would buy, and if not, great for hanging coats in the café.

'I'll take these, if you don't mind,' I said.

'Knock yourself out. At least you'll have some company.'

I tried to punch his arm, but he ran down the aisle of the shop, giggling. I ran after him and cornered him at the back of the shop. He put his arms up to surrender and I held his wrists against the wall, which brought my face uncomfortably close to his. I got a powerful urge to kiss him, but I chickened out and let my arms fall to my sides again.

'Coward,' he said.

I hit him hard in the arm, even though we both knew what he meant. I looked around the room and noticed three or four old mechanical Singer sewing machines. Glad of the distraction, I wandered over and tried the wheel on one. It turned smoothly, and the foot pedal moved up and down.

'I think this one works,' I said. 'I presume they would prefer manual ones.'

'It's better for villages where they don't have electricity. We can take all of them, even if they are not in working order. They have a technician who refurbishes the machines before they send them out in a container.'

'These stools are nice,' I said, feeling the smooth wooden tops, shiny with use.

'Many bottoms have shone those. Do you want to take them too?'

'If that's okay.'

'The new owner is going to rip out everything and start again. I think it's going to be a takeaway.'

'Can I take the counter? Those units sell really well to high end retailers once they've been buffed and oiled.'

'Take anything you want. I didn't have to pay for it. I'll give the rest to my mate.'

Once we had loaded everything into the van, we set off for the warehouse owned by the charity. Harry turned the music up too loud for conversation, a deliberate act on his part. Our near miss had brought me out in a cold sweat. But maybe I was the only one who thought about kissing. He didn't pursue the situation any further, nor did he initiate any further banter. After all the years of being married, I had no experience of flirting. George would have taken a very dim view of me practising on anyone else, and would have been astonished if I had tried it on him. George again. Stop wondering how George would react.

We hit green traffic lights all the way and arrived in record time at the warehouse in the west of London, and unloaded the sewing machines. After unloading them and receiving thanks from the woman in charge of the charity, I had the urge to go by Greg Summers' house.

'Why do you want to go there?'

'I don't know. I can't help feeling we missed something, and it wouldn't take us far out of our way. Do you mind?'

'Not at all. If your Spidey senses are tingling, I'm happy to detour via Greg's house. That man is hiding something.'

We were back on safe ground again. Eventually, we would have to broach the subject of our partnership and its boundaries, but we had this investigation in common. A good place to start.

There were no parking spaces big enough for the van on Greg's road so Harry parked on the parallel road and we walked through a gravel lane joining the two. Suddenly, Harry put his hand up and crouched closer to the wall. I know little about the army, but I've seen that gesture before in movies. I stopped still and made myself small behind him. He pointed at Greg's house, almost opposite us, and I noticed the 'For Sale' sign had gone. So why had we hidden? A few seconds later, Fiona Conrad walked across the road and rang the doorbell. Luckily, she didn't turn around or she would have seen our astonished expressions. The door opened and Greg Summers stood on the doorstep, a broad smile on his face.

'Darling,' he said. 'You came.'

He swept her into his arms and they kissed passionately before he carried her indoors, shutting the door behind him with his foot.

'Holy moly,' I said. 'Who'd have guessed it?'

Harry laughed and stood up again.

'If I had known you were Mystic Meg, I'd have asked you for your autograph.'

'If I had known, I'd have charged you for it.'

'Let's get back to the van. We need to get out of here before someone spots us.'

'Don't you think they'll be too busy to look out of the window?'

Harry didn't answer. We trotted back along the lane and got into the van.

'I think you could call that a turn up for the books,' said Harry. 'I certainly didn't see that coming. How on earth did you know?'

I smirked.

'I didn't. But there was something odd about their physical proximity at the church and then at the funeral. And he didn't talk about Mel, he talked about cricket. I just wanted to be sure that he'd actually left.'

'But he hasn't. And the estate agent's sign has gone. Has he come into money all of a sudden? I'll get my cousin to swing by Greg's office and see if his business partner is there. Maybe they got a cash injection from a client? I can ask Mouse to find out if you like.'

'Just don't tell him it's for me.'

'He has to stop sulking sometime. He won't be able to resist a bit of research.'

'Okay. But this brings Fiona and Greg sharply into focus as suspects for Mel's death, doesn't it? With Mel gone, Fiona inherits everything.'

'So how come she's linked up with Greg? He doesn't seem to offer anything.'

I laughed.

'What?'

'Honestly? Greg is a six-foot tall, blond bombshell with fancy manners, and a ticket to the upper classes. Just the thing for a middle-aged woman losing her looks as her aging husband refuses to die.'

'Oh, now that you put it like that, it all makes perfect sense.'

'Greg is the male equivalent of a dumb blonde. Every woman wants one to play with.'

'Do you?' he said, running his hand over his shaved head.

I took pity on him.

'Only in my dreams. I prefer something a bit more down to earth for my daily amusement.'

'I'll keep it in mind.'

'Do you want a coffee before we go home? I think we're pretty safe around here. I don't imagine Fiona will emerge again until later.'

'There's a café on the corner up there.'

We strolled in and ordered cappuccinos. The café looked similar to the one that had closed down on our high street and made me feel nostalgic. I wandered around and looked at the faded pictures of Italy on the walls, and inspected the notice board to see what services local people were offering. To my surprise, a newspaper article about Mel's death, with a pretty photograph of her, took pride of place. The owner saw me looking at it and shook her head sadly.

'Gracious lady, that. It's a terrible pity what happened to her. She used to live around here, you know?'

The hairs on my arms prickled.

'Did you know her?' I said, and I could see Harry leaning over to hear us.

'Oh yes. She started coming in recently, with her brother.'

'Her brother? Was he tall and blond?'

'Oh no, dear. That's her husband. They made her brother from a different mould. He had dark hair and a wiry body. He looked weather beaten. Shy. Wouldn't say boo to a goose.'

'Can you remember his name?'

She scratched her head.

'No. It's gone. It was a while ago now.'

But when she brought over our coffees, she beamed at me.

'Ronnie. Her brother. That's his name.'

I couldn't have been more astonished. I thanked her and turned to Harry my eyes wide.

'That means Mel hung out with Ronnie before she died.'

'Have you considered the possibility he really could have been her brother?' said Harry.

'What do you mean?'

'Well, Sarah Bingley spent many years in that household. Did she have an affair with William during his first marriage?'

'But why would Mel marry her brother?'

'Maybe she didn't know they had the same father?'

'Why did she tell the café owner Ronnie was her brother?'

'She could have been lying. Or maybe she found out recently. Could Ronnie have killed Mel to inherit William's money? Does William know he has a son? Does Fiona know? Why has Sarah kept this secret?'

'Okay, stop. My head is spinning. I've got to mull over this new piece of the jigsaw,' I said.

'Let me know if you work it out.'

Harry dropped me off when the street lights were already lit. I wanted to ask him in, but without the cushion of Mouse's presence, I wasn't sure I could cope with the attraction between us.

'If Mouse rings you again, can you tell him I'm in bits and I want him to come home, please?'

'Of course. I'll give you a tinkle when I know where the next clearance is. Keep me updated with the investigation.'

'I promise.'

Chapter 23

Mouse still hadn't returned by the time I got home. I stood in the doorway to his bedroom and surveyed the bombsite he had left behind. I had to resist the urge to pick up his dirty clothes, make the bed, and remove the used cups and plates. Most of his clean clothes still hung in the closet, giving me hope he might return. The Grotty Hovel seemed freezing and dark without Mouse in it. Hades refused to emerge from his basket and glowered at me when I left his food outside it. I wondered why he hated me so much. Most animals took to me in an instant. Maybe he thought I had shut him into the basket in the first place. Or disposed of his owner. I hadn't thought to check if someone wanted him back, but I put it on my list of things to do that never got done. I made myself a double gin and tonic and curled up in front of the television.

I tried to relax, but my mind raced, filled with circles upon circles of arguments that wouldn't resolve themselves. Maybe Mel had pretended Ronnie was her brother, so the café owner wouldn't be scandalised by Mel meeting him for cosy chats. And if William really was Ronnie's father, did Ronnie know that, or did he think Mel was pretending? As it stood, Sarah Bingley appeared to be the only person who could tell me the identity of Ronnie's father. That would clarify many of the scenarios in my head and eliminate others. What if I asked her directly? Again, I had the photos as an excuse to set up the meeting, but how to broach the subject? My head ached with the effort of trying to figure out this intractable puzzle.

I stood up to clear my head, and I noticed a large envelope on the floor near the front door. I must have missed it when I came in, still trying to get a last glance at Harry. Glad of the distraction, I leaned over to pick it up. At first, I thought the envelope might contain a catalogue of some sort, but as I ripped it open, I saw the manila folder with the sticker on the tab. Diane Conrad. Good old Flo had come up trumps. I sat back down and removed the folder from the envelope. It had faded with time and had several circular coffee mug stains intersecting on it. Someone had written 'Accident?' in the intersection of the stains. Several other names inscribed in the circles had been scrubbed out and I could not decipher them. So, they had not convinced everyone about Diane's death being caused by a fall. Maybe the roots of Mel's death went back further than anyone could imagine. But she was only a little girl at the time. What could it have to do with her recent death?

The folder contained a mixture of interviews, crude forensics, and some gruesome crime scene photographs, which left little to the imagination. Being married to George meant that I had seen worse before. It was against department policy to bring work home, but in the good old days, he had often slipped a folder in his briefcase when he wanted to pick my brains on a case. I reviewed the photographs first. Diane Conrad had died in October 1991. Killed by a blow to the head which caved in her skull. According to the report, she had been pruning the roses when she had slipped and fallen backwards onto the rock surround of the rose garden. The fall had killed her instantly. Fiona Dillon, the private secretary of William Conrad, who claimed to have been looking for the housekeeper, found Diane's body. Fiona found the body? It all seemed rather convenient, considering she married the grieving widower not long afterwards. I googled 'rose pruning' and discovered experts considered late winter or early spring peak pruning times. Would Diane would have got that so wrong? I rolled my eyes as I imagined the team agreeing to call it an accident. But no one questioned Fiona's motives. After all, she was only the secretary, and not worthy of notice, as women rarely murder anyone by violent means.

Could Fiona have murdered them both? After all, she would inherit all of William's wealth now they were dead. Ronnie represented the only fly in the ointment in this theory. If he was really Mel's brother, Fiona never stood to inherit anything, because he had already turned five when Diane met her fate. If, however, she hadn't known about Ronnie's parentage, she could have elaborated the plan to clear the way, without taking him into account. Fiona still had charm and looks, and her relationship with Greg suggested she used them to their full advantage. Had she persuaded Greg to kill Mel? After all,

Mel had already decided to divorce him, according to Fiona, cutting him out of a share in her inheritance.

It might have been Dutch courage, but I had the urge to find out the truth at its source. Fiona knew about Mel's marriage to Ronnie. She found Diane's body; she had seduced Greg, what else had she done? I dialled her number and waited. It rang out without Fiona answering it and went through to the answering machine. I took a chance and left a message.

'Fiona, it's Tanya. I saw you with Greg in London today, and I wondered if we might have a chat. Call me when you get this message.'

After I hung up, I wondered if I had made a mistake, but the gin had made me brave and there was plenty of time to repent. Still wondering about the latest revelations, I wandered into the kitchen to wash my mug. My cell phone vibrated in my pocket and I shook the suds from my hands. After giving them a brisk wipe with the dishcloth, I took the phone out and answered the call.

'Flo. I've been reading the file you dropped by. It's such an interesting read.'

'Oh, yes, about that. George—'

I rolled my eyes.

'George what?'

'I didn't drop it by your house. He did.'

'Seriously?'

'He spotted it under my arm when I brought it up from the stacks. You know what he's like when he thinks someone is stepping out of line. I explained you had asked to see it and he gave me a dressing down. He demanded to know what we were up to. I told him he really ought to talk to you about Mel's murder, as you had come up with some new ideas.'

'What did he say to that?'

'He sighed and said he'd give the folder to you himself.'

'Luckily for me, I wasn't in and he posted it through the door.'

'How long will your luck last, though?'

Even as Flo finished her sentence, the doorbell rang. Someone pressed the buzzer long and hard.

'Not very long,' I said. 'Someone's at the door.'

When I opened it, George stood outside, drumming his fingers on the door frame, and raising an eyebrow at me.

'I thought I told you to keep your nose out of this,' he said. 'But it was delusional of me to imagine that you'd listen to me any more than when we were married.'

He pushed past me and sat himself on the sofa. Without another word to me, he sifted through the file on Diane Conrad's death, and read the notes I had taken. Knowing it would be pointless to object as the file was technically police property, I made us both a gin and tonic.

'I hope that's not too strong. I'm driving home, you know.'

'It's one shot. I measured it.'

Mollified, he took a slug and wiped the back of his hand.

'Blimey, that's good. I really needed that.'

I almost made the mistake of sympathising with him, but then I remembered that was Sharon's job now.

Instead, I said 'want to know what I think?' To my surprised, he nodded.

'Make it concise. I have to go home soon.'

So, I told him about Greg and Fiona's affair, and the coincidence of Fiona finding Diane's body. I didn't mention Ronnie because we didn't know if he would turn out to be a red herring or not. As far as I was concerned, Fiona didn't know about him, and neither did I. George listened without interrupting, except to ask for one detail or another. Then he shook his head at me.

'The problem with your theory is that you're assuming everyone has told you the truth. People lie all the time. They're not like you, Tan. They lie to make themselves look better, or cleverer, or richer, or innocent, or to pass the blame onto someone else. The point of evidence is to prove or disprove what people tell you and work out who's lying and who isn't, and you don't have proof of any of this. Where's your evidence?'

For a moment, his piercing examination of me made me feel stupid, like the old days, but then I had a revelation.

'The handkerchief,' I said.

'What handkerchief?'

'The one found beside Mel's body. Flo said the impact on the ground scattered Mel's possessions.'

'Which she shouldn't have told you,' George interjected.

'Mel carried a packet of tissues everywhere. She had a runny nose, probably allergies, although in those days, nobody had ever heard of such a thing. A packet had fallen out of her handbag.'

'And your point is?'

'Flo mentioned a handkerchief too. Women I know don't carry handkerchiefs, unless they are ninety. And not if they already have tissues.'

George now gazed at me.

'So?' he said.

'Why didn't anyone question the presence of the handkerchief on the floor beside the body? It was very unlikely to be Mel's.'

'You may have a point. Go on.'

'Greg uses a handkerchief. I saw him dabbing his eyes with one at the funeral. It had some sort of red design on it.'

'A pimpernel?'

'I don't know. I couldn't see it clearly.'

George slapped his forehead.

'The Gentleman's Club that Greg belongs to is called The Scarlet Pimpernel. You might just be on to something here.'

'Won't there be DNA on it?'

'Unfortunately, you took those items back to Greg. It's likely he washed the handkerchief by now, and anyway, he might say he lent it to her, and we can't prove otherwise.'

'But it's a start, isn't it?' I said, elated.

'It's a start. Please, promise me you won't ask any more questions while I look into this?'

I crossed my fingers behind my back when I remembered the phone message I had left for Fiona and smiled.

'Okay, but you promise to keep me informed in return?'

He sighed.

'As you well know, I can't tell you anything about an investigation in progress. I'll take the folder back too.'

I must have looked crestfallen because his big mitt lifted my chin and he pecked me on the forehead.

'It's nice to see you're finally getting yourself back together again. I've missed you.'

And with that, he left.

Chapter 24

As hard as it was for me to back off, I took George's instructions to heart. Nothing remained to be done. Fiona did not call me back straight away, and as the days went by, my dread lessened. I vowed never to leave another message after a double gin. Perhaps my message had not been delivered to her? Maybe she was mulling a reply? I only knew I felt relief to my bones that she had decided not to respond to my challenge. George would sort it out.

The Vintage café continued to be popular, but it had lost its buzz since Mouse had left. He had a subtle way of flirting with every woman, no matter her age, that made everyone light up and buy cake to go with their coffee. Harry told me he had been in contact with Mouse and I should be patient, but I mourned his presence and Hades spent life in a permanent sulk, blaming me for the loss of another person he actually liked. Harry and I had done a couple of clearances where I could find nothing to salvage, and I wondered if I should continue. Only the prospect of seeing him kept me interested. I wondered if we would ever have the courage to raise the bar on our relationship, or would we just slip into the role of mates and get marooned there?

Then one day, Harry turned up at the shop unannounced.

'Any information on how the case is progressing?' he said.

'George's team is sealed tighter than a Kilner jar. Getting blood from a stone would be easier.'

'You'll find out eventually. For now, you need to come with me,' he said.

'I don't remember you telling me about a clearance for today. I'm alone in the shop.'

'Shut it. This is more important.'

'But what's going on?'

'You'll find out.'

His conviction overcame my reticence, and I turned the sign in the door to c*losed* with a theatrical sigh.

'Where are we going?' I said.

'It's a surprise.'

He gave me an infuriating grin and moved out of hitting range. He knew me too well. I followed him down the side street, out onto the promenade and down the pier towards the end, skirting the café, out into the buffeting wind of the English Channel. The seagulls whirled around above our heads, their beady eyes on the lookout for an emerging sandwich bag or discarded ice cream cone. The tide had almost reached its highest point, and the local anglers were gossiping in the café's shade while their lures dangled in the pier's shadow. Shoals of baitfish shimmered in the clear water and larger fish lurked between the rusty struts. One angler emitted a strangled cry as his rod jerked and slid along the boards. I was so distracted by the activity that I failed to notice Mouse and one of his friends waiting for us at the far end of the pier until I almost bumped into them.

'Well, look who it is,' said Harry, who is a terrible actor at the best of times.

I rolled my eyes at him and waited for a reaction. Mouse gazed at his feet and his friend with the weasel face pretended to be interested in the seagulls.

'Is there any point to this?' I said. 'I'm kind of busy.'

'This is Fergal. He's got something to say to you,' said Mouse, elbowing his friend, who sucked in his cheeks, and reached into his pocket. To my surprise, he produced my bracelet, which he dropped into my palm with disdain.

'I don't know what all the fuss is about for one crappy bracelet,' he said, sniffing. 'The fence wouldn't give me a fiver for it.'

He tried to leave, but Harry grabbed him by the ear and forced him backwards, his face hard. I had never seen Harry's ruthless side before. His eyes had lost their sparkle, and he didn't blink. Sharks look less scary. A shiver ran up my spine.

'Apologise, now,' he said.

'Alright. Alright. Let go,' said Fergal. 'I'm sorry. I saw it tossed on the shelf in the bathroom. I didn't realise it was so important. You've got lots of other stuff.'

I made a mental note to check what else he had taken, but it didn't matter anymore.

'That doesn't give you the right to take it,' I said. 'You're not welcome in my house anymore.'

'The next time something goes missing, I'll call the police,' said Harry. 'Now, get lost.'

Fergal shoved his hands in his pockets and sloped off. Mouse looked like he might go too, but I grabbed his arm and pulled him close to hug him before he could escape.

'Please come home,' I whispered in his ear. 'Hades misses you. He won't eat.'

'And you?'

'I'm missing the extra laundry and cooking.'

He hugged me back and Harry hugged us both. I felt like a bubble of love surrounded us and kept the wind off for a few seconds.

'Can we have something to eat?' said Mouse. 'I'm starving.'

'You're always starving,' I said.

'The café's open,' said Harry. 'I hear the lasagne is delicious.'

Life at the Grotty Hovel went back to normal for me with Mouse's return. Hades was ecstatic and followed Mouse everywhere. He sat outside the bathroom sulking when Mouse ushered him out to have a shower or use the toilet. He purred loudly when stroked and gave me a smug look whenever I caught his eye. I swear he did it on purpose. Cats like to make you grovel. No wonder the ancient Egyptians thought they were gods. It's the superior attitude that gets me. And the worst thing is that I still hope he'll forget his grudge and sit on my lap one day.

Mouse wanted to be brought up to speed about Mel's death and our investigations, so I told him all about

Fiona and Greg, and their unexpected affair. He found my abandonment of the case deeply disappointing, despite my impossible situation regarding his father.

'He still bullies you,' he said. 'You should tell him to get lost.'

'I'm not sure you understand the whole police thing. I can go to jail if I obstruct an investigation.'

'Prison's no big deal.'

'I suppose you'd know,' I said. 'I thought you only had a night in the local slammer.'

'Having a father in the force can be useful sometimes. I don't think he's ever forgiven me though, for his loss of face.'

'He hasn't forgiven me, either. He thinks depression is a sign of weakness. George can be tough on the people he loves.'

'He doesn't love me.'

'I'm afraid he does. His powerful emotions betray him.'

'But he has strong emotions about you too.'

'Not any more.'

'How come he turns up here to berate you? He could do that in the station.'

I didn't answer. I had questioned it too, but only in my head. Did George have residual feelings for me? Feelings he hadn't dealt with yet? I thought he had found happiness with Sharon, a woman for whom no cliché could be overused, and no toy too pink or fluffy. She'd probably get on great with Mel's landlady. They could have an entire cliché-based conversation together without ever saying anything in particular. It occurred to me I hadn't found out what happened to my lacquered Chinese box. Another mystery.

Chapter 25

My efforts to make a home for Mouse, re-enter the modern world, find Mel's murderer and forge a business relationship with Harry had caused me to neglect the mainstay of my income. If an inanimate object can project resentment, that must be what I felt when I opened the doors of the Second Home for business again. It had been closed for two days instead of the usual twenty-four hours to facilitate my latest clearance trip with Harry. My whole body ached with fatigue after helping him to load and unload the van of heavy hardwood furniture. I had been determined not to be seen as weak, which seemed to amuse, rather than impress, him.

George's veto on any interference in the re-opened investigation into both Diane and Mel's suspicious deaths frustrated me. I have had trouble sleeping at night as my racing thoughts competed to keep me awake. My insomnia sent me straight upstairs to the coffee machine. I almost had a heart attack as I walked straight into one of the tailor's dummies Harry had delivered to the shop. I had intended to use it for hanging coats, but Ghita had dressed it in a stylish 1940s man's three-piece suit to add atmosphere to the café. It worked a treat, but I swore at it as I attempted to slow my heart rate. A strong coffee would not help me calm down, but I needed it to wake me up.

I checked the fridge, and found that someone efficient, probably Roz, had already bought milk for the week. She had been out to sea more often recently as one of Ed's crew had resigned or gone off in a huff. Ed had a reputation as a hard taskmaster and often fell out with people. His good humour and generosity generally won them round again until his next tantrum. Roz adored him, despite their constant rows and his expectation that she would fill in for his crew every time they resigned or refused to work for him. There had been a storm brewing for a while at the county council, which threatened to upset more boats than Ed's. Some eco warrior had turned up and convinced them to open an inquiry into designating a section of the seabed as a marine reserve for regeneration of the kelp forest along the coast. The local fishermen were up in arms and other stakeholders had come out of the woodwork to muddy the waters. Since Ghita worked in the department allocated to overseeing the intended approval of the project, I could see trouble ahead.

Roz herself turned up at midday to help me at the shop, her cheeks rosy from her days at sea. She went straight upstairs for a coffee and I found her deep in conversation with Mouse who made some notes on his cell phone before putting it away.

'Am I allowed to know what you two are plotting?' I said.

'No,' said Roz. 'But I've got some gossip that might interest you. It's about Mel's death.'

I raised an eyebrow.

'I promised George I wouldn't get involved.'

'Nobody is asking you to interfere,' she said. 'This is straight from the horse's mouth.'

'You've been talking to George?'

'No, don't be silly, or I won't tell you what I heard.'

'Go on then. I'm all ears,'

'Sally Right on reception at the police station; you know her, the young blonde PC.'

'What about her?'

'She's friends with my niece, and told her things.'

'Okay, get on with it. What things?'

'Sally told her that Greg Summers and Fiona Conrad have both been in for questioning. She says she saw Diane Conrad's file on the table in the interview room when she took in the tea for Fiona Conrad.'

'Wow, that's interesting,' I said. 'Maybe the police will get to the bottom of it after all.'

'I'll let you know if she hears anything else.'

My trips with Harry had generated a decent amount of new stock, which we had stacked up at the back of the ground floor waiting for some TLC. As well as the tailor's dummies and the sewing stools, I had collected several Parker Knoll armchairs, some tiled coffee tables, and a selection of lamps. This haul added to the stock of untouched tables and chairs and cabinets piled in the back of the shop. As soon as I finished my coffee, I began to refurbish some of them by polishing and re-waxing table tops.

The physical act of infusing new life into these pieces made my love for vintage surge again over the next few days. I felt reinvigorated, sanding and buffing long after closing time, and talking customers' ears off if they showed the slightest interest in any article. Enthused, I searched car boot sales for antique fabrics to re-cover cushions in the correct era material. The early openings galvanised me and I soon found myself at the front of the queue in the still dark mornings, champing at the bit to get in and sort through the junk. I even found some classic pieces for the shop.

Ghita came a couple of times, but she found the combination of the early start and her shifts at the council untenable. I breathed a sigh of relief when she stopped coming, as I couldn't bear her enthusiasm over pieces of tat that I could never sell. Our ideas of what would sell were further apart than Venus and Mars. On one of our trips, she shoved the photograph of a plump, middle-aged man with a luxuriant moustache and kohl on his eyelids in front of me while driving.

'For heaven's sake,' I said. 'I almost crashed into that telegraph pole. Who is that, anyway?'

'Sorry,' she said. 'My mother's been to the matchmaker again. This is Rohan. I have to meet him next week.'

'He looks pleasant. Do you have much in common?'

'Both our sets of parents want us to get married.'

'Are you going to meet him?'

'I guess so. I have to pretend I'm trying.'

She sounded defeated.

'You don't have to get married if you don't want to. It's not compulsory.'

'But I want to.'

'Why don't you choose your own husband?'

'I'm afraid of getting it wrong. Then my family will have more reasons to despise me.'

I sighed.

'Marrying someone you don't know can go wrong too,' I said. 'It's a lottery whichever way you look at it.'

Ghita ran her finger over the screen.

'Will you come with me? If I meet him? I need a chaperone, but I don't want any of my family there. They make me too nervous.'

'Of course I will. What are friends for?'

She beamed and put away her phone.

'Excellent. I didn't want to ask Roz. I'm trying to make him feel comfortable, not terrified.'

I tried not to laugh, but soon we were both giggling away. Poor Ghita. I hope he's a nice man.

Chapter 26

As Spring took hold, my clientele emerged from hibernation and began to spring clean and redecorate their nests. The Vintage café became a hive of activity, filled either with students using social media, or office workers at lunchtime, slowly replaced by groups of mothers with their strollers in the afternoon. Even the Second Home experienced an uplift, as people searched for the ultimate vintage piece to finish their décor. All the hard work I had put into preparing my stock paid off and I felt the pressure release as bills went from red to black again. Mouse had got work helping people to design websites, and, I suspected, he had a side-line in hacking for information. As long as he didn't blackmail anyone, I let it go. After all, I had used him to get information on the Conrads.

Harry and I had got into a rhythm with our house clearances, and our friendship grew with each venture into other people's pasts. Some homes we cleared resembled time capsules, little changed since someone built them in the late 1800s. We found manual floor sweepers, the predecessors to vacuums, Bakelite dial telephones, some old valve radios, now covered in table cloths and used as a surface for balancing candlesticks and flower vases. Visit by visit, I tried to help Harry identify eras and fashions in furniture, how to tell a fake, and which pieces were the most profitable. He showed little inclination to learn, saying 'you know everything, I'm just the brawn'. He was more than capable of picking it up, but I flattered myself that he enjoyed having me around, even if just to help him transfer the furniture into the van.

With all the lifting I did, my bat wings disappeared, and I gained some more muscle. Pretty soon, my arms were the envy of the Fat Fighters Club. The ladies were also jealous of my new status as Harry's business partner. His brand of chirpy cockney meets army muscle had them day-dreaming he would offer to clear out their houses. Roz told me they all discussed my relationship with Harry when I wasn't there. The room often went quiet when I arrived, so I could believe it. I would have liked there to be some truth to the gossip, but Harry showed no interest in taking it to the next level. I contented myself with his occasional visits to the Grotty Hovel to cuddle Hades and tease Mouse. Mahatma Gandhi called patience and time the two most powerful warriors, and I fought dirty.

Fiona Conrad's call came out of the blue. I had been polishing an old wooden chair at the back of the shop when my cell phone vibrated. I had polish on my hands and didn't pick it up at first. Then I noticed who it was from and it jolted me out of my reverie. I picked it up and pressed the answer button.

'Hello? Tanya, is that you?'

'Yes. It's me.'

'I got your message, but I wasn't sure I should call you back. And now the police are involved, well…'

'I understand. There's no need—'

'Oh, but there is. I don't expect you to understand, but if you'd listen, you might understand what happened.'

'Shouldn't you be talking to the police about this?'

'I already have, but I doubt they'll tell you anything. Will you meet me?'

'I'm not sure you know this, but DI Carter is my ex-husband. He asked me not to get involved.'

'This is important. I think I know who killed Mel, but the police won't listen to me. I've realised it's been obvious the whole time. I want to show you first, since you were there with me when Mel and Greg came to Conrad House. Will you come?'

'Can't you tell me now?'

'It might not be safe. Please come. I'll wait in the hall where we first met at two o'clock.'

'Do you mind if Harry comes with me?'

'Not at all.'

But I couldn't contact Harry. And in the end, I decided it would be safe enough to meet her. It wasn't like I had any insider information on the murder. I texted Harry the time and place in case he got the message and told the girls where I was going.

'Take Mouse,' said Roz, who called me back immediately.

'But his father will kill me if anything happens.'

'It's less likely to happen if you take Mouse with you.'

'And if you think you're going without me, you've got a lot to learn,' said Mouse from the top of the stairs.

'You shouldn't be listening to my phone calls,' I said.

'You shouldn't go to deserted houses by yourself to meet a murderer,' said Mouse.

'She's not a murderer.'

'And how do you know that? The police aren't so sure. Anyway, I thought you and Harry suspected her.'

'We did, we do, I'm not sure.'

'I'm definitely coming with you.'

'Okay.'

We set out for Conrad House in plenty of time, but we hit traffic on the main road, and slowed to a crawl.

'Did I tell you Fiona helped Mel to marry Ronnie Barratt?' I said.

'No. Didn't you say Fiona hated Mel?'

'I'm not sure anymore. I think Fiona knew William would disinherit Mel, which he did. Fiona resented her coming back to claim her inheritance after all these years. William is a lot older than Fiona. Perhaps she hoped to inherit the fortune herself?'

'But doesn't that give her a powerful motive to kill Mel?'

'Then why would she call me, wanting to point me at the killer?'

'I guess we'll soon find out.'

The journey seemed to take forever, but, in reality, it only took fifteen minutes longer than usual. By the time we drew up to the house, both Mouse and I were on edge. The ludicrously aggressive dog I had seen the first time I saw Mel, again came running up to my car snarling and barking, but I had learned from Harry to ignore him. I stamped my feet, and he backed away, his ears flat to his head.

'Not much of a guard dog, is he?' said Mouse.

'He's probably quite sweet if he knows you.'

I looked around for Fiona. She had parked her car in front of the house, but there was no sign of her. I walked up to the front door and noticed that they had attached a new aluminium hasp and plate to the door and its frame. The door was ajar, and I pushed it open wider so light would enter the hall. I stood blinking, trying to adjust to the gloomy interior. Behind me, Mouse gasped. I turned to him and he pointed wordless to a bundle at the bottom of the staircase. I did not need to approach it to guess who lay lifeless on the ground, but I called out just in case.

'Fiona? Are you here? Do you need help?'

The house echoed with my voice, but the body did not stir. The angle of its neck suggested it might never move again. I could not risk contaminating what appeared to be a murder scene.

'Touch nothing,' I said, pushing Mouse out again.

'Is it her?' said Mouse. 'Shouldn't we check if she's still alive?'

'We need to wait for the police,' I said, dialling George's number. 'Don't go in whatever you do.'

'But—'

I shushed him and the cell phone rang loud in my ear.

'Tan, I'm busy right now. I—'

'George, I'm at Conrad House. There's a body at the bottom of the stairs, so unless you forgot to remove Mel, I think we have another murder on our hands.'

'Our hands? For heaven's sake, woman. How do you manage it? Don't go anywhere, especially near the body.'

I could almost hear the cogs whirring in his brain.

'Are you safe?' he said.

'What do you mean?'

'How do you know the murderer has left the scene?'

An icy chill worked its way up my spine and my stomach flipped as I backed away from the front door, guiding Mouse from the building with my arm.

'I don't.'

'Is the body warm?' said George.

'I haven't touched it, but if it's who I think it is, we were meeting her here at two o'clock.'

'We? Who's we?'

'Um, Mouse is here. I brought him for protection.'

'Bloody hell! Who's protecting him? Shut yourselves in the car and be ready to drive off if someone approaches. I'll be there as soon as I can.'

'Okay.'

'Do you know who it is?'

'I haven't checked, but I suspect it's Fiona Conrad.'

'Fiona? What on earth is she doing there? And how come you are at the house?'

'Well, it's a long story—'

'No, don't tell me. Stay there. I'll arrive as soon as I can.'

I hung up and dropped my head in my hands, groaning. Mouse patted me on the back.

'Let's sit in the car,' he said. 'Or I could get a bus back into town so George doesn't get cross with you.'

'And how do you know the murderer isn't watching us right now, waiting to pounce on one of us if we are alone?'

He blanched.

'Oh.'

'Get in the car. We'll lock the doors and stay put until George gets here.'

Chapter 27

The sound of a siren alerted us to the arrival of the cavalry. Mouse wanted to get out of the car, but I put my hand on his shoulder.

'Stay where you are for now,' I said. 'I don't want you to see the body. She may be badly injured.'

'But what about you?'

'This isn't my first rodeo. I was married to a detective for most of my adult life, and I don't want George to remember you are here.'

'Will you tell me all about it?'

'Of course.'

George's saloon car screeched to a halt, followed by Flo, and a squad car containing two police constables and a couple of forensic officers. The dog did not come out to bark at them. I guess the number of people intimidated him. George signalled for me to stay in the car, but I had no intention of missing the action. I had already left DNA at the scene, by my mere presence there, so if I didn't approach the body, I couldn't make any contamination worse. I followed him as far as the door, where he and Flo struggled into jump suits and put on forensic gloves and shoe covers. Flo raised her eyebrows as she saw me approach.

'We've got to stop meeting like this,' she said.

'I wish we would,' I said. 'It's not a habit I want to get into.'

'Talk me through it,' said George.

'Well, we arrived at about two fifteen—'

'All of it,' he said.

I swallowed.

'Um, I got a call from Fiona at about midday. I can check on my phone and give you an exact time if you like.'

George signalled for me to get on with it.

'She said she knew who murdered Mel, and she had proof.'

'What sort of proof?'

'She wouldn't tell me. She said someone might be listening. I thought she was exaggerating, but…'

'And then?'

'We arranged to meet here at two o'clock, but I got stuck in the traffic, and I didn't get here until quarter past. I went up to the house and found the door ajar, so I pushed it open.'

'What did you see?'

'Nothing at first. When my eyes became accustomed to the gloom, I could see what looked like a body at the bottom of the stairs.'

'Déjà vu,' said Flo.

'Quite,' said George. 'Flo, can you confirm the identification of the body, please?'

As if on cue, the arc lights set up by the crime scene technicians burst into life, blinding us all with their vicious white light. The body stood out in stark relief on the floor, throwing a gruesome shadow behind it. Fiona's dyed blonde hair stood out on the dusty floor. The sense of déjà vu only increased as I saw the contents of her handbag scattered on the floor, sending their own shadows in the startling light.

Flo made her way to the body, illuminated by the arc, throwing a monstrous shadow on the wooden panels under the staircase.

'Visually, I can confirm that it's Fiona Conrad, but I'll need to take her to the lab for confirmation tests. Her handbag has emptied onto the floor. I don't see any keys. Maybe she left them in her car.'

'Wouldn't she have needed them to open the padlock on the outside door?' said George.

'They might be under the body, but I won't know that until I move it,' said Flo.

'I'm going upstairs to have a look for signs of a struggle. I'll take one of your guys with me, if that's okay?' said George.

'Do you want me to stay here?' I said, feeling forgotten.

'Yes, please. Go back to the car. I'll be over when we've had a look.'

I stepped outside again, relieved to be out of the blinding lights. If it wasn't for them, I'd have imagined I'd entered Groundhog Day. How could this have happened again? The similarities between the two cases were ghastly. My mouth had dried and my tongue stuck to the roof of my mouth. I needed some water, and I had some in the car.

I found Mouse scrolling through his phone, a comfort mechanism I guessed. Something normal, in an abnormal situation. I searched in the glove box for a toffee and offered him the bag, taking a not very fresh bottle of water to quench my thirst. Mouse took a toffee and undid the crinkly wrapping with deliberate movements. Then he put it in his mouth and chewed it, shutting his eyes in pleasure at the sugar rush which flooded his body as he swallowed the resulting liquid. I did the same with my own, and we both sat in silence for a moment, waiting for the glucose to hit our bloodstreams.

'Is it her?' he said.

'Yes. I'm afraid she's dead.'

'Did someone push her?'

'I don't know. George is checking the landing for clues.'

'This is horrible.'

'I'm sorry. I shouldn't have let you come.'

'No, I didn't mean—'

'I know. But I shouldn't have agreed to come. What if someone heard our call and followed her to the house?'

Mouse tutted.

'That doesn't make it your fault, you know. She's the one who called you.'

'I should have refused and made her go to the police. I was too keen to be the one who solved Mel's murder. That makes it my fault, partially anyway.'

A knock on the window almost made me jump out of my skin. I wound it down and George loomed large in its frame. Mouse shrank in his seat as George leaned in.

'Andy, can you get in the back, please?' said George.

As usual, Mouse's real name made me look around for some bloke called Andy. I don't know why George wouldn't use his nickname. I suppose he had always called his son Andy, and had no intention of changing, but I wanted to correct him anyway. Mouse pushed through the gap in the seats, knocking over my bottle of tepid water, and slumped in the back with a sulky expression on his face. George walked around the car and sat in the passenger seat. He looked around, as if to check for eavesdroppers, and lowered his voice.

'This is top secret,' he said. 'If either of you breathe a word about this, I'll cut your tongues out.'

'Mum's the word,' said Mouse, with a hint of sarcasm that went right over George's head.

'Cross my heart,' I said, with the appropriate gesture.

'Fiona left a note,' said George.

'What sort of note?' said Mouse.

George sighed, a sigh that shouted 'amateurs'.

'Oh. That sort,' I said. 'What did it say?'

'She claimed to have murdered Mel for her inheritance. The note said she hadn't been able to sleep since the murder, and she had decided to kill herself when she discovered she wouldn't after all be inheriting the estate. It didn't say why.'

'Was it in her handwriting?' I said.

'I wouldn't recognise it, but she had written the note in capital letters.'

Capital letters? Who writes their farewell letter in capitals?

'Fiona murdered Mel?' said Mouse. 'I didn't see that coming. I thought it was Greg.'

'But why would she call me and tell me she knew who the murderer was?' I said.

'Because she knew who they were,' said George. 'Herself. She wanted her body to be found, so she called you.'

'That makes zero sense,' I said.

'Maybe. It's all we've got right now,' said George. 'Because if she didn't kill herself, the prime suspect for her murder would be you, a candidate for the last person to see her alive right here at Conrad House.'

'Awkward,' said Mouse.

'Very,' I said.

Chapter 28

Harry called me as we were driving away from Conrad House. I put him on speakerphone.

'Hi Harry. It's me and Mouse in the car. We're on our way home. Give me a second to stop the car.'

I pulled up in the driveway.

'Okay. We can talk now, and don't swear, you're on speakerphone.'

'Honestly,' said Mouse. 'I'm not ten years old.'

'Everything alright with you two?' said Harry. 'I'm sorry I didn't get your message. I had a funeral.'

'Oh, I didn't know. My condolences.'

'No worries. One of my army mates topped himself. It's a common occurrence, unfortunately. PTSD and all that. I didn't know him well, but I felt obliged to turn up and support his family.'

'That's awful. We had a suicide our end too. But don't tell anyone. The police haven't confirmed it yet.'

'What? I don't Adam and Eve it.'

'Fiona Conrad. We found her at the bottom of the same stairs where Mel had her accident.'

'Stone the crows. I can't leave you alone for one minute, Ms Bowe. Would you like me to come round and visit this evening?'

'If you're not too busy. Mouse and I had a nasty shock.'

'Mouse was there? Is he alright?'

'Yes, just shaken,' said Mouse.

'The coincidences are piling up here. And I can't work out what I've missed,' I said.

'I'm on my way. Shall I buy us some fish and chips?'

'Yes, please. I can't face cooking tonight.'

'Put on a kettle. I'll be with you both soon.'

Harry's voice had the effect of a fleece blanket on us both. He had that army air of authority, which made me feel safe and under the protection of a professional. Mouse patted my shoulder.

'Harry's got our backs,' he said. 'Nobody can harm us with him around.'

I pulled away from the verge and checked my mirror. I couldn't see any cars behind us. The light faded fast as we drove home. I made sure we weren't being followed, and I spotted Mouse checking too. We were both paranoid after George's warning. I wondered if Fiona really killed herself. It would have been easy to fake a suicide note. And what if the murderer had been in the house when we arrived? Did they see us? Would they think we knew what Fiona did about the murders? I speeded up.

Once we arrived home, I asked Mouse to light a fire, while I went around checking every window and door was securely locked. I gazed down at the tiny back garden from my bedroom. It had not been touched since I moved in and had become an urban jungle of shrubs and brambles under the previous owner. Hades used to disappear into the undergrowth for hours and emerge with half eaten carcases of small rodents and unfortunate sparrows which he dumped beside the fridge. I tried to peer into the darkness, to check for intruders, but I needed infrared glasses. Instead, I told myself to stop being paranoid. After all, Harry was on his way.

By the time he arrived, normality or what passed for it, had returned to the Grotty Hovel. Mouse had burrowed into a pile of furry throws and scrolled through TikTok, emitting the odd muffled guffaw. Hades soon joined him. He batted at the phone with his paws to attract attention. I saw my chance and grabbed the miniature fishing rod, which had a furry ball on a string. This I dangled in front of me on the couch and kicked at it, pretending to be entertained. The movement caught Hades' eye. I could swear he raised an eyebrow at my feeble attempts at playing with the ball. He crept out of the covers and landed on the floor, as soft as a duvet made of Icelandic goose down. I could never understand how a frankly sturdy animal like Hades could do that without making the slightest sound. He readied himself for a pounce, his shoulders quivering with excitement, having completely forgotten how much he hated me. I braced myself, ready to whip the ball out of his reach, just as the doorbell rang.

I jumped up, dropping the rod, and trotted to the door, salivating at the thought of fish and chips. I swung it open, and in walked George Carter. My jaw hit the floor with a clang.

'What are you doing here?' I said.

'That's a fine welcome,' he said. 'I just dropped by to make sure you both got home safe. It's not every day you find a body.'

'Did you discover any clues?' said Mouse.

George frowned.

'The poor woman killed herself. We weren't looking for clues.'

'But how do you know? Tanya says—'

George raised an eyebrow.

'And what does DI Bowe say?'

'Nothing. It's normal to speculate. This isn't the first death in the Conrad family. You used to say there was no such thing as a coincidence, but that seems to have gone out of the window,' I said, trying not to sound cross.

'It appears to be a cut and dried case, but we will follow procedure and examine all the evidence. Flo will perform an autopsy, just to be sure.'

'You're not convinced then?' said Mouse.

The doorbell rang again, making us all start.

'Who's visiting at this hour of the night?' said George.

I caught the expression of indignation on his face and couldn't help sniggering.

'It's Harry with the food,' said Mouse, opening the door.

Harry bustled in with a large bag full of fish and chips which emitted a fabulous aroma. He stopped dead when he spotted George. Honestly, they reminded me of two bull terriers meeting on the promenade. Their metaphorical hackles rose, and they looked each other up and down, their limbs stiffening. They were evenly matched. George was taller than Harry, but had gone to seed because of too many donuts and takeaways at the office. Harry had the stocky body of someone who spent his days lifting heavy pieces of furniture.

'Who's this?' said George, and I could see Harry thinking the same.

'George, this is Harry, my business partner. And Harry, this is George, my, um, Detective Inspector Carter.'

Harry grinned and relaxed.

'Your ex? Great to meet you mate. I'm surprised you survived such an ordeal.'

He pumped George's hand up and down, and George couldn't help smiling.

'Have you seen the state of me?' he said. 'I barely got out alive.'

Mouse appeared transfixed by this meeting and looked from one to the other in amazement. I pulled the bag out of Harry's hand.

'Well, we're about to eat,' I said. 'So, you need to go now…'

'That smells good,' said George. 'I've only had a coffee since lunchtime.'

Harry patted George on the shoulder.

'Come on, mate. There's plenty for everyone. You know how massive the portions of chips are these days.'

'Do you mind, Tan?' said George.

I let out an exasperated sigh.

'Of course she doesn't,' said Mouse. 'It will be great.'

A day which started out like any other, got progressively stranger, and ended up with me sitting down to supper with my ex-husband, my future boyfriend (a girl can dream), my stepson (sort of) and a neutered cat with a bad attitude. I don't suppose many girls had four men round for dinner that night. I seemed to make a habit of it. But as I watched them all eating and exchanging banter, and becoming friends, I realised just how lucky I had become in the last few months, murders aside. I not only had a coven of women friends to hang out with, but now I had my own team of tough guys too. Heaven help anyone who messed with me from now on.

Chapter 29

It wasn't until the next day that reality set in. Fiona had murdered Mel, and then she had killed herself when she couldn't stand the remorse. Despite my lurid imaginings; Greg was just a bankrupt loser, Ronnie a star-crossed lover, and Sarah a bitter single mother. I wondered how William would cope with the loss of Fiona. I felt awful for him as I remembered his tender expression as he perused the photographs of his family in the album. All the women from his family were dead now. What a terrible blow for one man. Maybe the shock would kill him. I resolved to take the album up to the house to pay my condolences and hand over the last memories he had of them all together. It would be a fitting gesture, and hopefully, one he would appreciate.

I drove past Second Home on my way to William Conrad's house in order to collect the album from safe-keeping under the cash desk. I found Ghita perched on the stool, flushing with pleasure as she read something on her phone. She looked up as I came in, cheeks scarlet as she shoved the phone under the desk. I tapped the side of my nose in jest at her panicked expression.

'Watching naughty movies on your phone? What would your mother say?'

Ghita jumped off the stool and flounced away from the desk, flashing me a resentful glance.

'Don't project your filthy habits onto me,' she said. 'I'm corresponding with Rohan, my, my…'

'Boyfriend?' I said, trying to help. 'And less of the aspersions. I was joking you know. Remember jokes? You used to like them last week.'

'Actually, he's my fiancé. And he respects me too much for any of that dirty stuff.'

'Your fiancé? Wow, congratulations! I didn't realise things had moved on so quickly.'

'That's hardly surprising, considering you are too busy playing Miss Marple to spend any time with your friends. You've missed two great step classes at Fat Fighters as well. I put a lot of work into those.'

The hurt in her voice cut me to the core. The curtains had parted on her resilient act and showed the tender heart underneath. Shame engulfed me. I needed to pay closer attention to her courtship, like any friend would.

'You're right,' I said. 'I'm sorry. But it's all over now, bar the shouting.'

'Really? What happened?'

'Fiona Conrad is dead. She killed herself and left a note describing how and why she killed Mel. Please don't tell anyone, especially not Roz, until the police make an announcement.'

'How terrible! At least Mel can rest in peace now. And I promise not to tell Roz,' she said. 'Thanks for letting me know.'

'After all that happened, I've got to pay my condolences to William Conrad, and then I promise normal service will be resumed.'

Ghita sniffed.

'Okay, I forgive you.'

She gave me a damp hug and looked at me from under her ludicrously long lashes. Think giraffe, and you'd be close. She shrugged.

'And he's not my official fiancé. I haven't met him in person yet. I've been waiting for you to come with me.'

'Now I feel guilty. Make a date, and I'll be there.'

'Really?'

'Cross my heart.'

I reached under the desk and pulled out the photo album, including William's clandestine copies of the beach sequence. Fiona wouldn't be objecting to them anymore, so I slipped it into my shoulder bag.

'I'll be back shortly,' I said. 'Bringing us some eclairs to have for tea.'

William's new house sat in the middle of an estate composed of villas similar to the one where George and I had lived, and where Sharon now occupied my place. For a while, I had been jealous of them living in the villa, surrounded by Smeg fittings and beige furniture, but since I had filled the Grotty Hovel with Art Deco pieces amid comfy chairs and charity shop paintings, this feeling had evaporated. It had been replaced with pride and contentment, and I now remembered our villa as a cold, soulless showroom for visitors I didn't even like. I shuddered as I drove up to William's villa and noticed his oatmeal curtains. Fiona's taste, no doubt. I'd seen a flash of William's Muppet-themed socks, and I was pretty sure the photographs weren't the only thing he'd been hiding from Fiona.

To my surprise, Sarah opened the front door to the villa.

'Tanya,' she said. 'I suppose you've come to see William. He's indisposed today, but I don't suppose he'd mind a quick visit. It might even cheer him up.'

Before I could demure, she ushered me across the bland carpets and up the stairs into William's bedroom. He had slumped against his pillows, staring at the ceiling, and for a moment I thought he had died of his sorrow. However, he hauled himself into a sitting position when we entered. He still had crumbs from breakfast toast on his chin and appeared much diminished in spirit. At least he had eaten something. I approached the bed and took his bony hand.

'I'm sorry to disturb you,' I said. 'Please accept my deepest condolences on Fiona's death. You must be devastated after so much tragedy in your family.'

He nodded, but didn't speak. Then I took the album out of my shoulder bag and put it on the bed beside him.

'I thought you might like this,' I said, kissing his wrinkled cheek. 'I added the photographs you gave me.'

He patted the album with his hand.

'Thank you. They'll be a great comfort for me. Are you sure you don't want to keep them?'

'Absolutely certain. Mel would want you to have them.'

'You're a kind girl,' said William. 'I can see that. You were a good friend to Mel. The police told me you were the one to find Fiona's body. They won't tell me what happened yet. Can you?'

His distress radiated from him, and he sank into his pillows again. I opened my mouth to give him a gentle refusal, but Sarah put her hand on my shoulder and shook her head.

'Don't go getting upset again,' she said to William. 'They'll tell you when they know. Tanya's not allowed to talk about it, I'm sure.'

I mouthed a thank you to her. William sniffled, and I stood up again.

'I'm so sorry for your loss,' I said. 'I need to go now.'

'Will you come back?' said William.

'Of course.'

I left the room with Sarah close behind me.

'I've got to go,' I said. 'William isn't ready for visitors.'

'Don't leave yet. We need to talk. Have a cup of tea with me.'

I couldn't think of anything I wanted to do less. The house smelled of decay and misery. Panic gripped me and adrenaline coursed through my veins, making me feel like running.

'Are you okay, dear? You've gone white as the proverbial.'

'Yes, I'm fine. I'd love a cup of tea.'

We walked into the gleaming kitchen, which looked like no-one had ever burnt a lamb chop within its pristine walls, and sat on some uncomfortable stools at the breakfast bar. I had a feeling of déjà vu as I remembered trying to persuade George to let me have a small breakfast table and chairs in ours. Not a battle I won.

While Sarah made us a pot of tea, I scanned the kitchen, noting the touches Fiona had made to de-beige it. The colourful spice rack and the twee key storage board on which hung many sets of keys. Among them, I recognised the bronze letter S keyring from Greg's description of the one he lent to Mel. She must have left them behind her when she went to the Conrad House on the day of her death. I resisted the temptation to ask for them, as it felt inappropriate. I'd mention it another day. Sarah poured the tea into the tiny floral cups she found in a cupboard. I sipped mine cautiously.

'It's okay, love. I bought some breakfast tea,' she said. 'I'll be staying here for a while to get William back on his feet.'

I smiled. She knew exactly what I was thinking. Now or never, I guess.

'Why didn't you tell me you were Ronnie's mother?' I said.

She stiffened and narrowed her eyes.

'How did you know?'

'I didn't realise it was a secret. The photographs made it obvious,' I said. 'I don't know why I hadn't seen the family resemblance before.'

'He looks like me, doesn't he? He doesn't look like his father at all.'

'Doesn't he?' I said, and waited.

'You might as well know. It will be common knowledge soon, although I'd like you to keep it quiet for now, until I've told Ronnie.'

Suddenly I knew.

'William?'

She laughed at my surprise.

'William and I go way back. I started working for him before he married Diane. We've always been close. Fiona got rid of me because she didn't like us being friends.'

'Did Fiona know William was Ronnie's father?'

'Nobody ever guessed. Not even Diane. William was the only one who knew.'

'So that's why Fiona helped Mel to marry Ronnie, even though he's Mel's half-brother?'

'Correct. Fiona's plan was to force William to disinherit Mel for marrying against his will, but she didn't realise why he was so against the marriage.'

'And Mel?'

'I had to tell Mel the truth.when I found out she had married Ronnie in secret.'

'Is that why she ran away?'

Sarah sighed.

'I'm afraid so. I didn't tell Ronnie the truth, because I thought it would traumatise him more if he realised he had been intimate with his half-sister.'

'Shouldn't you tell Ronnie about his father, now that Fiona is dead?'

'I intended to, but I was hoping to get the chance to tell Fiona first. I thought if she lost her hope of receiving the inheritance, she'd run away with Greg. How was I to know she'd kill herself?'

'She killed herself? I thought the autopsy was still pending?'

'She left a note saying she couldn't live with the guilt of killing Mel.'

How on earth did she know that? The police station must be as leaky as a sieve. I nodded, but alarm bells rang in my head. According to the café owner near Greg's house, Ronnie already knew about his father from Mel. Hadn't he told his mother about it yet? Didn't that give Ronnie a motive to kill Fiona too?

'Life's full of surprises,' I said. 'I never had her as the murderer on my Bingo card. I'm sorry, but I have to go now. Ghita's minding the shop, and she has a shift at the council later.'

'You can't tell anyone about this yet,' said Sarah.

'Don't worry. I'm not in the habit of gossiping. Everyone will find out soon enough. I expect the local papers will have a field day.'

Chapter 30

When I arrived back at the Second Home, carrying a box of four conciliatory eclairs, Ghita had joined Roz, who had been doing some digging on the case. I'm constantly amazed at her persistence. She's been out at sea with Ed fishing for mackerel, and somehow without the internet or a phone signal, she'd dug up information on a man called Dennis Barratt, an ex-boyfriend of Sarah Bingley. She's asked Mouse to investigate his whereabouts in the year before the birth of Ronnie Barratt, and I found them all upstairs discussing the case.

We made ourselves a coffee each, and I handed round the eclairs. They were beyond delicious. Why can't foods high in fat and sugar be slimming? I like meat and vegetables, but I could easily cut down on them if they were fattening. From the contented sighs around the table, the others felt the same. Ghita wiped a blob of cream off her upper lip.

'Is that the case over then?' she said.

'If the police decide Fiona committed suicide, they will tie it up with a neat bow. But I don't buy the suicide thing. Fiona told me she knew who the murderer was. Why would she call me, of all people?'

'Maybe she knew you were the only person who might believe her. Do you want me to stop researching Dennis Barratt?' said Roz.

'We probably should, but Ronnie's the only loose end the police haven't dealt with yet. I can't help feeling he's the key to everything, so I might meet him again.'

'You can't go alone,' said Roz. 'If he's the murderer, it might be dangerous.'

'Oh, don't worry about that. My last visit to Conrad House spooked the hell out of me. I keep checking I've locked all the windows in my house.'

'Why can't you leave it alone?' said Ghita. 'Haven't you done enough?'

She turned her back to me and I could read the deep resentment. I stood up and put my arm around her shoulders. Then I hugged Roz too.

'I've neglected you both. I know it's hard for you to understand my obsession with this murder, but I had a career I loved once and I lost it all when I got depression. Well, everything except my precious friends, who pulled me through when I thought my life had ended. Mel's death has given me the opportunity to see if I've still got it. Don't you see? I must find out who did it, even if it turns out to be Fiona. I can't leave any stone unturned.'

'You're brilliant at this,' said Mouse. 'Even I'm impressed. But you drive too fast when you're in a panic. We're lucky we didn't get a speeding ticket on our way back from the Conrad house.'

Roz snorted.

'Rather you than me, but it's true.'

'White knuckle rides,' said Ghita.

I beamed.

'If you've all had your say on my driving, I'd like to ring Harry and see if he wants to solve this last puzzle with me.'

'When are you going to ask him out?' said Mouse.

'Isn't it about time?' said Roz. 'My networks are overheating with anticipation.'

'He's my business partner.'

'Well, if you ask me,' said Ghita. 'It's high time you got down to business with this partner.'

We all sniggered together.

'Just don't let him get away,' said Roz. 'They don't make those by the dozen, mores the pity.'

'Who says I even like him that way?'

'The blush on your cheeks whenever he's around,' said Roz. 'You don't fool anyone.'

'I've been thinking about Fiona,' said Mouse. 'If she killed Mel, maybe she killed Diane?'

'But how would we find that out?' I said. 'It happened decades ago.'

'You need a haircut,' said Roz.

'What's that got to do with Fiona?'

'Do you remember when William came here to see the photographs? You told me he could only come because Fiona went to the hairdresser to see her long-time stylist. I bet she knows a lot about Fiona that we can't find out anywhere else.'

'Now, that's a genius idea.'

'And you need a haircut,' said Ghita. 'It looks like you have a crow's nest on your head.'

'Thanks a bunch,' I said, but I knew it was true.

I looked up the number of the salon and dialled it. A bright voice answered almost immediately.

'Hairways, how can I help you today?'

'Good morning, my late friend Fiona Conrad had her hair done at your salon the other day, and she looked fabulous. I wondered if I might make an appointment with the same stylist?'

'That'll be Marge. She's been here since the Ark. Mrs Conrad wouldn't use anyone else, God rest her soul. But Marge only works two days a week. Tuesday and Thursday.'

'So, she's there today?'

'Yes. And, give me a minute, um, she's free at two-thirty. Shall I book you in?'

'Great. The name's Tanya. I'll be there.'

I rang off and pulled at my hair in the mirror. It had originally been chestnut, but in my various attempts at cheering myself up, I had had several goes at highlighting it. Not successfully, I might add. It would be nice to have a classic cut to distract from the Jackson Pollock effect. I should really get it coloured professionally too, but I found sitting down for so long agitating because of my tendency to brood.

When I got to the salon, I spotted an older woman I assumed was Marge putting the finishing touches to a pink rinse at the far end.

'Our Marge is a Seacastle institution, like the pier or the Shanty pub,' said the receptionist. 'She'll be with you in a minute once she's happy the client is satisfied.'

'That makes a pleasant change,' I said.

The remark didn't go down too well with the receptionist who took to filing her nails with vicious intent and ignored me from then on. I breathed in the smell of hairspray and pushed some amputated curls around the floor with the tip of my pixie boot. The indistinct murmur of women swopping details of their forthcoming or latest holidays filled the air. One stylist attempted to subdue a young woman's sophisticated coiffure with a fixer. It looked like a helmet by the time she had finished, but the recipient looked ecstatic.

Marge swirled me around in the chair and gave me a critical once over.

'Did you let your daughter colour your hair?' she said, pulling at different coloured strands.

'I'm not married,' I said.

'Oh well, there's still time. Get a wash and we'll see what we can do for you.'

Several minutes later, I returned to her chair, my hair wrapped in a tight turban on my head. Marge waited for me; arms crossed. I wondered if the receptionist had repeated my comment to her. I noticed her cardigan had a homemade look, so I went for broke.

'That's a fabulous cardigan,' I said. 'Is it made by a designer?'

Marge's plump face flushed with pleasure.

'Good heavens no, I knitted it myself.'

'You had me fooled,' I said. 'It's gorgeous.'

Marge ran a comb through my hair.

'Thanks. Mrs Conrad used to love my cardigans too, you know. It's such a shock to hear that she passed on.'

'Dreadful, wasn't it? Did you know her long?'

'Years and years. I knew her before she became Mrs Conrad, you know.'

'Gosh, that's a faithful client. You must be amazing at your job.'

'I like to think so.'

'Did she fall for Mr Conrad when she went to work for him?'

'Oh no, dear. She lost her father early, so Mr Conrad was more like a father figure to her. She didn't particularly like him. He begged her to marry him and help him with his daughter after Diane died. And she liked the luxuries too, of course. She came from a poverty-stricken background.'

'Did you know Diane?'

'She used to come here too, but we didn't get on so well.'

'Why was that?'

'She was the most tremendous snob. She looked down her nose on everyone. Even the housekeeper, who had been with Mr Conrad since he inherited the house from his parents.'

'You mean Sarah Bingley?'

'Yes, dear. She was a real looker too. I always wondered about her and Mr Conrad.'

'So how come Sarah left when he married Fiona?'

'I think Fiona wanted things done her way. Sarah didn't like that. Do you want it dried?'

'Yes, please,' I said, without thinking.

My mistake. Marge turned on a turbo dryer and all conversation ceased due to the wall of noise. I rolled my eyes inwardly and watched as she performed her magic on my hair. She wielded the dryer like a magic wand. By the time she had finished, I looked like a princess, a middle-aged princess, but nonetheless royal for it.

'Wow. That's fantastic. Thank you so much.'

'You're welcome. Come back and get your hair coloured when you have more time.'

'Will you tell me more about the Conrads?'

'Probably not. I've been indiscreet enough already. Next time I'll ask you if you're going anywhere nice on your holidays.'

She gave me a wicked grin, which thrilled me. Marge was quite a girl. I hoped she could become a source in the future. If I started investigating again.

After I had paid the still grumpy receptionist, and given Marge a generous tip, I walked back up the high street towards the Second Home. I tossed my head and pranced down the street like a prized pony in pleasure at my new haircut. I almost walked straight into George who had stopped dead in the street and stared at me in amazement.

'Hello Tan,' he said. 'I came to find you. I…'

'What did you want?' I said.

'I've forgotten. You look different, like before. What—'

'Oh, my hair. Nice, isn't it?'

George pulled himself together.

'I came to tell you we've declared Fiona's death a suicide. The Chief Constable has lost patience with the whole saga. He won't allow us to investigate what seems to be an open and shut case. It's over.'

I tried not to lose my cool.

'I don't believe that. And neither do you. Can't we do something? The loose ends around this case are so compelling.'

'Hearsay is always compelling. We don't have any evidence. And you don't have any either. Give it up. You're making a fool of yourself. And me.'

George enunciated the last words slowly, as if to a child. I felt my blood boil, but I knew he had no choice. The word of the Chief Constable trumped everything. The buck stopped with him and that gave him the right to decide. I left George mid-pavement and strode down the street to the Second Home, stumbling through the door of the shop to cries of approval for my new haircut. In my stunned state, I hardly heard them. I noticed Harry standing beside Mouse. They both had their mouths open.

'Your hair looks amazing,' said Ghita.

'You look like a film star,' said Mouse.

'I didn't realise I had been working with Rachel Weisz,' said Harry.

I should have been thrilled that he noticed, but George's news had so depressed me, I hardly acknowledged him.

'The police have closed the case of Fiona Conrad,' I said, to a general gasp of disappointment.

'But they can't have,' said Mouse. 'There's no way she killed herself. She told you she could identify the murderer.'

I shrugged.

'George says there is zero proof of anybody else being involved. I'm sorry, but that's me done,' I said. 'All our suspects are non-starters. I need to do something more constructive.'

Mouse's face fell.

'But Harry and I have found out where Dennis Barratt hangs out. It's not over yet.'

'It is for me. Ghita, can you close up please?'

I'm not sure why I collapsed in a heap at that juncture. Perhaps the sudden spate of activity after so long had exhausted my reserves. Maybe I felt like an imposter. Depression does that to you. I had been the best investigative journalist of my era. My abilities had not evaporated because I had been ill, but I couldn't quite believe in myself. I suddenly felt the urge to go home and abandon shop. I turned around and started off down the street, my chest tight. Tears rose unbidden to my eyes. What on earth had happened to me? Why was I so deflated and confused?

Rain fell, first as a drizzle and then as a deluge, but I walked on regardless. I needed to be home, in my house, with the door shut. My wet trousers clung to my legs and my glamorous hairdo dissolved like the cake in MacArthur Park. The water gathered in the gutters and in shallow pools on the pavements. After a while, I stopped trying to avoid treading in them. By the time I reached the Grotty Hovel, the rain had penetrated as far as my underwear and my feet were sloshing in my pixie boots. I staggered inside and up the stairs, straight into the shower where I removed my clothing under a stream of hot water, rinsing it out as I took it off.

After drying myself with a towel and putting on a baggy tracksuit, I stuffed a newspaper into the boots and balanced them on a radiator. I took a deep breath and pulled on some thick slipper socks from Norway. My mood had lifted somewhat, as if the rain had washed some of it down the drains of Seacastle. I looked at myself in the mirror and mourned my elegant hairstyle. I brushed my hair off my face and blow dried it over a brush, but somehow the salon magic had dissipated and it looked as it always did.

Once I had finished my ablutions, I went back downstairs, where I had left damp footprints on the floor. I looked around the little sitting room, noticing the piles of paper and notebooks and photographs on every surface. Suddenly, my mind cleared, and I stuffed a cardboard box with my notes on Mel's murder. I admitted defeat and felt foolish in the extreme with my obsession. Fiona had pushed Mel down the stairs, end of story. I had wasted my time, and everyone else's when I should have been getting my life back on track and building up my antique business. Mouse needed me. Harry needed me. My friends needed me. Mel did not. I had allowed my ego to get the better of me. Past glories were just that. No more investigations for me.

Chapter 31

The next morning, I debated putting the boxes of research into the outside dustbins, but I decided not to bother as they had forecast more rain, and I wasn't sure how pleased the binmen would be to deal with boxes of soggy paper.

Mouse had turned in late and I left him sleeping when I set out for the shop. I intended to ask him to continue running the Vintage full time as we needed money to pay the bills. The increased footfall had lifted sales of antiques as intended, and I need to restock as soon as Harry got his next clearance contract. The café being Mel's idea; she had certainly played her part in saving my business and I wished I could have done more for her. She had grown on me more since dying. The irony was not lost on me.

The town still shone wet after some early morning showers and a keen wind blew from the northwest as I walked into town. In the distance, flocks of seagulls mobbed the small boats as they arrived from night-fishing with their holds full of crabs and white fish. I thought of Ed and Roz battling their way through life, and felt a tinge of jealousy. At least George and I seemed to be talking again, although we had our awkward moments. My new haircut had definitely thrown him. I chuckled out loud as I remembered his face.

'What's so funny then?' said a voice behind me.

Harry. I turned around, beaming.

'Nothing. Just life.'

'What happened yesterday? You turned up looking like royalty and swept out like a wet weekend without saying goodbye.'

'I know. I'm sorry. George is a real downer sometimes.'

'That's why you divorced him, remember? Anyway, I have big news about Dennis Barratt.'

'I'm not doing this anymore.'

'Don't be silly. We're so close.'

'Seriously, Harry. I just want to make a living at the shop and forget all about sleuthing.'

'Are you sure?'

I nodded.

'Okay. I won't tell you. But you and I have another clearance today, if you're game?'

'Now you're talking. When do we go?'

'After you get me a latte and a gigantic piece of coffee cake from my favourite café.'

We both had coffee and cake upstairs and I pointed out the different styles of table to Harry who made sarky comments and refused to take the lesson seriously. I felt a rush of emotion towards him, as he fought to cheer me up in the only way he knew how. We might be an unlikely pair, but we needed each other for lots of reasons.

Mouse turned up, looking bed-rumpled and sleepy, and took the reins from me. He even gave me a quick hug that made me gulp and bite my lip. Harry pulled me outside and pushed me along the pavements to his van.

'I've got some great music today,' he said. 'If you like Fleetwood Mac, you must love this.'

Soon Dire Straits blasted out of the speakers with both of us singing at full volume.

'How did you know Making Movies is one of my favourite albums of all time?' I said, in a break between songs.

'Because it's about many types of love,' he said.

I had to look away, because my eyes had filled with tears. I knew exactly what he meant to say, and I thought my heart might break with sorrow and joy. We certainly had that in common. I saw him struggling too. I wondered if Mel and Ronnie had that kind of relationship. All kinds of love.

We pulled up in a side alley beside a dive bar in a cellar.

'This is a musicians' hang-out. It used to be called the Fix,' said Harry. 'But the police raided it so often it went bankrupt. The owner told me the original idea had been to get your fix of music and companionship, but some of the clientele interpreted it differently.'

I laughed.

'I'm not surprised,' I said. 'It looks like the sort of place I used to go as a teenager. A place where being underage went unnoticed in the dim lighting, as long as you didn't get pissed and vomit everywhere.'

'That's why my father frogmarched me to the Army recruitment office. I showed too much promise as a delinquent. Do you worry about Mouse?'

'Not at the moment. He enjoys his work at the Vintage and seems to have abandoned his erstwhile buddies on the pier. But he's still liable to go off the rails from time to time.'

'Does George get involved?'

I barked out a laugh.

'Only to criticise. That's why Mouse and I get on so well. We were both criticised and abandoned. George can be harsh on those he perceives as weak.'

'He's afraid someone might spot the man behind the bluster.'

I waited, but Harry didn't elaborate. The owner turned up in an old Ford Escort which looked as if the next MOT would be its last. He had long, stringy hair with a beaded plait and a wispy moustache. His eyes were bloodshot in his sun-tanned face. The jeans he had on hadn't been washed since the 1980s and he wore an Afghan jacket that hadn't been cured properly. He held up two fingers in a V-sign.

'Peace and love,' he said.

Harry slipped me a look.

'Peace, brother,' he said. 'What've you got for us today?'

'My whole life. And it's all got to go.'

'How much?'

'Nothing. I've taken the things that will fit into my digs and my storage cabinet. The rest must go.'

He stumbled down the steps, leaving the faint smell of weed behind him, and with shaking hands, he unlocked the door.

'Voila,' he said. 'I'd appreciate it if you took everything you can manage. Leave the door open when you go. Maybe someone else will find joy in what's left.'

We thanked him as we squeezed past him in the stairwell. The odour of marijuana clung to his clothes and made me wrinkle my nose. After he had gone, I turned to Harry.

'Did you smell that guy? I almost got high myself,' he said.

'I tried weed twice.'

'Only twice?'

'The first time I had a white-out and vomited everywhere.'

'And the second time?'

'Same.'

'They say the third time's a charm.'

'I've never been able to face it.'

'Lightweight.'

'Have you ever smoked it?'

'Nope.'

He winked at me and picked up a barrel which had acted as the base for a table. I scoured the room, finding it hard to believe there could be anything worth salvaging in this relic. Then I spotted a tower of disco lights. I plugged it in, sure it wouldn't work, but it lit up. Suddenly the bar filled with coloured lights. Harry lifted his head to gaze at the ceiling.

'I never went to the sixth-form hop at my school,' he said. 'I had already signed up by then.'

He scrolled through his phone and perched it on the bar. Then he stretched out his arm to me.

'May I have the pleasure of this dance?'

The phone's tiny speakers emitted a song that brought back a million memories; Ten CC's *'I'm not in love'*.

I took his hand, and he pulled me close. His familiar odour filled my senses, and I shut my eyes, allowing the bar to morph into the school disco in my imagination. We moved around the small space, my face in the crook of his neck. I could feel his broad hand wide across my back and his heart beating almost synchronously with mine. The song ended, and we stood in silence for a moment. When I opened my eyes, he was gazing at me.

'I really like you,' he said. 'I hope you know that.'

An enormous lump formed in my throat so I just nodded.

'But it's too soon,' he said, his voice croaky. 'I need time to get over Cathy. You understand that, don't you?'

I swallowed.

'We both do. You've seen how much of a hold George still has over me.'

'But you like me too?'

'More than chocolate.'

He let me go and a feeling of intense loneliness coursed through me. I wanted to pull him back into my arms, but I just stood there.

'Let's get on with it, then. The furniture won't pack itself.'

'Harry?'

'What's up?'

'I love working with you. It would be a shame to ruin what we've got already. Why don't we call a moratorium?'

'A what now?'

'You know what I mean. Let's just have fun together, like Mel and Ronnie when they were children.'

'Love can wait until I'm ready?'

'Until we're ready.'

'I'd like that.'

'Me too.'

Chapter 32

Love seemed to be high on the agenda at Second Home, as Ghita had turned into a fifteen-year-old schoolgirl with a first crush. I don't know how she behaved during her shifts at the council, but she floated around the shop about a foot from the floor. She had put henna in her hair and fallen asleep, so it now looked like a forest fire. Her eyes sparkled, and she stood taller. Roz found Ghita's transformation quite disconcerting.

'Who is this weird apparition and what have they done with Ghita?' she said.

'I hope Rohan can live up to the hype,' I said, crossing my fingers.

Finally, after weeks of procrastination, Rohan had asked for a person to person, and Ghita roped in both myself and Roz as chaperones. She would have co-opted Joy and Grace too, if they had been willing. In fact, it wouldn't have surprised me if she had asked all the members of Fat Fighters.

As it was, only Roz and I accompanied her to Brighton on the bus along the coast, which stopped right outside the Pavilion. Rohan had suggested tea at the Royal Pavilion Café and Ghita had jumped at the chance. The café sat on the first floor overlooking the gardens and was unrivalled in its oriental splendour. The wind had picked up while we travelled on the bus and, by the time we arrived, could have classified as a near gale. It buffeted the seagulls on the beach where they had congregated on the sand. As we approached the Pavilion, I wondered, as I always did, if the architect had been tripping on some exotic narcotic when he designed this festival of domes, balconies, and archways. The domed roofs of the Pavilion with its many folderols and plaster scrolls covered the seaside pleasure palace built for King George IV. The outside shell looked like an Indian temple. The rooms inside are mostly decorated in the Victorian version of Chinese style. Winged dragons roam the walls and hold up chandeliers in opulent yellow and pink rooms unmatched in their elaborate and expensive décor.

Luckily, Rohan had booked a table indoors, so we could look out over the terrace where the wind threatened to blow the chairs into a heap at one end. The palace lost none of its glamour despite the awful weather. The table Rohan had booked featured four purple velvet bucket seats which matched his rather lurid jacket. He did not shake our hands, but nodded gravely as Ghita introduced us. Rohan had jet black hair and neat eyebrows. He had kohl on his eyelids and his skin looked as soft as a baby's. This should have rung alarm bells, but I dismissed my fears as old-fashioned. Men of his age often groomed themselves with excessive care.

Rohan had ordered afternoon tea for four, which the waitress brought over on a tiered cake stand lined with paper doilies. The tiers groaned with miniature cucumber sandwiches, chocolate eclairs, cherry scones, and various decorative petits fours; a veritable Ghita banquette. Her eyes opened wide as she gazed at the sugar explosion in front of her.

'I hope you like it,' said Rohan. 'I got the idea you were keen on cakes. Like me.'

Ghita nodded, unable to articulate her happiness. Roz raised an eyebrow at me as Rohan flicked his napkin to open it and draped it on his lap.

'Tuck in, ladies,' he said.

There's nothing more delicious than a cream tea. I love scones with clotted cream and jam with a passion. I would travel all the way to Devon just to eat a cream tea. All four of us emitted sighs of ecstasy as we reduced the layers of goodies to a mere memory and a scattering of rumpled paper cases. I folded one to distract myself from the remains of the feast. Ghita and Rohan were getting on a storm, giggling, and having bites of each other's treats. At one stage, Rohan wiped some icing off her cheek with his linen handkerchief and she blushed prettily. She stood up and went to the bathroom to check her face. I think she expected us to follow her for a debrief, but we missed the cue. Rohan sighed with contentment and rubbed his rotund belly.

'Which of you is her partner?' he said, peering at us through his sugar haze.

'Her what?' said Roz.

'Oh, I see,' I said. 'She works with me in the shop, but she's not a business partner.'

Rohan laughed.

'I see what you did there,' he said.

Roz and I looked at each other in confusion.

'I don't think I understand,' I said.

'Are you both gay?'

'Neither of us is gay,' said Roz. 'None of us, and that includes Ghita.'

His face fell.

'Oh,' he said. 'That's awkward. Because I am.'

Our jaws hit the table together.

'But why are you courting Ghita?' said Roz.

'I thought she understood. I told her I lived with a man. We live in Brighton, for heaven's sake, the gay capital of Britain.'

'Ghita is a little sheltered,' I said. 'I have a feeling she didn't understand what you were signalling to her.'

'But I thought our union would be a marriage of convenience. I expected us to go to weddings and christenings together, but live apart.'

'The perils of conducting a relationship by text,' muttered Roz.

Rohan stood up, brushing the crumbs off his purple smoking jacket.

'I'm sorry,' he said. 'I can't do this.'

He shot off like a scalded cat. Before either of us could react, he had reached the door of the café and disappeared into the storm. At the same moment, Ghita emerged from the toilets, floating along on her happy cloud. When she got to the table, she sat down and looked around.

'Where's Rohan?' she said. 'Did he go to the bathroom too? How cute.'

Roz bit her lip and pointed discreetly at me. I shook my head vigorously.

'What's going on?' said Ghita, looking at me. 'Is he gone?'

I shrugged, unable to tell her the truth.

Ghita turned to Roz, her face pale.

'What did you say to him?'

'Whoa! I said nothing. Why are you blaming me?' said Roz?

'Because it's always you. What nasty piece of information did you tell him to make him leave? How could you do that to me?'

'Ghita, sit down. You've got this all wrong. Roz said nothing. Rohan—'

'And you're worse than she is. You let her get away with it. I thought you were my friends, but you're cruel and sarcastic and you don't care about anyone except yourselves. I'm going home now, and I never want to see either of you again.'

'Ghita, you need to listen. It's nothing to do with us,' said Roz.

But she stalked out of the café without a backward look, leaving us sitting there in shock.

'He'll tell her,' I said.

'Let's hope so. We really need Fat Fighters after that tea,' said Roz.

'That's not funny. She's got a broken heart.'

'I'm sorry. I can't help making jokes, and it really isn't our fault.'

'I know, but it feels like it is.'

Chapter 33

I tried to call Ghita multiple times after the disaster at the Pavilion, but she wouldn't answer her mobile phone. When I rang her at the County Council, they told me she couldn't come to the telephone because she had a meeting. Roz didn't have any luck either, so we let Ghita come to us in her own time. I was certain Rohan would tell her the truth if we didn't. I couldn't imagine he would just cut her off after they had got on so well. It made me sad to lose her friendship over something I had no control over.

Despite my feeling about Fiona Conrad's suicide, I had finally accepted the police's verdict on the matter. George had made clear to me we had nothing that could class as evidence. They did not win cases based on he-said-she-said arguments. The boxes of papers on the Conrad investigation still lurked behind the couch in the sitting room, but I couldn't bring myself to throw them away just yet. Mouse still wanted me to investigate the Dennis Barratt angle, but I imagined we would just get more hearsay testimony, which just wouldn't hack it.

Mouse had gone to the arcade with some friends, and I had the house to myself for a change. I had slumped in front of the latest police procedural with a glass of rosé and a bag of nachos when the doorbell rang. I did not expect anyone, but I balked at opening the curtains to check who it could be. Instead, I took a deep breath and opened the door. To my surprise, George stood outside, his face a mixture of embarrassment and appeal. I must have looked surprised. I certainly felt it. He put a hand out to grab my arm.

'Are you alright?' he said. 'You look like you've seen a ghost.'

'What are you doing here?' I said. 'Isn't it a bit late for house calls?'

'Can I come in? I want to talk about the Conrads.'

'I thought the case was dead and buried.'

'So did I. Believe me. But there's been a development.'

'What sort of development?'

'Let me in and I'll tell you.'

I groaned and opened the door wider, waving him in. He scanned the room and spotted the cardboard box containing my research.

'May I?' he said, but he didn't wait for a reply.

He lifted it onto the table and flipped through the contents. Before I could stop him, he reached into it and pulled out the photograph of Mel, Ronnie, and Sarah at the beach.

'And where did you get this from? I thought I told you to stop investigating.'

His words were hostile, but his face creased into a smile when he saw mine.

'I couldn't help it. I felt so sure, but not anymore.'

'What if I told you I had come across evidence that Fiona Conrad's death might not be an accident after all?'

'You mean we have a double murder on our hands?' I said, my heart racing.

'I didn't say that. But I need to apologise to you first, because I found this at home.'

He reached into the poacher's pocket of his raincoat and handed me a parcel addressed to me at the old address (his house). Somebody had already opened and then resealed the parcel. I raised an eyebrow as I examined the rough edges.

'Who opened it?' I said.

'Sharon. I don't know why. I'm not sure she knows either. Anyway, she opened it, and then felt guilty and hid it in the hall cupboard. I found it there when I was looking for my golf shoes this evening.'

'What's in it?'

'I haven't looked. I didn't think it was any of my business.'

I tore open the package and pulled out a square box, whose shape I recognised, my lacquered Chinese box, wrapped in a piece of paper. I unfolded the paper and read the note written on it out loud.

'Tanya, I'm feeling a little insecure because of the complications I mentioned to you the other day. I have enemies, and they don't want me discovering the truth. I think they may try to kill me and frame someone else who is involved, so I'm sending back your box. It contains evidence of past sins which may be of some use, if anything should ever happen to me. If not, I'll come to the Vintage with a bottle of bubbly and tell you all about it soon. Love Mel. X.'

'Holy shit,' said George. 'What's in the box, Tan?'

I opened it with trembling fingers. A small object enveloped in a wad of toilet paper fell into my hand.

'What's that?' said George.

'Hang on.'

I unravelled the paper, and a wedding band fell into my hand. On closer examination, I noticed some lettering on the inside, but I couldn't read the tiny writing. I had become longsighted, but vanity prevented me from getting reading glasses. My desk contained a magnifying glass I had taken home from the shop. I held the ring under the light and focussed on the inscription.

'It reads Mel and Ronnie 4 Ever.'

George sat down heavily on the sofa and wiped his brow.

'What the hell?' he said. 'Give me the note and the ring. I want a closer look.'

I sank to the sofa beside him, stunned.

'We need to open the cases again,' I said.

'We?' said George. 'You're not a police officer.'

I sighed.

'Listen. You need to call a truce with me. I'll show you everything I've got if you will include me in your investigation. I can probably get more out of the suspects than you can. They trust me.'

'That's not possible. Officially.'

He rubbed his chin.

'Why don't you open a bottle of wine and we can go through the evidence you've collected together? Once I see where you've got to, we can formulate a plan.'

'Do you still think Fiona did it?'

'She confessed in her suicide note. But there's no proof, and people often confess to murders they didn't commit.'

'But why do they do that?'

'Mostly to protect someone else. Either someone they know has motive, or someone they love who actually carried out the crime.'

'Maybe the suicide note is a forgery.'

'That's another possibility. But why would someone kill Mel in the first place? Fiona wanted Mel's inheritance, but if she didn't kill her, who else had motive?'

'Let's go over the facts. I'll get that bottle.'

Chapter 34

I know I shouldn't have waited until George left, but something stopped me from opening the secret compartment in the lacquered box until he had gone. We had drunk the bottle of red wine between us, but he swore he had only drunk a glass himself, because he had to drive home. I don't remember it that way, but I imagined trying to get the DI to do a breath test might test most junior officer's resolve. I decided George could police his own life. We had a great couple of hours together. I had gone through all the different scenarios with him, and explained whom we had talked to and the conclusions we had reached in each case. The solution to the murders ultimately revolved around Mel's marital status. If she and Ronnie were siblings, it conjured up different suspects than if they were not.

Mouse had produced the key lead to unravelling Ronnie's parentage. He had tracked down Dennis Barratt, who also had a strong claim to being Ronnie's father. If not, why on earth had Ronnie changed his surname to Barratt? Since the cases were still closed, George gave me permission to chase down the lead, but only on condition I told him everything I learned. He promised to re-examine the Diane Conrad case and find out which of our prime suspects had the opportunity to murder her too. We were dealing with someone unscrupulous enough to murder three people to get what they wanted. But we needed the motive. Why did they kill three people (or two) over such a long timeframe? I could not discount Fiona, as she was already in the picture when Diane died. But she was not the only one.

By the time George left, he had moved quite close to me on the couch, and I got vibes from him I had not felt in years. I don't know what would have happened if he hadn't gone home, but I suspect Sharon would not have approved of the slightly febrile atmosphere generated by the wine and the intrigue. I wished he had hung in longer before dumping me. The old chemistry still lingered even if he had shacked up with someone else. I felt relieved that Harry and I had been platonic for now. I'm not sure I could deal with two heartaches at once.

Once I had made certain George had driven off into the windy night, I sat back down on the couch and picked up the box from among the papers. I popped open the secret compartment and let out a pleased exclamation as I saw another handwritten note inside it. It had been read and refolded until it was coming apart so I unfolded it with caution. The handwriting did not belong to Mel. It had a sharp forward slant, a masculine scribble, which made it hard to decipher. It looked like a doctor's writing on a prescription. I made out the sender after staring at it for a while. To my surprise, it appeared to be from Dennis Barratt, confirming their appointment to meet. The hairs on my arms stood to attention when

I noticed the time and date of their meeting. Mel had an appointment with Dennis Barratt on the day of her death, before she came to the Vintage for coffee. I discounted him as a suspect, as it seemed pretty obvious that he could have killed her then if he had intended to harm her. But he may have told her something that got her killed later on.

Mouse stumbled in late and found me asleep on the couch. He woke me by tapping my shoulder, lifting his finger to his lips, and pointing at my feet. Hades had snuck into the space on the cushions and curled up to sleep. I grinned and signalled for him to come into the kitchen with me. Hades woke when I moved and slunk off in a sulk to his basket. Mouse had his sleepy and slightly drunk face on, but when I told him about Mel's final meeting, his eyes opened wide.

'Are you going to meet him?'

'George said I could.'

'But what if he's dangerous? You'll take Harry with you, won't you?'

'If he'll come.'

'Call him now.'

'It's too late. I'll call him tomorrow.'

'I will then,' he said and took out his phone.

Before I could stop him, he had dialled Harry and put the phone on speaker. It rang several times before a grumpy voice answered.

'Mouse, what the hell? This better be important.'

'It is. Speak to Tanya. She's on speaker phone with me.'

'What are you two up to now?' said Harry, amusement creeping into his voice.

'The missing Chinese lacquered box has turned up, and it had a note in the secret compartment from Dennis Barratt,' I said.

'Holy crap. I'm awake now. What are we going to do?'

'I thought we'd see him together, if that's okay with you?'

'Well, there's absolutely no way on earth I'd let you go alone.'

'Okay, I'll call him tomorrow. Sweet dreams.'

'Night, you two vampires. Get some rest.'

It's all very well telling me to get some rest when I'm as excited as a child the night before Christmas. When I drifted off, I had lurid dreams about George and Harry, which made no sense, but I needed to forget immediately. I tossed and turned and threw my blankets off, giving myself cramp when my legs turned to ice. I stared down at the jungle in my backyard and considered cutting back the brambles with my secateurs. Finally, I slept for a couple of hours, and woke when Mouse came into my room.

'Have you called him yet?'

'What time is it?'

'Quarter to eight.'

'Go back to bed.'

I got into the shower and washed myself awake, taking my time while I waited for a decent hour to call Dennis Barratt. I kept telling myself that even if I got hold of him; he didn't have any obligation to speak to me. And even then, perhaps he had no time. I considered asking

Ronnie if he would call Dennis for me, but Ronnie had to be on the list of suspects for now. Even if he couldn't have murdered Diane, a jealous rage over Mel's marriage to Greg, or greed if he might be the heir to William's money, could not be discounted as a motive for the other murders. I would call him directly and hope he would speak to me.

I forced myself to eat a bacon sandwich to cure my hangover. Maybe George had only had one glass after all. I had an evil headache. I wondered if I had reached the age when I would control my drinking, not by common sense, but by the fear of horrible hangovers lasting for days. At nine o'clock on the dot, I dialled Dennis Barratt's number. It rang out twice with no sign of him answering. He probably screened his calls, and he wouldn't recognise my caller ID. I sent him a brief text telling him Mel had been a friend of mine and asking if he would talk to me.

'Hasn't he answered yet?' said Mouse.

'No. Maybe he's not interested in raking over the past.'

'Or he's got things to hide too.'

'How frustrating.'

I walked to work along the promenade, stopping halfway to sit in a wind shelter and gaze out over the sea towards the wind farm. The morning sunlight hit the steel stems, highlighting them in the grey waters. The colours of the sea were a constant amazement to me. Just when I thought I knew all its moods, it would surprise me again. I noticed a juvenile seagull sidle up to me, his head cocked in inquiry. Herring gulls are massive close up and always make me feel nervous about their razor-sharp beaks and evil eyes. I patted my pockets and found a half-eaten biscuit, likely the result of my drunken stumbling around the kitchen the night before. I dropped it on the pavement in front of me and watched as he debated the likelihood of it being a trap in his pea-sized brain. It occurred to me that Dennis Barratt might do the same. I did not know how he fitted in to this story. Perhaps I'd never get an answer.

I kicked the biscuit towards the seagull who grabbed it and flew off to be mobbed by bigger seagulls who made him drop it among the pebbles. He landed on the bank and wandered around for a while before flying away. Bummer. Then my phone pinged at me. A text had arrived in my inbox from Dennis Barratt. I opened it with my fingers crossed. The message said 'where and when?' I pumped my fist and whispered 'yes' to myself, before calling Harry to find out when he might be free. I could sit down no longer and jumped up to walk to the shop, humming to myself as Harry's number rang in my ear. About ten minutes later, I got confirmation from Dennis Barratt that he would meet us for a cup of tea in a greasy spoon in Shoreham at midday. I gave Mouse a lie in of an hour before I called him and told him to spring clean the house.

'Find every scrap of information and put it in the boxes.'

'What shall I do with them?'

'George will pick them up later. Just leave them on the side.'

'Are we finally going to catch Mel's murderer?'

'Maybe.'

Chapter 35

Harry sounded the horn outside the Second Home and I ran out and jumped into the cabin. Mouse gave us a thumbs up as we drove off, looking forlorn at being left behind. Since Ghita has stopped coming to help, the shop has lost its sparkle as if Tinkerbell had left the building. Roz had taken it pretty hard and disappeared off to sea with Ed to get it out of her system. We all tried to contact Ghita without success, but unless Rohan told her the truth, she had no intention of speaking to us again. We needed to talk to Rohan and ask him to explain what had happened, but I didn't hold out hope of finding him again.

We drove along the coast road to Shoreham, getting stuck behind the Brighton bus, which halted at every single stop, as if on purpose. How do buses know when you are in a hurry? Despite my agitation, we arrived only two minutes late and found Dennis Barratt outside the café smoking a Rothmans. For an instant, I felt tempted to cadge one from him, but I reminded myself how much more attractive it was to smell like Eau de L'Orangerie instead of a full ashtray. I contented myself with taking a long and deliberate breath of the smoke, which made me cough like mad. Dennis Barratt raised an eyebrow and stood on the butt. He pushed the glass door open.

'After you,' he said, patting my bottom as I passed him.

This creeped me out, and I put Harry between me and him when we sat down. I examined Dennis with a jaundiced eye, noting his comb-over, his nicotine-stained fingers and his ravaged smoker's skin. He must have been handsome once, but now he exuded dodgy vibes from every pore and his shifty eyes made me twitch. I half expected him to offer me some cheap branded perfume, or some silk stockings which fell off the back of a lorry. We ordered a pot of tea and some tea cakes which turned out to be as hard as the pebbles on Seacastle beach. I left my bun on my plate, intending to wrap it in a napkin and give it to the seagull at the wind shelter. Barratt asked for a fizzy drink. He took a swig and letting out a loud belch, daring me to comment. When I ignored him, he pinched the bridge of his nose and leaned back in his chair, his legs akimbo.

'How can I help you?' he said. 'I couldn't believe you tracked me down after all these years.'

'My stepson found you. He's a bit of a whizz with computers,' I said.

'He must be.'

'We're interested in your relationship with Sarah Bingley,' said Harry.

'Ah, the lovely Miss Bingley. One of my first conquests. You can't beat a bit of posh totty.'

I squirmed at his casual boast, but I knew he wanted a reaction, so I kept my disgust off my face.

'Did you go out with her for long?' I said.

'Long enough,' he said, and winked at me.

'Long enough to get her pregnant?' said Harry.

Barratt roared with laughter.

'It only takes one go, you know, if you're unlucky.'

'Are you Ronnie Barratt's father?' I asked.

He rubbed the lower half of his face with his hand and pursed his lips.

'It depends who you ask,' he said.

'What do you mean?' said Harry.

'Sarah told me Ronnie was mine, and she told him that too. He even took my surname, despite me having almost nothing to do with him. He's a likeable lad, actually.'

'We like him,' I said. 'Are you definitely his father?'

'You'd have to ask Sarah.'

'We're asking you,' said Harry, a slight edge to his voice.

I noticed him stiffen slightly, the way a dog does when it is threatening another. Barratt noticed too. He licked his lips and shifted in his chair.

'The way I heard it,' he said. 'Sarah Bingley blackmailed William Conrad for years about being Ronnie's father; first to keep the truth from Diane and later from Fiona. The thing I don't understand is why she told Ronnie that I was his father. That's why he changed his surname to Barratt. He asked me for permission, and I couldn't see any reason to stop him.'

'When was this?' I said.

'Soon after Mel left him. He married her using his mother's surname, but after what happened, he changed his name to Barratt.'

'Who is Ronnie's father?' said Harry

'I don't know, but if it's William Conrad, Ronnie would be his heir.'

'That's a powerful motive to kill Mel,' I said.

Barratt laughed.

'Ronnie's as soft as a white bap. He couldn't kill a fly. He would never be capable of murder.'

'Why did you see Mel the day she died?' said Harry.

Barratt's cheek muscles stood out as he fought for self-control. His cocky air vanished, and he deflated. Just for a second, I recognised a resemblance to Ronnie.

'Who told you that?' he said, finally.

'She did. We found a note from you in her belongings.' I said.

He shrugged.

'So, I saw her. That proves nothing.'

'We're not accusing you,' I said.

'We just need to know what you talked about,' said Harry. 'It may have got her killed.'

Barratt blinked and swallowed.

'Killed? She fell, so I was told.'

'Somebody pushed her. And they murdered Fiona Conrad to stop her identifying them.'

Barratt's head dropped into his hands.

'I did not know that,' he said. 'Mel didn't tell me it could be dangerous.'

'What did you do for her?'

'Nothing. She wanted to find out if Ronnie could be her brother. She asked me for a sample of my DNA.'

'And you gave it to her?'

'Of course. I wanted to know too.'

'What happened to the sample?'

'Your guess is as good as mine.'

Chapter 36

On our drive back from Shoreham, I mulled over the facts of the case, certain I had missed something.

'Well, that wasn't what I expected,' said Harry. 'Dennis Barratt is some piece of work. Do you think he's telling the truth about the DNA sample?'

'Maybe Mel and Ronnie planned to get back together? If Barratt is Ronnie's father, they weren't related.'

'Perhaps. But I wouldn't trust Dennis Barratt as far as I could throw him. He may be on the phone to the murderer as we speak.'

'Possibly. Although he seemed more bewildered than vengeful to me. Anyway, there's something else bugging me. I found a DNA result from a laboratory concealed in Mel's room, but it reported that there were no family ties between the two samples submitted. Why would she test him twice?'

'Didn't Ronnie pay a visit to Mel's room after she died? Maybe he wanted the results.'

'They had fallen down behind the cabinet drawer when I found them, so whatever he needed from them, he didn't get it.'

I looked out at the blur of water as we passed along the coast and breathed in the air, thick with beached seaweed as my hair struggled to escape from its bun. In the back of my mind, I caught a glimmer of something I had missed. I took a deep breath and let it out in increments. Think woman, think. I slapped my forehead as it came to me.

'What's up?' said Harry.

'The timing of the samples is wrong. If Barratt gave Mel a sample on the day she died, the results I found in her room couldn't possibly be from him.'

'She tested someone else?'

'It looks like it. Unfortunately, the subjects who she got tested didn't get identified in the document. But I just remembered something important. Before she died, Mel asked Flo to do her a favour. Flo wouldn't tell me what it was, but I think I've guessed. I've got to check with her. It's time to finish this puzzle.'

'Please be careful. There are now three accidental deaths which appear more likely to be murders. If somebody killed three people already, they'll have no compunction about finishing you off too. Don't go anywhere alone.'

I rang Flo as soon as Harry dropped me back at the shop. She couldn't come until the following day, because George had reopened the cases on Mel and Fiona, and she had to review the autopsies. Flo could wait, but I needed to talk to Ronnie Barratt again. He had two strong motives to kill Mel. If he was William's son, he would inherit the Conrad money with her gone, and if he wasn't, he might have killed her in a jealous rage over Greg. Dennis had told us he wouldn't kill a fly, but I wasn't so sure. Maybe his acting skills were better than we imagined.

The door bell sounded downstairs, and I leaned over the banister.

'You can have a look around if you like,' I shouted. 'I'm upstairs having a coffee if you have questions.'

'It's me, Ronnie Barratt. Do you mind if I come up?'

I couldn't believe it. Why would he come here? I hesitated. Surely he wouldn't attack me in broad daylight?

'Not at all. Come and have a coffee with me,' I said.

I sent a frantic text to Harry telling him to come back. Ronnie's strained face appeared as he mounted the stairs. He came to sit beside me on the banquette seat, his anxious hands twisting in his lap, as I kept my screen out of his line of vision.

'I was hoping to have a chat with you about Mel,' he said. 'I haven't been entirely honest with you, but it's time I came clean.'

'About what?' I said. 'Shouldn't you be talking to the police?'

'They don't seem to care about Mel. If you knew what I know, perhaps the clues you already have would fall into place.'

He obviously hadn't heard about the case reopening. I bet Sarah Bingley knew.

'Go on,' I said.

'As I told you before, Mel and I were brought up together. We were almost the same age; she beat me by a few months. We fell in love as children and our relationship only grew stronger as we became teenagers. Mel had lost her mother, and I had no father, so we bonded over that. Anyway, when we were both sixteen, we decided to get married, and told Mr Conway who flew in to a terrifying rage. He told Mel he'd cut her out of his will if she married me. But Fiona encouraged us. She even signed the paper for the civil service. I've never been so happy as that day we said I do.'

'What went wrong?' I said, although I already knew.

'We had made plans to run away together, but Mel disappeared without telling me why. Our marriage was annulled. I searched for years, but I never found a trace. I began to think someone had murdered her and hidden her on the property. After she disappeared, Mr Conrad took me on as a gardener. I guess my mother had something to do with that. He could never refuse her anything, even though Fiona got rid of her. Whenever I dug up a flower bed, I expected to find Mel's bones hidden beneath the soil. But I never did.'

'But she contacted you recently?' I said.

'Yes, she told me she had married Greg Summers and lived in London, but she wanted to come home. I met her a few times in the café at the end of her road. She told me we were half-siblings and that Mr Conrad was my father too. I found it terribly shocking, but it also made sense. My mother and Mr Conrad were always close, despite everything Fiona could do. He supported us for years without telling her. Mum said he was just generous, but I never really believed that.'

'Where does Dennis Barratt come into this?'

His mouth fell open. For a second, the weak mask fell, and I had a glimpse of the hatred and pain behind it.

'How did you…?'

'I am, was, an investigative journalist, and I haven't given up on finding out what happened to Mel.'

'So, you realise Mel got it wrong about us being siblings? I don't know who told her that awful lie. She divorced me, and married Greg because of it. They broke my heart.'

'That must have been devastating for you. What happened when she came home?'

'I only found out from Dennis. I couldn't believe she hadn't contacted me.'

He rubbed his face with his hands and ran them through his hair.

'I'm sorry. But the last time we spoke, you said you were supposed to meet up before she died.'

'Did I? I must have been confused. We never spoke after the last time in London.'

'Was that because of the row?' I said.

He froze.

'What row?'

'The café owner near Greg's house told me you had an argument with Mel and stormed out.'

Ronnie stood up, his hands balled up into tight fists. The muscles on his jaw stood out white on his face and icy fear gripped me.

'I didn't do it,' he said. 'You've got to believe me. I loved her.'

He took a step towards me just as the shop bell jangled downstairs.

'Tanya? Are you still here?'

Harry's voice. Thank goodness. A cold sweat which had dampened my t-shirt. Ronnie's shoulders slumped.

'I've got to go,' he said, and ran down the stairs, almost knocking Harry back down them.

'Steady on,' said Harry, but Ronnie had gone.

I got up and reached out for Harry, trembling as he wrapped his arms around me.

'You're so stubborn,' he said. 'You could have been killed.'

'He just turned up,' I said. 'I thought you were too far away to rescue me.'

'I stopped for a Mr Whippy on the promenade, but I jumped on my white horse and charged over.'

I laughed.

'De-stressing after hanging out with me.'

'You could say that. Ronnie looked like he's seen a ghost. What happened?'

'I asked him about the row with Mel and he freaked out.'

'Do you think he's involved in her death?'

'Before today, I'd have been certain he wasn't.'

'And now?'

'And now I'm not so sure.'

Chapter 37

Mouse had failed to start on the planned clear up when I got home, so I told him that if he wanted to avoid paying rent, he would take his finger out and get on with it in the morning. He went to his room in a sulk, but I had no intention of letting him get away with it. The next morning, I shook him awake and left the vacuum cleaner outside his bedroom door so he would walk right into it when he left his room. I stuffed the stale bread into my bag and strode off down the promenade. I took out the bread and tore it into pieces. I didn't have to wait long for the herring gulls to spot me. They wheeled in over my head, yelling their determination to claim the lot. Their shrill cries attracted others and soon the pebble bank became blanketed in their white bodies with the silky grey wings. Their bright yellow beaks with the peculiar red spot that looked as if they had been pecking at bloody corpses always made me shiver. I flung the bread into the air and watched as they fought over every scrap.

Afterwards I walked to the local Spar supermarket and bought milk and teabags, and some chocolate digestive biscuits for sustenance. The café had become a port of call for many office workers on their break and I liked to give them a sweet treat with their coffees. I let myself in and, after stowing the supplies, I began to remove some of my latest finds at the boot sale from a cardboard box.

I lined up a set of pretty glass lampshades that needed a hot soapy wash to remove years of nicotine and fly excreta. As I filled the sink, the doorbell jangled and Grace Wong came in waving a piece of paper.

'I nearly forgot,' she said. 'We sold the silver you gave me for a great price. Seeing as it's for the cats' home, we only took fifteen per cent, so here's a cheque for the rest.'

I wiped my hands on my trousers and took it from her. My eyes almost popped out of their sockets.

'Seriously! It's far more than I imagined.'

'A few clients were interested, and we let them fight it out. I love an auction.'

I gave her a hug.

'Thank you. I'm sure the old lady would so appreciate her money going to keep her cats. I'm sorry she isn't compos mentis any more.'

'We'll all be like her one day,' said Grace. 'You're doing the right thing.'

'Can you stop for a coffee?'

'Not today, but I'd like to discuss the annual antique fair with you sometime, if you're interested.'

'Isn't it impossible to get a table there?'

'That's what they say,' she said, and grinned.

At that moment, Flo burst in puffing and panting as if she had run all the way. She recovered by pottering around the stock on the ground floor, as I bid goodbye to Grace. Then we mounted to the café where I made her a coffee with our machine. I even got the milk to froth correctly for once. I served the coffee to her with a generous slice of carrot cake.

'I shouldn't,' she said, but she immediately took a large bite, as if I might believe her and withdraw it.

'How have you been?' I asked. 'It must be weird to deal with three murders in the same family.'

'It has been a little stressful, but I talk to the bodies first, before I start the autopsy, and explain what I'm about to do. They don't mind.'

'I'm sorry you got into trouble with George. He really can be a pig when he wants to.'

'Not surprising, considering who he works for,' said Flo, taking another large bite of her cake. 'The Super's much worse than George.'

Large crumbs fell into the lap of her tweed skirt and a small fleck of icing stuck to her upper lip. I handed her a napkin and pointed at my lip with my index finger. She wiped it off, blushing.

'I'm the real pig around here, but your cakes are so delicious,' she said.

'I know they have reopened the case, but I'd like to ask you something anyway, if that's okay?'

'Fire away. I can't guarantee I can tell you the answer, though.'

'It's been playing on my mind. You told me on the way to Conrad House, on the day she fell down the stairs, that Mel asked you for help, but you refused her. What did she want?' I said.

'She asked me to carry out a DNA test on something. I still can't figure out why.'

All the hair on my arms stood to attention and an ice-cold chill crawled up my back.

'A DNA test?'

The alarm bells went off in my head. Think, Tanya, think. 'But that's… Oh my, it's been staring me in the face the whole time.'

'I'm sorry Flo. I've got to call Mouse. Give me a minute.'

I keyed in Mouse's number, but the call went to his voicemail. I tried again, twice, but he wouldn't take my call. Was he in a snot because I had made him do the housework for his keep? I turned to Flo, urgency in my voice.

'We've got to go to my house. Right now.'

'Okay, give me the keys to the shop. I'll shut up while you get the car.'

Flo flagged me down as I rounded the corner and squeezed herself into the front seat.

'Remind me not to eat anymore cake,' she said.

My heart thundered as I drove towards the Grotty Hovel. Mel had tested the DNA for a reason. It had to be connected to the murder. Maybe I could get to the bottom of this case after all.

A local bus pushed in front of us, and then halted, for what seemed an age, at every bus stop all the way home, with no way of passing it on the narrow streets. I felt like I had been stuck behind a bus all my life. My knuckles whitened on the steering wheel as I muttered, 'come on, come on' to myself.

'Are you going to tell me what's wrong,' said Flo. 'Is it Mouse? Is he in trouble again?'

'No, well, yes, he's always in some sort of scrape, but that's not the problem. I asked him to clean the house from top to bottom to make sure he had gathered the case information together, and I'm afraid he may tidy away the vital clue we have been looking for.'

'You mean you've had it all the time?'

'I think I might have.'

I parked outside the house and ran inside, leaving Flo to heave herself out and lumber after me. Mouse did not hear me as the vacuum cleaner blocked out all the other sounds. I tapped him on the shoulder and he spun around in fright.

'Whoa! When did you get here?' he said. 'I'm not finished yet.'

'This second. Can you switch that off, please?'

'Keep your hair on. Oh, hi Flo.'

Mouse leaned down to turn off the vacuum cleaner.

'So, where's the fire?' he said. 'Am I in trouble again?'

'You might be,' I said. 'During your efforts at cleaning the sitting room, did you come across a Ziploc bag with an empty can of Fanta in it?'

'I did.'

'Where is it now?'

'It's in the rubbish bin outside.'

I dashed out to the back door and tore open the sack of rubbish uppermost in the wheelie bin. The Ziploc bag nestled among the discarded plastic trays and cardboard boxes at the top of the sack. To my relief, it still appeared to be sealed. I removed it and took it back indoors, where I found Mouse putting on the kettle, and flirting with Flo, who was pink cheeked with pleasure.

'It's here,' I said.

'And what is that, besides being a sticky plastic bag with a fizzy drink can in it?' said Flo.

'I found this in Mel's room after the funeral, when I went to collect her things. The proprietor had thrown it in the bin, but I took it out again. I felt sure Mel had kept it for a reason, but, at the time, I couldn't figure it out.'

Flo's eyes opened wide.

'But whose DNA is it?'

'I'm pretty sure it belongs to Dennis Barratt, who may or may not be Ronnie's biological father. She saw him the day she died, and he told me she took an empty drink can back to the guesthouse.'

'Oh, my goodness gracious. That would change the complexion of things, wouldn't it?'

Mouse whooped and bounced all around the kitchen, sending Hades scampering for safety to sulk on the windowsill.

'Can you run the test? And cross check it against the Conrad DNA samples? Tell George what you are doing.

I think it may be vital information. Maybe Mel will solve her own murder.'

'I can. I'll put a rush on the results. They'll take forty-eight hours, though. May I have a cup of tea first?'

'You can have one after we've dropped you off at the station. This is life or death now.'

Chapter 38

After Flo had left, I called Roz and Harry and asked them to come to my house. I sent a text to Ghita too, telling her we had almost solved the case and asking her to come and discuss it with us. She had nothing to contribute, but I hoped she might find the chance of being in on it too tempting to turn down. Our little group had missed her. As I sent it, I remembered Ghita's mother must have Rohan's telephone number since she set them up. I texted her too, pretending he had something for me to collect. Almost immediately she texted me his contact details, and I dialled his number with my fingers crossed. He answered.

'Hi Rohan, it's Tanya. We had tea the other day. Please don't hang up, this is important.'

'What do you want?' he said.

'Ghita won't speak to us. She thinks we said something to make you leave. She won't answer our calls or texts. We miss her, and she hasn't got many friends. Please, can you tell her the truth about you?'

'I already did.'

'I know you think you did, but she didn't understand what you meant. It would be wonderful if you would do this for us. Please, Rohan.'

'I didn't mean to hurt her, you know. I thought she understood.'

'We believe you. Unfortunately, she is hyper-sensitive and she won't speak to us ever again, if you don't tell her in words of one syllable.'

'How about I'm gay and I live with my partner?'

'That should do it, but let her down gently.'

'Okay, you've guilt tripped me into it.'

'Thanks Rohan. Bring him to the Second Home for coffee sometime. We'd love to meet him.'

'I'm not sure Ghita would, but thanks for the invite.'

A wave of relief swept over me as I waited for the others. Our lives weren't the same without the companionable shambles of the Fat Fighters Club. I doubt anyone ever lost a pound, but we learned to accept ourselves and have fun, which was more important in the long run, and Ghita had made it happen by the sheer force of her willpower.

Mouse, with Hades snuggled in his arms, came down from his room as the doorbell rang. I opened it to find Roz and Harry on the doorstep. Roz had dyed her hair green, and she looked like a mermaid. She breezed in, smelling of the sea, and a slightly fishy aroma which I could not place. Harry winked at me and held his nose behind her, making me bite my lip to prevent a guffaw.

Once we were all seated and Hades had chosen Harry's sturdy lap to sit on, I realised that, despite my suspicions, I didn't have any way of proving them.

'I think I know who killed Mel, or at least I've narrowed it down to two possible suspects,' I said. 'But I don't know how to prove it. We don't have enough evidence.'

'Why don't you give us the timeline first?' said Harry. 'That way we can see how we got here.'

'Okay, this is what I think happened. William Conrad had an affair with his housekeeper, Sarah Bingley, while married to his first wife, Diane. After Diane died in a supposed accident in the garden, William fell for his secretary, Fiona, a year after Diane's death and they married and brought up his first wife's daughter, Mel, together.'

'Was Sarah still working there all that time?' said Mouse.

'No. Fiona fired Sarah at some stage. We don't know why. Fiona didn't realise that Sarah had been blackmailing William about him being the father of her son Ronnie. Despite the blackmail, Fiona and William were happy for a decade or so until Mel started to go out with Ronnie, the son of Sarah, who had convinced William that Ronnie was his son. Fiona knew nothing about this. William threatened to disinherit Mel if she married Ronnie, but Fiona helped Mel, because she thought William was being unreasonable. Mel and Ronnie got married in a secret ceremony, and William cut Mel out of his will. Then Sarah told Mel that William was Ronnie's father, and Mel left home for good without telling Ronnie.'

'No wonder Ronnie had such a broken heart. He couldn't imagine why Mel dumped him,' said Harry.

'Especially as Sarah had convinced him that Dennis Barratt was his father.' I said.

'Oh, that explains the surname,' said Roz.

'Anyway, Mel stopped coming home and made a new life in London where she met and married Greg Summers. Greg worked as a commodities broker and talked a big game, but he made some disastrous investments and needed to cover his loans before he went bankrupt. He didn't tell Mel about his parlous state of affairs. Mel became unhappy with her marriage, and when Ronnie turned up, she decided to find out if he really was her brother. Greg persuaded Mel to return home and reconcile with her parents, so she would inherit William's money. She didn't want to go, but then heard from Sarah who told her that William was frail.

Maybe she also told her about Fiona working on him to change his will?'

'Was that even true?' said Roz.

'Probably just a way to get Mel within striking distance,' said Mouse.

'This set the cat among the pigeons. Someone arranged to meet Mel at Conrad House and they pushed her down the stairs. As we know, the death got labelled an accident, but when Fiona discovered proof of who did it, the murderer overheard her planning to meet me and tell all. The same person pushed Fiona down the same stairs as Fiona waited for me there.'

'They killed two people?' said Mouse.

'Three, if you count Diane,' said Harry.

'But I have no definitive proof of who it was,' I said.

'If what you say is true, there are two suspects left. Sarah has been clearing the way for Ronnie, whether or not he knows it,' said Roz. 'Or Ronnie has been ploughing his own path.'

'In that case, there's only one obstacle in their way,' said Harry.

'William Conrad?' said Mouse.

'Exactly. Sarah has moved back in with William who thinks Ronnie is his son. We've got to get him out of that house before one of them kills him too,' I said.

'But do we have any proof that either of them was in the house on the day Mel died?' said Roz. 'You said the door had a padlock on it.'

'Not yet, but there must be something we've missed,' I said.

'Walk us through what you saw on the day of the murder,' said Harry.

'Okay.' I shut my eyes as I imagined us sweeping up the driveway to Conrad House with the building illuminated in our headlights. 'Once we parked the car, we walked up to the front door. Flo changed into her jumpsuit. The front door hung open, and someone had pulled the hasp out of the frame and it swung from the padlock. I noticed it because I'd hurt my shoulder on it the last time I went in, and I wanted to avoid doing the same thing.'

'Wait. Didn't you tell me the padlock on the backdoor of the cat-owner's house was the same make?' said Harry.

'Yes, I don't see what—'

'The person who shut the lock needed the key. That's why Mel's keys were missing from the scene.'

'So, whoever locked the door killed Mel and might still have the key? But the keys are hanging in William's kitchen. I saw them when I went to offer my condolences. They must be a trophy from the kill hidden in plain sight. By returning them to the kitchen, the killer wanted the police to think she had forgotten her keys, but they didn't take the padlock into account. It makes me sick to think of the murderer gloating every time they walk past and see them hanging there.'

'And William would be the last piece of the puzzle. If the murderer could get him to rewrite his will in favour of Ronnie, William would be next,' said Roz.

'It's all about Ronnie,' I said. 'Although he may not even be aware of it.'

'You're not suggesting William's the murderer?' said Harry.

'Of course not. It's got to be Sarah or Ronnie or both. They'll force him to change his will and then get rid of him. We need to get William out of that house before he dies too,' I said.

'But how do we do that?' said Roz. 'Sarah won't let him out of her sight.'

'He asked me to come and see him. I'll tell her I want to take him for coffee at the Vintage to give her a break.'

'You're going to kidnap him?' said Mouse.

'Not exactly. Just save his life.'

'What about the keys?' said Roz

'I'll slip them into a Ziploc when she's not looking. They may have the murderer's DNA on them. She's unlikely to miss them. George will have to act when he sees the keys. It's the last piece of the puzzle, when added to the DNA evidence.'

'It's risky, but it just might work. Why don't I come with you in my van? We can wheel William into the back and secure him there. If Sarah knows I'm waiting, she won't dare touch you, even if she guesses something is up,' said Harry.

'That sounds good. Hopefully, George will get the DNA results tomorrow. We can hand over the keys and tell him our theory.'

Chapter 39

It all seemed so simple in theory. March up to William's house, try to persuade Sarah to let me take William for a coffee, and steal Mel's keys from the kitchen. But as we drove up the cul-de-sac towards the villa, my stomach bucked and churned with dread.

'Are you okay?' said Harry. 'You've gone as white as the wall of an Irish cottage.'

'Fear,' I said. 'She's may already have killed three people, and I know she doesn't like me much.'

'She won't kill you in William's house while I'm waiting outside. You just need to hold your nerve. If anything happens, yell blue murder and I'll be there before you've run out of breath.'

I managed a smile and approached the front door. Despite signs of occupation, nobody came to answer when I rang the doorbell. After a few minutes, I made signals at Harry and slipped down the side of the house and made for the back patio door. I tried the handle, and it opened. I poked my head into the kitchen and called out. No-one answered. I hovered; uncertain, but then I spotted Greg's key ring hanging on the keyboard in easy reach. I crept across the linoleum floor and took a Ziploc bag out of my pocket, turning it inside out without touching the inside of the bag. I reached out and grabbed the keys, using their weight to send them to the bottom of the bag and sealed the top. I put it back into my pocket just as footsteps sounded on the stairs.

'Hello,' I said. 'Is anyone at home?'

Sarah Bingley's face passed through a range of emotions from surprised to furious as she entered the kitchen. I smiled at her as if I hadn't noticed.

'How did you? Oh…'

'I'm sorry. The door was open,' I said. 'Harry and I were in the neighbourhood and we thought William might like a breath of fresh air.'

Sarah did not answer, the muscles in her face taut with fury.

'Well,' I ploughed on. 'Actually, I thought you might appreciate the break. The last few weeks have been very tough on everyone.'

I waited. The tick of the electric clock seemed to echo through the kitchen.

'He's already got a visitor. Ronnie is with him,' she said, at last. 'And he needs to rest afterwards. We have to visit the solicitor's office tomorrow, so I can't have him tiring himself out.'

'That's a pity,' I said. 'We thought a quick jaunt would do him good.'

'You thought wrong. I need you to leave. Now.'

Her tone did not leave room for argument.

'Another time then?' I said, stepping out onto the patio.

'We'll see,' she said, shutting the door and locking it behind me.

Slightly shaken by the encounter, I returned to the van, where Harry drummed his fingers on the steering wheel.

'I almost broke the door down,' he said. 'Where's William?'

'He's with Ronnie upstairs. Sarah's taking him to the solicitor's office tomorrow. She has no intention of letting him out of her sight.'

'And the keys?'

I allowed myself a grin.

'Right here,' I said, patting my pocket.

'Call George.'

'Can we get out of here first?'

'I'll drive and you dial.'

George picked up on the second ring.

'Hi. How's the investigating going?'

'I've found an important piece of the puzzle at William's house.'

'And what in God's name were you doing there?'

'Don't be cross. You told me I could help.'

'You should have told me about it. I could have sent in a team.'

'On what grounds?'

'Don't get smart with me. I'm at another investigation in Shoreham right now. I'll come and see you later tonight. And whatever you do, don't let anyone in.'

I rang off and sighed.

'What's up?' said Harry.

'Just George being George.'

'He's not a bad person.'

'I didn't say he was. He treats me like I'm an infant sometimes.'

'Sometimes you deserve it.'

I sulked all the way home. Harry ignored my tantrum and put on some Led Zeppelin which I couldn't help enjoying.

'He's right though,' he said. 'Stay at home and don't let anyone in. That family is dangerous.'

'I promise.'

I got out of the van with a grunt. And I fully intended to keep my promise, until Ghita turned up on my doorstep, as forlorn as Little Bo Peep without her sheep. I had already cleaned the kitchen and sitting room in a fit of boredom, and spent hours trying to engage Hades in a game. His expression suggested that his metaphorical eyebrow had been raised to high mast at my antics with an empty cardboard box. I was crawling on my hands and knees with my head halfway into the box when the doorbell rang. I froze, checking my watch. Seven-thirty. Could George have got back already? It seemed unlikely. I crawled over to the window and peeped through the curtains. Ghita stood on my front doorstep, chattering from the cold. I couldn't leave her out there. I clambered to my feet and opened the door.

'Hello stranger,' I said, but my intention of cracking some witty remark got stymied by a wave of tears and patchouli. When she finally released me, Ghita's mascara had run down her cheeks and she couldn't look me in the eye.

'Rohan told me the complete story,' she said. 'I'm so sorry. I don't know what came over me.'

'That's okay. You had every right to be upset. We've missed you more than you can imagine.'

Soon, we were ensconced on the couch with a pot of tea and some chocolate biscuits. Hades watched us chat and laugh with a slightly miffed air, which made me gloat. When we had ignored him for too long, he got up and stretched and headed for the back door, where he sat meowing piteously. I rolled my eyes.

'Do you want to see the garden?' I said. 'His majesty needs a pee.'

'You should put in a cat flap.'

'He's so stubborn. He'd probably refuse to use it.'

We stood at the back door and I peered into the undergrowth while Hades stalked invisibly through the brambles.

'I like what you've done with the garden,' said Ghita.

'It's jungle chic, the latest thing.'

After a violent tussle in the dark, Hades scampered back inside with his ears flat. He headed straight for the refuge of his laundry basket. I thought I spotted a pair of eyes low down in the brambles. No wonder Hades had made himself scarce. Foxes are not fussy eaters.

'I'd better go,' said Ghita with a sigh.

'Are you sure?'

'Yes. I've still got to apologise to Roz, and I'm in the mood for grovelling, so no time like the present.'

After she had gone, I cleared away the tea things and debated the wisdom of uncorking a bottle of wine for George's visit. I wandered into the kitchen and had pulled out a couple of bottles in order to select the best one, when I heard a noise in the garden. I peered through the window and imagined I glimpsed a shadow outside. But I didn't hear another sound and I couldn't be sure I'd actually seen anything. It's amazing how paranoid you could get when you lived on your own. I wished George would hurry. I felt like a sitting duck and my bravado faded. Then I heard a noise in the sitting room like the door opening. Had I forgotten to shut the front door when Ghita left? I swallowed my fear and left the kitchen to check the front door. The sitting room appeared to be empty. I sighed in relief and shook my head. I was about to return to the kitchen when a shadow fell on the floor in front of me. I looked around to see Sarah Bingley, standing in the back doorway, pointing an ancient pistol at me. In my shock, I let out a guffaw.

'This isn't a joke,' she said. 'It works.'

'What are you doing here?'

She sneered.

'As if you didn't know. I want my keys back.'

'They're not yours though, are they?'

'You think you're so clever, but you're no cleverer than any of them, and they're all dead.'

'But why? I don't understand.'

'For my son, Ronnie, of course. William wouldn't acknowledge him officially, so I had to blackmail him for money. And then I discovered he'd left everything to Fiona. That was the final straw.'

Her face contorted with hatred and I felt a shiver run up my back. If I was about to die, I wanted her to know she wouldn't get away with it, and her plans had failed.

'But Ronnie isn't even William's son,' I said. 'Dennis Barratt's DNA is with the police lab getting analysed as we speak.'

The colour drained from her face and her mouth fell open. I continued.

'So, everything you've done is for nothing.'

'You bitch. You'll die for your interfering.'

She raised the ancient gun and held it away from her body, her hand shaking. Time stopped for an instant. She stepped closer to me and I froze, looking around frantically for something with which to defend myself. Suddenly, Hades emitted an unearthly yowl. He had emerged from his basket expecting to find Mouse, his favourite person, and she had stamped on his tail. He wrapped himself around one of her legs in fury, biting and scratching. She twirled around, trying to kick him off, but he clung on. With her distracted, I picked up a wooden candlestick from the rolltop desk and hit her over the head with it. She dropped to the floor as if felled by an axe; Hades still attached to her leg. He let go as he felt her fall and leaped into my arms with an expression of total panic on his bewhiskered face. I don't know who was more surprised. I folded my arms around him, holding him close as I had once read about cats liking to be confined. It's why they squeeze into small cardboard boxes. Anyway, he went floppy and let out an enormous sigh, almost as big as mine.

I wanted to phone George, but I gave Hades a few more seconds to get used to my smell before I let him loose. He sat on the floor beside me, washing his paws, unconcerned by the drama. I kept a sharp eye on Sarah's body, which lay crumpled on the floor. I could see the rise and fall of her rib cage, but she did not stir. The doorbell rang, making me jump. I pushed myself away from the prostrate body and towards the door, keeping a wary eye on her.

'Tanya?'

George's voice, concerned. I staggered over and opened the door, intending to take refuge in his familiar arms, but he hadn't come alone. PC Brennan, who I'd last seen at Conrad House, peered over George's shoulder. Sarah moaned and tried to right herself.

'What the hell?' said George.

'You'll need an ambulance,' I said. 'I hit her quite hard. But she attacked me first and threatened to shoot me. There's a gun lying around somewhere.'

'Are you hurt?'

'No, a bit shocked.'

'Why did you let her in?'

'I didn't she—'

Mouse and Harry rushed up behind George and PC Brennan who had not entered yet.

'Don't go in. It's a crime scene,' said George, holding out his arm to stop them. 'Tanya, can you come out? PC Brennan will make the arrest.'

I tottered out and Mouse hugged me tight. Harry stood to one side, grinning awkwardly.

'Thank goodness you're okay,' he said. 'I don't know where I'd find someone to value the furniture if anything happened to you.'

George's face showed the myriad of emotions going through his mind. He coughed loudly.

'It's like Piccadilly Circus here. I need you all to leave right now, except Tanya. She's got to give us a statement.'

Mouse and Harry muttered and groaned, but ended up going off together to have a takeaway. Their cheeky smiles as they walked off together made me happy, despite the frightening experience I had just had.

By the time they had taken Sarah to A&E and I had given my statement, it was almost midnight. I realised I had nowhere to go, since they had sealed off my house for crime scene work. The long day had left me wrecked and I could hardly stand up anymore.

'I've got to go,' said George. 'Sharon will have my hide. Do you have somewhere to go?'

'I'll stay at the local Premier Inn. The rooms have a superb view of the sea, and I need a quiet night. Can you ask the crime scene boys to feed Hades for me, please?'

George laughed.

'Only you would name a cat Hades.'

'He's a hellcat. It fits.'

'But now he's a hero.'

'He sure is, but I won't change his name.'

'See you tomorrow.'

Chapter 40

There's something about being exhausted that prevents me from sleeping. I think it's the desperation to get eight hours of rest before it's too late. I stayed awake for ages that night trying to figure out how I'd missed the clues about Sarah Bingley. I suppose I presumed the murderer would be male at first. Middle-aged women are not obvious candidates to be serial killers and people's behaviour made them suspects. I wondered how Ronnie would feel when the full extent of his mother's deception came out. His happiness depended on Mel, but Sarah had manipulated and schemed until he had nothing left. When I finally got to sleep, weird nightmares about man-eating cats did not help me feel rested.

As I lay groggy in bed the next morning, George texted me to say he would be over to the Vintage later to fill me in on developments. The crime scene boys let me know mid-morning that they had finished up at my house, and I let myself in for a shower. Hades ran up to me purring, but hissed when I bent down to stroke him. Ratbag! Soon I stood under the stream of hot water and washed the previous day out of my hair. The smell of my clean towels made me feel alive as I buffed my skin to a pink hue. I dressed in a colourful outfit and threw on my big winter coat to walk to the shop.

The sea gleamed in the spring sunshine, but the chill wind took any heat out of the sun's rays. My hair whipped around my face until I put it into a ponytail and stuffed it into my collar. The seagulls whirled above me, looking for evidence that somebody had food they might discard. The smell of seaweed drifted up the beach from the rock pools exposed by the low tide. Several people walked their dogs along the shoreline and I wondered if Hades could be persuaded down to the beach. I felt sure he'd enjoy the adventure. As I gazed upwards at the vapour trails left by airliners taking off from Gatwick, a wave of tiredness swept through me. I speeded up, suddenly gasping for a milky coffee at the Vintage.

The shop felt like a refuge as I entered and looked around at my treasures. The glass buoys twinkled in the sunlight and threw coloured shards of light around, which picked out shiny tabletops and mirrors. I climbed up the stairs to the Vintage and felt a swell of pride as I sat down with my coffee and looked around the room. Mel had been right about everything and it made me sad to think of her losing her life because of greed. She had been on a long journey, provoked by the lies of Sarah Bingley, and had finally found her way home. Maybe she could finally have settled down with Ronnie. She had also helped get some of my old self back, for which I would always be grateful.

And then there was George. Mel had also made him see me as my true self again. During my illness, he drifted away, unable to comprehend the change in my character, unwilling to compromise. Sharon had been a straightforward choice for him, comforting in her familiarity to me, but tougher inside. Now, I could build a new friendship with George. The danger of awakening old feelings lurked in the background, but I had never stopped loving George, he had stopped loving me. The doorbell clanged, and I leaned over the bannister. George came into the shop as if he had been reading my thoughts.

'I'm upstairs having a coffee. Come on up,' I said.

He came over to me and hesitated, unsure how to greet me. I took pity on him, pecked him on the cheek, and made him a cappuccino to break the ice.

'I wanted to fill you in,' he said. 'Sarah is in the cells and we will charge her this morning. I don't expect her to get bail. She's too dangerous.'

'Have you spoken to Ronnie?'

'He's at the station. We won't have any problems with him. He's horrified by the whole situation. He had no aspirations to be rich.'

'And William?'

George stirred his coffee and pursed his lips.

'I'm afraid he's dead.'

'Dead? Did she…'

'No. They think he died of old age, but I'm sure the stress of the past couple of months took its toll.'

'What will happen to Conrad House?'

'I'm really not sure. If Fiona was still his heir, the state will inherit it. But we haven't got a copy yet. How are you holding up? Last night must have spooked you.'

'I'm okay, actually. It seems more like a bad dream than something that actually happened.'

'Maybe you should take the day off. Tuesday isn't peak for sales, is it?'

After George had gone, Roz and Ghita turned up and I related a blow-by-blow account of the night's drama to them. Ghita couldn't believe how close she came to being in the house with Sarah.

'Was it my fault she came in the back door?' she said.

'I think we can blame Hades for that one,' I said.

Roz stroked my hair and gave me a hug, which made me glad of my friends. I shut the shop early and went home to find Mouse and Harry making a massive lunch from the contents of the fridge. Mouse almost burst into tears when I came in and held me tight like a small child when they haven't seen their mother for hours. Harry stood awkwardly in the kitchen, a half-peeled cucumber in his hand. I felt like making a rude joke to break the tension, but I put on some music instead. After lunch, I sat on the sofa with Harry. Mouse disappeared into his room almost immediately. I knew he was trying to give us space. Harry kissed me on my forehead and pulled me against his chest. I could feel his strong heart beating against mine.

We lay like that for ages and eventually slept, only waking when Mouse came downstairs again. Harry looked at his watch.

'Is that the time?' he said. 'I've got to see a man about a dog.'

He kissed my cheek and shook Mouse by the hand. They looked as if they would hug, but Harry got embarrassed and left. Mouse came and sat with me on the sofa. He played with Hades for a while, but I could feel he wanted to say something, so I waited. Finally, he took my hand.

'Will I have to move out if you get together with Harry? I don't want to be a gooseberry,' he said.

My heart almost broke, and I gulped down a sob as I read the fear of rejection in his eyes.

'Don't you dare leave me, you little sod,' I said, shaking with emotion. 'How would I cope with modern technology if you leave?'

'But Harry—'

'But Harry nothing. He and I are friends, that's all. We're both getting over horrible emotional trauma, and need to deal with that before we launch into a relationship, if ever. You, me, and Harry are a team. No matter what.'

Mouse sniffed, but he smiled.

'What about Hades?' he said.

'Him too, the ratbag.'

We both jumped as the doorbell sounded. I couldn't imagine who it might be. Surely George hadn't turned up again? Or maybe Harry forgot something? I opened the door a crack, and my sister Helen stood on the doorstep.

'Aren't you going to welcome me in?' she said.

The next book in the series is **Eternal Forest**. You can order the ebook now by going to this link https://bookgoodies.com/a/B0C6MYBR9G

I hope you have enjoyed Deadly Return. I would very much appreciate you leaving a review. It doesn't have to be a thesis. A couple of lines would be great. It helps me to sell more books. Thank you.

You can buy all my books in paperback direct from my website. Use this QR code to get there.

Other books in the series

The Seacastle Mysteries - a cosy mystery series set on the south coast of England

Eternal Forest

What if proving a friend's husband innocent of murder implicates her instead?

Tanya Bowe, an ex-investigative journalist, and divorcee, runs a vintage shop in the coastal town of Seacastle. When her old friend, Lexi Burlington-Smythe borrows the office above the shop as a base for the campaign to create a kelp sanctuary off the coast, Tanya is thrilled with the chance to get involved and make some extra money. Tanya soon gets drawn into the high-stake arguments surrounding the campaign, as tempers are frayed, and her friends, Roz and Ghita favour opposing camps. When a celebrity eco warrior is murdered, the evidence implicates Roz's husband Ed, and Tanya finds her loyalties stretched to breaking point as she struggles to discover the true identity of the murderer.

Other books by the Author

I write under various pen names in different genres. If you are looking for another mystery, why don't you try **Mortal Mission,** written as Pip Skinner.

Will they find life on Mars, or death?

When the science officer for the first crewed mission to Mars dies suddenly, backup Hattie Fredericks gets the coveted place on the crew. But her presence on the Starship provokes suspicion when it coincides with a series of incidents which threaten to derail the mission.

After a near-miss while landing on the planet, the world watches as Hattie and her fellow astronauts struggle to survive. But, worse than the harsh elements on Mars, is their growing realisation that someone, somewhere, is trying to destroy the mission.

When more astronauts die, Hattie doesn't know who to trust. And her only allies are 35 million miles away. As the tension ratchets up, violence and suspicion invade both worlds. If you like science-based sci-fi and a locked-room mystery with a twist, you'll love this book.

The Green Family Saga (written as Kate Foley) – a family saga set in Ireland

Rebel Green – Book 1

Relationships fracture when two families find themselves caught up in the Irish Troubles.

The Green family move to Kilkenny from England in 1969, at the beginning of the conflict in Northern Ireland. They rent a farmhouse on the outskirts of town, and make friends with the O'Connor family next door. Not every member of the family adapts easily to their new life, and their differing approaches lead to misunderstandings and friction. Despite this, the bonds between the family members deepen with time.

Perturbed by the worsening violence in the North threatening to invade their lives, the children make a pact never to let the troubles come between them. But promises can be broken, with tragic consequences for everyone.

Africa Green – Book 2

Will a white chimp save its rescuers or get them killed?

Journalist Isabella Green travels to Sierra Leone, a country emerging from civil war, to write an article about a chimp sanctuary. Animals that need saving are her obsession, and she can't resist getting involved with the project, which is on the verge of bankruptcy. She forms a bond with local boy, Ten, and army veteran, Pete, to try and save it. When they rescue a rare white chimp from a village frequented by a dangerous rebel splinter group, the resulting media interest could save the sanctuary.

But the rebel group have not signed the cease fire. They believe the voodoo power of the white chimp protects them from bullets, and they are determined to take it back so they can storm the capital. When Pete and Ten go missing, only Isabella stands in the rebels' way. Her love for the chimps unlocks the fighting spirit within her. Can she save the sanctuary or will she die trying?

Fighting Green – Book 3

Liz Green is desperate for a change. The Dot-Com boom is raging in the City of London, and she feels exhausted and out of her depth. Added to that, her long-term boyfriend, Sean O'Connor, is drinking too much and shows signs of going off the rails. Determined to start anew, Liz abandons both Sean and her job, and buys a near-derelict house in Ireland to renovate.

She moves to Thomastown where she renews old ties and makes new ones, including two lawyers who become rivals for her affection. When Sean's attempt to win her back goes disastrously wrong, Liz finishes with him for good. Finding herself almost penniless, and forced to seek new ways to survive, Liz is torn between making a fresh start and going back to her old loves.

Can Liz make a go of her new life, or will her past become her future?

The Sam Harris Adventure Series (written as PJ Skinner)

Set in the late 1980's and through the 1990's, this thrilling series follows the career of a female geologist. The first book sets the scene for the career of an unwilling heroine, whose bravery and resourcefulness are needed to navigate a series of adventures set in remote sites in Africa and South America. Based loosely on the real-life adventures of the author, the settings and characters are given an authenticity that will connect with readers who enjoy adventure fiction and thrillers set in remote settings with realistic scenarios. Themes such as women working in formerly male domains, and what constitutes a normal existence, are developed in the context of Sam's constant ability to find herself up to her neck in trouble. Sam's home life provides a contrast to her adventures and feeds her need to escape. Her attachment to an unfaithful boyfriend is the thread running through her romantic life, and her attempts to break free of it provide another side to her character.

Fool's Gold - Book 1

Newly qualified geologist Sam Harris is a woman in a man's world - overlooked, underpaid but resilient and passionate. Desperate for her first job, and nursing a broken heart, she accepts an offer from notorious entrepreneur Mike Morton, to search for gold deposits in the remote rainforests of Sierramar. With the help of nutty local heiress, Gloria Sanchez, she soon settles into life in Calderon, the capital. But when she accidentally uncovers a long-lost clue to a treasure buried deep within the jungle, her journey really begins. Teaming up with geologist Wilson Ortega, historian Alfredo Vargas and the mysterious Don Moises, they venture through the jungle, where she lurches between excitement and insecurity. Yet there is a far graver threat looming; Mike and Gloria discover that one of the members of the expedition is plotting to seize the fortune for himself and is willing to do anything to get it. Can Sam survive and find the treasure or will her first adventure be her last?

Hitler's Finger - Book 2

The second book in the Sam Harris Series sees the return of our heroine Sam Harris to Sierramar to help her friend Gloria track down her boyfriend, the historian, Alfredo Vargas. Geologist Sam Harris loves getting her hands dirty. So, when she learns that her friend Alfredo has gone missing in Sierramar, she gives her personal life some much needed space and hops on the next plane. But she never expected to be following the trail of a devious Nazi plot nearly 50 years after World War II …

Deep in a remote mountain settlement, Sam must uncover the village's dark history. If she fails to reach her friend in time, the Nazi survivors will ensure Alfredo's permanent silence. Can Sam blow the lid on the conspiracy before the Third Reich makes a devastating return?

The background to the book is the presence of Nazi war criminals in South America which was often ignored by locals who had fascist sympathies during World War II. Themes such as tacit acceptance of fascism, and local collaboration with fugitives from justice are examined and developed in the context of Sam's constant ability to find herself in the middle of an adventure or mystery.

The Star of Simbako - Book 3

A fabled diamond, a jealous voodoo priestess, disturbing cultural practices. What could possibly go wrong? The third book in the Sam Harris Series sees Sam Harris on her first contract to West Africa to Simbako, a land of tribal kingdoms and voodoo. Nursing a broken heart, Sam Harris goes to Simbako to work in the diamond fields of Fona. She is soon involved with a cast of characters who are starring in their own soap opera, a dangerous mix of superstition, cultural practices, and ignorance (mostly her own). Add a love triangle and a jealous woman who wants her dead and Sam is in trouble again. Where is the Star of Simbako? Is Sam going to survive the chaos?

This book is based on visits made to the Paramount Chiefdoms of West Africa. Despite being nominally Christian communities, Voodoo practices are still part of daily life out there. This often leads to conflicts of interest. Combine this with the horrific ritual of FGM and it makes for a potent cocktail of conflicting loyalties. Sam is pulled into this life by her friend, Adanna, and soon finds herself involved in goings on that she doesn't understand.

The Pink Elephants - Book 4

Sam gets a call in the middle of the night that takes her to the Masaibu project in Lumbono, Africa. The project is collapsing under the weight of corruption and chicanery engendered by management, both in country and back on the main company board. Sam has to navigate murky waters to get it back on course, not helped by interference from people who want her to fail. When poachers invade the elephant sanctuary next door, her problems multiply. Can Sam protect the elephants and save the project or will she have to choose?

The fourth book in the Sam Harris Series presents Sam with her sternest test yet as she goes to Africa to fix a failing project. The day-to-day problems encountered by Sam in her work are typical of any project manager in the Congo which has been rent apart by warring factions, leaving the local population frightened and rootless. Elephants with pink tusks do exist, but not in the area where the project is based. They are being slaughtered by poachers in Gabon for the Chinese market and will soon be extinct, so I have put the guns in the hands of those responsible for the massacre of these defenceless animals.

The Bonita Protocol - Book 5

An erratic boss. Suspicious results. Stock market shenanigans. Can Sam Harris expose the scam before they silence her? It's 1996. Geologist Sam Harris has been around the block, but she's prone to nostalgia, so she snatches the chance to work in Sierramar, her old stomping ground. But she never expected to be working for a company that is breaking all the rules. When the analysis results from drill samples are suspiciously high, Sam makes a decision that puts her life in peril. Can she blow the lid on the conspiracy before they shut her up for good? The Bonita Protocol sees Sam return to Sierramar and take a job with a junior exploration company in the heady days before the Bre-X crash. I had fun writing my first megalomaniac female boss for this one. I have worked in a few junior companies with dodgy bosses in the past, and my only comment on the sector is buyer beware...

Digging Deeper - Book 6

A feisty geologist working in the diamond fields of West Africa is kidnapped by rebels. Can she survive the ordeal or will this adventure be her last? It's 1998. Geologist Sam Harris is desperate for money so she takes a job in a tinpot mining company working in war-torn Tamazia. But she never expected to be kidnapped by blood thirsty rebels.

Working in Gemsite was never going to be easy with its culture of misogyny and corruption. Her boss, the notorious Adrian Black is engaged in a game of cat and mouse with the government over taxation. Just when Sam makes a breakthrough, the camp is overrun by rebels and Sam is taken captive. Will anyone bother to rescue her, and will she still be alive if they do?

I worked in Tamazia (pseudonym for a real place) for almost a year in different capacities. The first six months I spent in the field are the basis for this book. I don't recommend working in the field in a country at civil war but, as for many of these crazy jobs, I needed the money.

Concrete Jungle - Book 7 (series end)

Armed with an MBA, Sam Harris is storming the City - But has she swapped one jungle for another?

Forging a new career was never going to be easy, and Sam discovers she has not escaped from the culture of misogyny and corruption that blighted her field career.

When her past is revealed, she finally achieves the acceptance she has always craved, but being one of the boys is not the panacea she expected. The death of a new friend presents her with the stark choice of compromising her principals to keep her new position, or exposing the truth behind the façade. Will she finally get what she wants or was it all a mirage?

I did an MBA to improve my career prospects, and much like Sam, found it didn't help much. In the end, it's only your inner belief that counts. What other people say, or think, is their problem. I hope you enjoy this series. I wrote it to rid myself of demons, and it worked.

Box Sets

Sam Harris Adventure Box Set Book 2-4
https://bookgoodies.com/a/B07LH8G6BG
Sam Harris Adventure Box Set Book 5-7
https://bookgoodies.com/a/B09411NQHW
Sam Harris Adventure Box Set Books 2-7
https://bookgoodies.com/a/B0BR8F9NDK

You can order any of these books in paperback direct from my website. Please go to the <u>PJSKINNER</u> for links or use the QR code below.

Connect with the Author

About the Author

I write under several pen names and in various genres: PJ Skinner (Travel Adventures and Cozy/Cosy Mystery), Pip Skinner (Sci-Fi), Kate Foley (Irish contemporary), and Jessica Parkin (children's illustrated books).

I moved to the south coast of England just before the Covid pandemic and after finishing my trilogy, The Green Family Saga, I planned the Seacastle Mysteries. I have always been a massive fan of crime and mystery and I guess it was inevitable I would turn my hand to a mystery series eventually.

Before I wrote novels, I spent 30 years working as an exploration geologist, managing remote sites and doing due diligence of projects in over thirty countries. During this time, I collected the tall tales and real-life experiences which inspired the Sam Harris Adventure Series, chronicling the adventures of a female geologist as a pioneer in a hitherto exclusively male world.

I worked in many countries in South America and Africa in remote, strange, and often dangerous places, and loved every minute, despite encountering my fair share of misogyny and other perils. The Sam Harris Adventure Series is for lovers of intelligent adventure thrillers happening just before the time of mobile phones and the internet. It has a unique viewpoint provided by

Sam, a female interloper in a male world, as she struggles with alien cultures and failed relationships.

My childhood in Ireland inspired me to write the Green Family Saga, which follows the fortunes of an English family who move to Ireland just before the start of the troubles.

I have also written a mystery on Mars, inspired by my fascination with all things celestial. It is a science-based murder mystery, think The Martian with fewer potatoes and more bodies.

Follow me on Amazon to get informed of my new releases. Just put PJ Skinner into the search box on Amazon and then click on the follow button on my author page.

Please subscribe to my Seacastle Mysteries Newsletter for updates and offers by using this QR code

You can also use the QR code below to get to my website for updates and to buy paperbacks direct from me.

You can also follow me on Twitter, Instagram, Tiktok, or on Facebook @pjskinnerauthor

Made in the USA
Monee, IL
13 August 2023

40965267R00166